PRAISE FOR *THESE PEOPLE ARE US*

"Every page has a sentence worth reading over again just to savor the image." —*Winston-Salem Journal*

"George Singleton has the singular voice of a down-home schizophrenic. His stories are crazy mad fun." —*Playboy*

"George Singleton writes about the rural South without sentimentality or stereotype but with plenty of sharp-witted humor . . . A raconteur of trends, counter-trends, obsessions and odd characters." —Morning Edition, NPR

PRAISE FOR *THE HALF-MAMMALS OF DIXIE*

"A miasma of flea markets, palm readers, bowling alleys, and alligators, offering a disturbingly askew—at times, downright surreal—vision of the South." —*Entertainment Weekly*

"When was the last time you sat reading, in a beach chair, and started laughing out loud? . . . George Singleton keeps the humor volume on high." —*Seattle Times*

"Sly, intelligent, hilarious." —*The Charlotte Observer*

"George Singleton is a madman. He's also one of the most talented American writers the South has turned out in decades." —*The Post and Courier* (Charleston, SC)

MORE . . .

PRAISE FOR *WHY DOGS CHASE CARS*

"This is a South that knows something of suburbia and while the characters may not be in the best circumstances, this is a great new take on the hard-drinking, hardscrabble Southerner."

—*Raleigh News and Observer*

"Singleton's hilarious insights come early and often."

—*New York Times Book Review*

"Singleton's style lies outside the usual briar patch. It's a cross between, say, Ralph Ellison and Molly Ivins . . . Singleton isn't just a killer at the hilarious one-liner, he can keep riffing on something good paragraph after paragraph, page after page."

—*Atlanta Journal Constitution*

PRAISE FOR *WORK SHIRTS FOR MADMEN*

"If there is a fiction genre blending the riotous, bleary-eyed excess and absurdity of gonzo journalism with the rather earnest sensitivity of a John Irving hero—who always does right by his wife in the end—*Work Shirts* belongs to it . . . it's a fun read . . . an adventure to be undertaken."   —*Newsweek*

"Smackover funny and rare, many of Singleton's laughs come from deep wit and not easy Southern eccentricities and the rough-screeching Skoal crowd."

—Barry Hannah, author of *Yonder Stands Your Orphan*

BETWEEN WRECKS

BETWEEN WRECKS

stories

George Singleton

DZANC BOOKS

DZANC BOOKS

5220 Dexter Ann Arbor Rd
Ann Arbor, MI 48103
www.dzancbooks.org

BETWEEN WRECKS

Book design by Steven Seighman.

Published 2014 by Dzanc Books

ISBN: 978-1-938103-79-7
First edition: April 2014

This project is supported in part by awards from the National Endowment for the Arts and Michigan Council for Arts and Cultural Affairs.

Printed in the United States of America

10   9   8   7   6   5   4   3   2   1

TABLE OF CONTENTS

In Memory of Harry, Barry, Larry, and Lewis

BETWEEN WRECKS

NO SHADE EVER

Because I'd seen part of a documentary on gurus who slept on beds of nails, and because I'd tried to quit smoking before my wife came back home after leaving for nine months in order to birth our first child—though she would come back childless and say it was all a lie she made up in order to check into some kind of speech clinic up in Minnesota to lose her bilateral lisp—I had a dream of chairs and beds adorned entirely with ancient car cigarette lighters. This wasn't the kind of dream a person could forget or disobey. In the dream, I stood in the middle of a giant room filled with my handcrafted furniture. I didn't remember making the works, but I understood that it was an art show, that I was the center of attention, and that I was going to make 14.5 million dollars. I kept thinking, Who would pay that much money to sit on chairs and beds that could offer only a tiny strange cushion effect? There were famous rich people at the opening, namely Ted Turner and the vice president of the United States. I thought in my dream, I don't care that they're probably not on speaking terms, as long as they buy my work. Some professional basketball players and golfers stood around wearing their uniforms and outfits. Hollywood starlets stood on the perimeter, but I could tell that they wanted nothing more than to grab me by the arm and tell me how they wanted their mansions out in California completely covered in car cigarette lighters, or at least the shiny silver ones found in 1960s models. A group of Japanese business-men fought over a banquet table I'd drilled a thousand holes into in order to glue in Cadillac lighters. Of course, everyone wore tuxedos and evening gowns, and I stood around in my underwear pretending that I knew what I was doing, that it was some kind of statement, that I thought it important to show up at my first art opening clad in my work clothes. When I woke up alone, I certainly didn't feel good about myself, and before I had my first cigarette of the morning—who could quit smoking with dreams like this?—it came to me that maybe I'd taken yet another wrong-headed turn over the last year.

I'd given up on finding one more thesis-worthy subject for my low-residency master's degree in Southern cultures studies at Ole Miss-Taylor. But I'd learned enough along the way to under-stand that the subconscious—or what one of my ex-interviewees called "the sumconscious"—held more power in Southern cul-ture studies than in other branches of academia. So I got out of bed, walked down to the Unknown Branch of the Middle Saluda River, lifted a giant flat rock, unearthed a metal ammo box, and pulled out a pack of American Spirits I'd hidden from myself. I got back to the kitchen, poured bourbon in my coffee, poured bourbon and Pepsi into my Thermos, and drove straight down Scenic Highway 11—then south on 25, to where it no longer seemed scenic—to Doc's Salvage in Traveler's Rest. From the as-phalt it appeared that Doc only had a collection of snail-back trailers, battered ski boats, a couple school busses, and a few Buicks without their hoods, but down the clay-rutted road leading to his raw-wood office there must've been enough wrecked cars to fill a mall parking lot. I did my best to dodge or straddle every nail, bolt, hinge, snake, rat, or hubcap along the way, and pulled up front, next to a moped leaning against a three-wheeled shopping cart leaning against a mound of crushed beer cans.

Getting out of the truck, I tried to remember that experience of accomplishment and euphoria that I had felt in the dream. I tried to envision enrolling in a low-residency furniture-making class, or maybe an art school one rung above the ones advertised on matchbook covers, then constructing a giant chair bejeweled with car cigarette lighters in a way that would match a petty dictator's jungle-house's throne. As I scraped my shoes on a rough-hewn welcome mat that read Beware of Junkyard God, I imagined my wife Abby and our child, who I still had reason to believe existed up there, standing around in one of my outbuildings converted to an art studio, watching me manufacture car cigarette lighter chairs and daybeds suitable for Hollywood movie sets and vacation homes alike.

"Doc's out back," a man said when I finally got inside. "Doc's out looking for a carburetor. You looking for a carburetor?"

I assumed it was the guy with the moped. I said, "No. No, no carburetor for me."

"I ain't Doc. He's out in the yard. I'm Bobby Suddeth, but they call me Freebird. I might as well be Doc, much as I spend time here."

I said, "I'm Stet."

"I might as well be Doc, much time as I spend here," Suddeth said. I wondered if he suffered from echolalia, and kind of saw him crashing off his moped one too many times without wearing a helmet. "Doc's getting a carburetor. And I'm hoping he runs across a kickstand."

The room was like any other salvage-yard main office I'd ever encountered. There were a few pin-up calendars scattered on the walls from the 1960s up until the present. All of them came from a place called S & M Towing, and I made a mental note to search this place out some time. Doc had written various notes to himself in ink, lead, and Magic Marker—"Coy needs Caliente pump 1964," "Darryl Starter Mustang GT," "Preston Alternator Lincoln," plus enough telephone numbers to make up a small town—and the requisite dirt-, grease-, and oil-smudged paperback parts and price list directories atop the chest-high service counter. There were boxes of bolts scattered on the floor.

The place smelled like a mixture of cilantro and fruity candle.

"Got to get me a kickstand for my bike out front. I keep forgetting, and it falls over. In time I guess I'll have to get me new grips on my handlebar, and then a new handlebar if it gets bent."

Normally I would know what to say to a man who liked to be called Freebird. I'd lost my touch. I said, "If gas keeps going up I guess we'll all be riding scooters." I couldn't imagine any sane person in a three-state area saying such a thing. I hadn't used the term "scooter" since about second grade.

Bobby sat down on a sawed-off end to a telephone pole Doc had wedged in the corner of his office. I sat down on a brown vinyl-covered loveseat of sorts. There were no magazines scattered about. "I know about every square inch of this salvage yard," Bobby said. "Tell me what you came for, and I can send you off in that direction."

I didn't want to explain to this guy how I'd had a dream, and so on. Already this feeling of being an outsider started creeping up on me. It's not like I didn't have that feeling about every day while trying to conduct a thesis-worthy interview for my low-residency master's. Believe me when I say that I finished more than a few, and although they weren't exactly "scholarly" or "awe-inspiring" or "relevant" or "spectacular" or "research-laden" or "filled with forward-thinking relevance" according to my mentor Dr. Theron Crowther, I had placed them in various literary journals and quarterlies that published rhetorical nonfiction. Maybe my subject matter wasn't on par with what's expected of a southern culture studies master's degree recipient, but it was good enough to get me anywhere from ten to fifty dollars a printed page, plus a year's subscription. I've had profiles of a woman who thinks she met the devil working as a cemetery caretaker, and a man who thinks he can touch the image of a televangelist and make the guy ask people to send donations to the Humane Society, and a man whose wife is obsessed with putting "Before" photographs all over her kitchen before she remodels, and suburban meth labs and their importance to making people in the neighborhood getting friendly again, and a family that traveled all over the world trying out mission work before ending up in Las Vegas. There are others, too. Believe me when I say that whenever those essays get published and I get paid, it'll be more than nice to show Abby how I can support a for-real newborn seeing as I kind of let my river rock business dry up even more so since she left.

I didn't want to explain any of this, but luckily Doc walked back in holding what ended up being the carburetor for a Ford Pinto. He limped visibly. I thought, Who would want to fix up a thing like that? but didn't say anything. I said, "Hey, man."

"Freebird, buddy, I'm gone tell you one last time—I don't have a kickstand for your moped. I don't carry moped parts. I never have and I never will. You either have to walk to the moped store's parts department and order one up new, or figure out a way to weld your own on. Like I said before, a length of rebar with some kind of swivel joint should work."

Doc didn't seem to be in the best of moods. He was a tall man, and he moved as though he once owned a belly that made all the decision-making as to where his body might follow. He had a receding hairline on only one side, which made him look as though he'd recently undergone brain surgery.

Bobby said, "You never know."

I said, "Hey, man," again, like an idiot. "You wouldn't mind if I walked around your property getting cigarette lighters, would you?

How much would you sell me car cigarette lighters for?" I reached in my pocket, pulled out a cigarette, and put it in my mouth. There were six ashtrays scattered around the room, and I'd found out early while doing research for my low-residency master's degree in Southern culture studies that my particular lot of people felt more comfortable talking to strangers who cared zero about their health.

"You want the shiny silver ones from days gone past?" Bobby Suddeth said. "Doc can tell you where they located. Doc has a phonographic memory."

I didn't acknowledge Bobby. I kept eye contact with Doc. Phonographic memory!

Doc said, "It's true that I have a phonographic memory. I've told this story many times. I've never seen you around, so I've never said it in your presence. It'll be something new. See, when a car comes in, the first thing I do, if the battery still works, is I turn on the radio. Whatever song's playing, I'll remember where that particular car's parked. You say to me '1968 Corvair,' and I'll remember 'Bone Dry,' George Jones, Section 14. Oh, I keep a written record, too, just in case the Gift leaves me, but right on up till now I can still think back at songs and remember where cars are parked. My only problem is those times when I turn on the radio and it's a good year for a hit single, you know. Then it might take me some time seeing as I'll have about forty cars with, like, 'Proud to Be an American' stuck up here." He touched the hairless side of his upper forehead.

Bobby Suddeth said, "He's got a good rememory."

Well, Goddamn, I thought. Anyone with that freakish mnemonic device won't think anything weird about my dream. I told it. I told it all, including how my missing wife always wanted to be a TV anchorwoman but that she had a bilateral lisp that kept her from getting jobs. It might've taken me ten minutes to complete the story. If either Doc or Bobby had the wherewithal to undertake a low-residency master's degree program in Southern culture studies, he might've perked up his ears and asked to interview me.

Doc said, "I've never priced those things out. I have no clue. Maybe I should just sell them to you at scrap metal price, what I get for scrap metal."

Bobby said, "You should line a casket in cigarette lighters. You know, in case the guy went to Heaven and he was a smoker. Hell—you wouldn't need lighters in Hell. But Heaven, who knows about that place?"

I thought about a pine box covered entirely with car cigarette lighters. It would be cushiony. I wished that I had my notebook to write down such an idea, or maybe a radio playing a song so I could try out Doc's method. I thought about covering an entire car with lighters—one time I went to an art car show and saw a woman who'd glued her cats' toenails all over the hood of her Dodge or whatever—and then I started thinking about collecting the hotels and houses from Monopoly games and gluing them on, say, model airplanes.

I thought too much. I lit my cigarette.

"It seems like I should get at least a dollar each for a cigarette lighter, but if you wood-bored one down into a chair seat and sold it, who's going to pay two hundred dollars for an old-fashioned ladderback chair?" Doc said. "Shit. I can't imagine. Well, I can—there seems to be way too many people with way too much money down here these days, and way too many people with exactly zero money. Like Freebird. Freebird?—If I had a kickstand for your moped, could you pay for it?"

Bobby said, "It's not a moped. I like to call it a 'Harley Light.'"

"Could you pay for it? If you say 'yes,' then I'm gone think you the man talked me into taking pictures of my valuables, developed the things, then broke into my house, even though I'm pretty sure you've never held a job at One-Hour Snapshots."

There were no flies around. This was mid-summer, and there were no flies. That says something. Doc leaned hard on his counter, keeping weight off of his bad leg.

"I've had jobs in the past, for your information," Bobby said.

"You ain't part of this conversation," Doc said to him. "Go find something to do. Go ride your moped down into the slope where I keep the Chevelle parts. There's a job for you. Bring me back the sound of a car horn. Not the horn itself, just the sound."

Miss July 1972 on the S & M Towing calendar looked a whole lot like a really sexy Dorothea Dix. She was in a nurse's outfit, for one. To Doc I said, "What? Say that all again, about the man breaking into your house?" No matter how much I tried staying away from Southern culture studies, I couldn't help but notice a probable good scam. And in Southern culture studies, daily life pretty much depended on scams of one sort or another.

Freebird left the building. Doc said to me, "What did I do to deserve his hanging around every day? Listen, like I said, I'm about broke, so I'll do you a deal. In all these years—I worked here with my daddy, too—I don't remember anyone ever wanting to buy one car lighter, much less an armload. I'll sell by weight. There's got to be some copper in those lighters, so I'll sell you at the going rate of copper."

I agreed to Doc's offer. He asked if I wanted to take along a pistol. I said I wasn't scared of snakes, and that I wasn't a great shot. He asked if I'd be willing to shoot Bobby Suddeth.

Doc didn't lock his office door. We started down a trail of Plymouths and Chryslers. With each step Doc pointed at a car hood and either sang out some lyrics or hummed. We went from "Achy-Breaky Heart" down to "Stairway to Heaven." Doc stopped and looked down in a valley of dead cars, then said, "I think some of your best car lighters came out of your Oldsmobile, so let's walk on down this way."

I picked up a stick along the way. Though I wasn't afraid of snakes, I wasn't all that familiar with the audacity of feral cats. Doc, I noticed, no longer limped. I said, "How long you had this salvage yard?"

"The thing is, you see, with Bobby Suddeth—you have to let him start feeling comfortable. He's a lot smarter than he comes off, you know. I'm just biding my time."

As it ended up, there were forty acres of junk cars and trucks. In the distance I heard doors creaking open, slamming shut. Gulls circled overhead and mockingbirds flew by us at head level. I said, "He's a character." I knew from experience that it wouldn't take prying to get back to Doc's housebreaking story.

"What happened was, I took photos of my valuables should there ever be a break-in or fire. I had double prints, you know. I got a set of prints in a fireproof lockbox, stashed in the trunk of an old Renault back thataway." Doc didn't turn his head but gestured to the left. "Then I got the pictures hidden in a file cabinet in my house. I had the photos done, and I told people, I guess, all about it. I told Bobby Suddeth—or I told someone in my office, and Bobby was standing there like always."

I veered over to a Saab, reached in, and pulled out a nice lighter. I put it in my pocket. "Sometimes I wish I didn't have dreams," I said.

Doc slicked back his already slicked-back hair. He said, "I made Bobby believe that I believed that the photo shop boy developed my pictures, saw what I had, then came over and robbed my house. It was all made up. I said, 'The guy had my phone number and address from having to fill out that little envelope where I dropped in the film!' So Bobby, he says, 'That's exactly what happened. You need to tail the guy.' And I said, 'I ain't got time to tail the guy, Freebird. But I know someone who does—you.'

Next thing you know, Bobby's on his moped hanging out in the parking lot, waiting for the guy to get off work. Or that's what he says he's doing. Of course he doesn't have to, seeing as he's the one who broke in my house, and so on."

I thought about how good poker players slow play a hand. Doc had that game plan down. I pushed aside some cobwebs on the passenger window of an MG Midget, reached in, and extracted the car lighter. "It's hot out here. It's got to be ten degrees hotter out here than in town. Is it all this metal?"

Doc looked up at the sky. He said, "No cover available."

I tried to think of anything else to talk about. Doc didn't look like the kind of man who'd follow baseball stats. He didn't look like the kind of man with whom I'd want to bring up politics. I said, "No cover."

He began laughing. "Listen, I've learned that to run a good scrap metal operation, you need to know how to act. I mean, you need to have some acting skills. I could've told you all about how car cigarette lighters is the new fashion, you know. I could've made up a story about three, four men and women coming down here weekly for car cigarette lighters. But I knew your daddy. Soon's you come in, I said to myself 'That's old Looper's boy.' You look just like him. One time your daddy sold me some river rock for next to nothing. I used it for a fence"—Doc pointed to nowhere—"I thought I needed. I didn't. It's over there covered in kudzu, near where Bobby Suddeth's hidden three watches, my wife's engagement ring and wedding band that she should've been wearing in the first place, my silver dollar collection, two shotguns, most of my home tools, my collection of silver certificates, and a little urn with the ashes of my favorite dog, which Bobby Suddeth probably thinks is a genie."

We turned, finally, to walk toward the Oldsmobiles. Along the way I reached in and pulled out anything metallic. I refrained from pulling out newer, plastic-handled lighters. I said, "I know what this is all about. I'm with you on this one, Doc."

"You a smart man. I knew I could count on your understanding."

"In a weird way you're not really that pissed off at Bobby Suddeth. He shined a light on something." Let me say right here that I wasn't all that smart, and that I only tiptoed around hoping to set foot on solid purchase. I kind of wanted out of there. From this point on, I told myself, I wouldn't follow through on any dreams as being omen-worthy.

"Bobby Suddeth showed me my wife was having an affair, that's right. She wasn't home. She wasn't wearing her wedding band. I looked into the situation. She was out. Me, I work my ass off all day, grimied up, and there she is saying she's spent the afternoon at Wal-Mart or the Dollar General, when she's really going over to this tree farmer's nursery place, swishing her tail around amongst the Leyland cypresses. I don't see that fellow buying her a new refrigerator freezer. I don't see him putting in new flooring. But she's over there. She's over there right now as we speak, I'm betting. It's why she always says she doesn't want a cell phone. I mean, she says she doesn't want one because she'll always lose it. What woman doesn't want a free cell phone? I'll tell you—the kind of woman who won't pick up 'cause she's in the middle of laying down."

At the Oldsmobiles Doc sang "Little baby born in the ghetto." He sang, "We're caught in a trap." He sang, "I turned twenty-one in prison." I kind of wondered if his "phonographic memory" was just one more notion of "acting." Those songs didn't come out at the same time, I thought. Wouldn't cars get parked one after another, day after day, kind of like soldiers at a national cemetery?

Doc said, "This is where I think we'll find what you're looking for, more or less. Tell me again about this dream. Why would you dream about car lighters? What a weird dream! Me, I always dream about getting sucked up into the sky by giant magnets. Always. Every night."

I said, "No way. You're acting. I'm on to you."

Doc nodded. Doc lifted his chin. He said, "Yup. And let me tell you another thing: I don't think the Oldsmobile car cigarette lighter is any better than the Cadillac or Buick or Dodge. It's certainly no better than the couple Hudsons I got lodged back here somewhere." He walked over to the car next to the one where I stood. He lifted the trunk and pulled out a Mason jar. "I just wanted a drink, more than anything else. What with what's going on in my life, I just wanted a drink."

Doc unscrewed the lid of what I knew was a particular favorite style of moonshine called Peach Bounce, what with the bloated piece of bruised fruit sagged to the bottom. He drank from it, then offered it my way. I said, "I got me a thermos of bourbon back in the truck, but what the hell."

"You goddamn right, what the hell. What the hell! We might get seen, you know, what with no cover available out here in the fucking middle of dead Detroit, but I don't give a woodpecker's vibrating ass." Doc handed over the jar. He reached in the trunk and got another. He said, "My wife's name's Gloria. G-L-O-R-I-A. That song came on one time when I backed a Duster in. I can't look at a Duster these days without singing that song."

I said, "Abby's mine." I said, "She might be cheating on me with a guy who likes hockey. She's been up in Minnesota for some time. What could I do?"

"Abby," he said. "Women. I don't want to make any suppositions about your wife, but saying her name sounds like a type of blood. A blood type."

I drank from the Mason jar and tried not to think of Southern culture studies, or what teleological connection Doc made with my wife's name.

"Teleological" is not a word I learned in my low-residency master's degree program at Ole Miss-Taylor. I got it either from the crosswords, or my short stint as a philosophy major way back before in undergraduate school. Three sips into the moonshine and I understood how I should've been a philosophy major. How many philosophers found themselves stuck at the back corner of a junk yard, drinking blind-worthy white lightning with a man destined to kill a tree farmer and a man without a kickstand?

Bobby Suddeth held his hands cupped together when Doc and I stumbled back to the office. Bobby opened them up quickly and said, "Uh-oh. I had that horn sound for you, but I guess the battery's dead." Then he haw-haw-hawed a bunch. "Let me see the lighters you picked out."

I unloaded my pockets, Doc unloaded his, and then I emptied a plastic Spinx station bag I'd found stuck on a briar along the way. I had a good hundred lighters, with which I knew that I'd never do anything. No, I would go home eventually, sleep one off, wake up, then start doing research on the importance of car junk yards in the South. I'd try to make a connection between junk yards and Antietam, or Bull Run, or Andersonville Prison. Then I'd send it off to Dr. Crowther and he'd say it wasn't a very good idea. By that time I'd have another dream, or begin obsessing more so on Abby and the child I thought she had but never really did, et cetera.

Doc said, "I got an idea. I got a great idea. Since most of my valuables got stolen, and since I got some insurance money for them, why don't I give you all these lighters here. You make me a special chair or bench—yeah, make a bench so I can get rid of this telephone pole stool—and then I'll let you go out and get another sack of lighters for free. How's that sound?"

Bobby Suddeth said, "You should make a chair that only has one lighter sticking straight up from the middle. It could be called the Happy Chair for Women, you know."

"Or the Happy Chair for Bobby Suddeth's Ass," Doc said. He exhaled loudly.

Bobby Suddeth said, "Y'all been drinking without me? I smell it on both y'all. Where'd y'all get the liquor? I didn't hear y'all leave."

I started laughing. I said, "We got it over by the collection of kickstands Doc has piled up." I felt like I had the right. I felt like I belonged in the club. "Hey, I got a thermos of bourbon out in my truck. Let me go get it. Damn it to hell, I know better than to start. If I start drinking, I can't stop until I'm asleep."

"Yeah. I'll drink some bourbon," Bobby Suddeth said.

I looked at Doc. He took up his limp again and scooted two stand-up ashtrays against the wall. He said, "I guess. Normally I'd say 'no,' but this seems like a different kind of day." He took his leg and scooted the loveseat back against another wall. Was he expecting us to need room for a bigger dance floor? I thought. Was he later going to sweep his office?

When I got to my truck I could hear Bobby Suddeth saying, "You crazy, man. Doc, Doc. You crazy, you old crip." It was what they might call, in the Southern culture studies world, a "plaintive cry." He yelped it out quickly.

By the time I picked up the thermos—this was one of those nice ones, with the plastic cup that screwed to the top—I expected to hear two pistol reports. Instead I only heard some pings. Ping, ping, ping. Ping-ping-ping-ping. Because I'd not lived long enough with car cigarette lighters in my possession, I didn't connect the sound with that of lighters being thrown hard and ricocheting off of Bobby Suddeth's forehead, the cash register, windows.

My first thought, of course, was to get in my truck and drive off fast. I'd done it before. I had sprayed gravel out of the Modestine Duncans' trailer park with all their weird Book of Revelation quotes printed on their mobile homes, and out of the barren fat lighter farm, and out of the He's Out Casting bar when I got the pet monkey, all in the name of a low-residency master's degree. I'd been spraying gravel directly or metaphorically since birth, I realized, and it didn't seem to matter. It was like I took off out of one trouble spot only to arrive at another. I could never find a place to flat-out hide.

But I didn't drive away. I sauntered back inside Doc's Salvage to find Bobby Suddeth smiling—was there a trick being played on me?—and Doc picking up my car cigarette lighters from the floor. He said, "I'm just frustrated, you know. You imagine how frustrating all this can be."

Bobby Suddeth said, "Hey," to me, as if we'd never met before. I could tell that he almost said, "You looking for a carburetor?"

I said, "Here's some bourbon." I said, "What's going on in here?"

"So after about a year what you can do is get me to go sell off that silver and that paper money. And you already got the insurance money. I don't want to brag none, but I would think that this is a good idea, and for it you'd give me a cut, you know," Bobby said. "If I leave here tomorrow," he sang out, "and you go turn in the silver, somehow you're going to get caught for insurance fraud." He said, "Hand me that thermos."

"I'm serious when I say I want that bench," Doc said. He reached behind the counter and pulled out two coffee mugs. Bobby Suddeth poured Doc some, then poured himself to the rim, then handed me back the Thermos. "Jesus S. Christ."

We drank. Bobby said something about how those cigarette lighters hurt. He said it reminded him of playing dodgeball with rocks and hardboiled eggs back when he was a kid. I couldn't wait any longer and said, "What's that mean, Doc? Tell me what 'Jesus S. Christ' means. I've never heard it that way before."

He wouldn't make eye contact. He limped over to the counter, picked up the phone, and said, "I'm calling Gloria." I could hear it ring a good ten times. No answering machine picked up. "She must be at Wal-Mart again. That woman won't be happy until she buys one of everything sold at the Wal-Mart."

I sat down on the loveseat. I wanted to go nowhere. For a second I thought about asking Doc if I could rent out some space here, maybe set up a studio, maybe in one of the junked buses. Then I thought about Abby up in Minnesota, and imagined her strolling around the baby section of Wal-Mart, picking up bibs and whatnot. Why hadn't she called me? Why had she asked that I not contact her, ever?

Doc said, "Shade. It stands for 'Shade.'"

I nodded. I thought about Jesus on the cross, probably hoping that there was some shade to comfort him a little. The three of us sat in silence for an uncomfortable amount of time. Doc said how he couldn't be selfish anymore, and pulled a brand-new bottle of bourbon from beneath his counter. We passed it around. He said, "I'm not going to kill you, Bobby, though I ought to. I know you're living back there." He pointed with his thumb.

I said, "I need to get home," but didn't move.

I didn't move, for I knew that our story together wasn't finished. I closed my eyes and inhaled the odd smell of cilantro and candle. Later on, I knew, we would get in my truck and drive to that nursery. Doc would ramble around pretending to buy a couple saplings to plant around his salvage yard, but really he'd be taking mental notes. Bobby Suddeth would look for things to steal while no one watched him. I'd end up maudlin, remember too many songs that played back when my wife and I underwent rites of passage, then make some more promises to myself I would never keep, and from which I'd never be able to escape.

TRADITIONAL DEVELOPMENT

Mal Mardis spun two spent rolls of color film on the bar, didn't look up at Gus, and realized that cutting basic cable alone wouldn't solve the problem. He'd also have to find a way for his wife to quit subscribing to the magazines. This morning's mission was no different than when Brenda renovated their bathroom, den, or what used to be a two-car garage. Mal was supposed to drop off the film at any of the one-hour developers twenty miles from their house, use that time to buy at least two dozen frames, go back to the developer—Eckerd, Jack Rabbit, Wal-Mart, One-Hour Photo—select the nicest shots, and ask that the person behind the counter now blow them up into 8 x 10s. Then Mal, according to his wife, could use that hour to visit Gus, have two non-brown liquor drinks, return to get the enlargements, and come home. Soon thereafter, Brenda would nail up on available wall space twenty-four photographs of the old kitchen, all of which looked down on the new tiled countertops, the laminated flooring, the new cabinets that replaced a gigantic island that once took up so much space they had to move the table outside to rot. Mal didn't get it.

Keeping pictures of old rooms on the wall pretty much, to him at least, kept the new room looking old.

"You don't see women getting face lifts then plastering pictures of their old selves all around the vanity," Mal said to Gus. He sat at the counter. At the far end sat a man known as Windshield, who claimed that he still had tiny fragments of glass imbedded in his face from when he took a hard exit out of a Ford truck. Gus's bar had a sign out front that only read "Gus," for back when he bought the place he couldn't remember if it should be "Gus's Place" or "Gus' Place." Neither looked correct. No one who ever came into Gus Place knew the grammatical rule or cared. One time some fraternity boys came by and painted an H on the end of his name. Another time somebody from the Latin Club came and changed it to read "Caesar Augustus," which Gus kept for a good month until Mal told him that it might be an omen that he was going to get stabbed by an everyday regular drinking customer.

Mal tried to think of another analogy about the new kitchen, something about a hip replacement.

"Missed you at Frankie Perkins's funeral Sunday," Windshield called over to Mal.

Mal spun a roll of film then set it upright next to the other. He said, "I didn't know Frankie Perkins."

"Well he was asking about you," Windshield said in a voice that started off a baritone and ended up so high he could've done a Memorex commercial for breaking wine glasses.

Gus leaned over to Mal and said, "Don't mind him. He said the same to me. For some reason he thinks this dead guy used to frequent the bar. Anyway, Brenda called and said you weren't allowed bourbon. She said you can have two vodkas." He laughed. He poured a jigger and a half of bourbon, placed it in front of Mal, then reached down and got him a can of Pabst. "I'm just kidding. She ain't called this time. Yet."

"Those fuckers on TV. How many shows are on about renovating or redecorating or do-it-yourself-ing? There's got to be
twenty of those shows on nonstop between channels 70 and 80.
Who are these people? I'm surprised there are any contractors left
out there doing real work."

Gus stood up straight and half-turned. "I been thinking about
changing around the bar. I'm getting tired of y'all getting to stare
down at the water. Some kind of flood or freak tidal wave shows
up, I ought to be the first to know about it, not my customers."

Mal stood up from his stool and craned his neck to look at
the Saluda River. He said, "Beavers still working hard down there.
Maybe Brenda can come on by and help them out with the inte-
rior of their den. I guess she'd have to use some kind of underwa-
ter camera for the before-and-after shots."

"Lodge," Windshield bellowed out. He stood up and looked
out of the plate glass window too. "Beavers live in something
called a lodge. Moose don't, even though they call it the Moose
Lodge. My daddy used to be a member. I didn't notice neither of
y'all at his funeral neither."

Gus said, "Don't make me cut you off, Windshield. I'll cut you
off. You know that."

Windshield grabbed his can of Budweiser and stood still.

Mal drank the bourbon in two gulps. "I wish to God I'd never
won that money from the scratch ticket. Who wins money off a
scratch ticket? Back in the old days renovating the kitchen meant
getting a new toaster oven."

Gus poured Mal another bourbon. He said, "You should've
quit your job. Then you'd be home more to take the distributor
cap off Brenda's car so she couldn't go down to Lowe's or wherever."

"I should've. I could hide the mail when those magazines
show up and I could monkey with the TV and say the cable's out."

"Where you work?" Windshield said. He sat back down. "Where you work, Frankie?"

Mal said, "Home Depot. I'm in charge of the garden center at Home Depot."

When the door to Gus opened, Mal Mardis looked down at his two rolls of film. He should've at least taken them by One-Hour Photo and left them and then come up with some kind of excuse. He could've said that the digital camera boom finally caused the death of traditional development. Or Mal could've at least placed the rolls in his pocket so that when Brenda stormed into Gus he could say he'd been by the film place, that they were backed up, that they apologized for having to become Six-Hour Photo.

Mal tensed, waiting to hear his wife's voice. Instead, a man who sounded already drunk called out, "You mind if I bring me a video recording device in here on a tripod?"

Gus looked up. Windshield smiled, and Mal turned around to find a stranger. Was this some kind of joke? he wondered. Is somebody playing a trick on me? Gus said, "What?"

The man walked in. He wore cowboy boots. "Pat Taft," he said, as if everyone should recognize him. He stuck out his hand to shake with Gus. "Prison Tat Pat, they call me. I need to film myself everywhere I go. It's a long story that involves an ex-wife."

Mal said, "Okay. Funny. I don't get it yet, but I know that Brenda's behind this somehow."

Gus said, "Long's it don't end up on *Cops* or *America's Most Wanted*, you do what you want."

"It'll end up on one of the goddamn home decorating shows, believe me," Mal said. "Ha ha ha. I get it. Brenda's gone too far this time."

Prison Tat Pat seemed to have a thyroid problem, which made the regulars think that he kept a look of surprise on his face. He said, "I've been doing it between here and Nashville. Everywhere I go. I just set up the camera and prove that I act and react normal with people. My ex-wife says she left me 'cause I couldn't act and react properly in public. I'm going to send her the video, when the time's right." He screwed the camcorder onto a miniature tripod and placed it on the far end of the bar, opposite of Windshield. He got behind it and looked through the eyepiece, focused.

Windshield said, "This ain't ever happened here. You gone be famous, Gus."

Gus said, "Tell me again what this is all about? There's a six drink minimum for capturing our essence."

Mal looked at Gus and squinted. " '*Capturing our essence*'? What'd you do, go to perfume college?"

Pat Taft said, "Okay. Here we go. Mind if I sit down?" He sat two stools away from Mal and stuck the knuckles on his right hand out. "This is why they call me Prison Tat Pat."

Where most people have L-O-V-E or H-A-T-E tattooed in India Ink or cigarette ashes across their knuckles, Pat Taft had a crude G-O-L-D. Windshield got up from his seat to examine it. He said, "Cold."

"*Gold*," Pat Taft said. "It says '*Gold*.'"

"That's a good idea," Windshield said. "You could put 'Hot' on the other hand, and then you'd always remember which handle on the sink meant what. Like if you got All-timer's you could remember what was hot and what was cold." He lost interest and returned to his seat.

Mal Mardis placed the film in his right side pants pocket. He said, "It kind of does look like C-O-L-D."

"Well it's not. Anyway, I'm from Nashville. Just quit my job working as a stockbroker, you know. Been with Edward Jones for sixteen years. Company didn't like what I was doing, letting my clients get all rich and all. They said that the last thing a brokerage firm needs is people making so much money that they can afford to buy a computer and start trading online, you know. I wouldn't toe the company line. No, sir. They'd tell me to push Putnam Voyager mutual funds, or Doubleclick, and to not let anyone buy a stock under four dollars a share. Let me just say that I got people into Amazon and Google when they went public going for nothing." Gus cleared his throat and didn't make eye contact with anyone.

Mal looked past Prison Tat Pat at the red light on his camcorder. He brushed hair out of his face. He said, "I work for Home Depot. I get stock options, but I don't trust the market."

"He won $250,000 dollars playing one them scratch cards," Gus said. "Now he's got a house that's worth eighty grand on the outside, and about two hundred grand on the inside."

Prison Tat Pat didn't respond. He said, "So I lost my job—and I used to be the stockbroker for the likes of Sheb Wooley and Porter Wagoner and Boxcar Willie, you know—and Emma left me, and I decided that I was going to do what I've always wanted to do. I sold my house, bought an RV, and am on my way to Myrtle Beach. I tattooed myself on the right hand, but I can't decide on what I want to do with the left. Maybe I'll print out B-R-I-C-K. Or S-O-L-I-D. Or C-O-I-N. Not only am I going to prove that I can keep up a conversation with normal people, but I'm going to prove I have a dangerous side to me. Emma said she thought I was too safe, too absorbed. So here we are." He turned to Gus and said, "If you got moonshine, then I'd like to buy some moonshine. If you don't, then I guess I'll take a Miller Lite."

Windshield got up off his stool and looked down at the river. He said, "Is that your Winnebago nose down in the river? That ain't safe."

Prison Tat Pat hadn't used the parking brake. He said, "I would cuss, but I don't want it on camera."

———

Mal Mardis's cell phone began to ring in his left side pants pocket. It came out James Taylor's "Fire and Rain." Brenda was always changing his ringer tone, as a joke. He spent a month showing people plants at work while his pants rang out "Parsley, Sage, Rosemary, and Thyme" before he figured out what his wife was doing.

Mal pulled his phone out and read "Brenda" on the readout. It kept ringing. He shrugged, looked at Gus, and answered. He said, "Man, you won't believe what happened down here. I went down to the One-Hour Photo place—they're closed because the UPS guy didn't bring the right chemicals or something—so I stopped by Gus's place to ask if he knew another photo shop, and this guy walked in saying he's the reason why Merle Haggard and George Jones have so much money, and the next thing you know his RV's in the river. You wouldn't believe it!"

Brenda listened. She said, "I just realized that I don't have enough grout. I need more grout. Now, sometimes they don't have it marked right, so I want you to go into Lowe's and open up the ten-pound bag of Keracolor Gray. It's supposed to be something called 'Gris Gray.' But I opened up some Gris Gray that ended up being red. Originally I thought about using red, but I looked at it and didn't like it. They got some kind of grout they call Rouge Red, but I don't want that. I want Gris Gray. I need one more ten-pound bag of Gris Gray."

Mal held the phone away from his head. Down on the riverbank, Prison Tat Pat and Windshield looked at the Winnebago. Brenda didn't seem upset that he was in the bar already. He said, "I'll get right on it. This might take some time. Gus says the next closest one-hour picture place is about thirty miles away."

"Have you got the frames yet?" Brenda asked.

"Yes. Yes, I got the frames. I went straight to the Kmart and got the frames. Noir Black, just like you said."

After he pressed the hang up button he pushed it down hard so as to turn off the phone altogether. Gus said, "It ain't called 'gris gray,' you idiot. That just means French gray, English gray. It means gray-gray. Just like 'noir black' means black-black. French black, English black."

Gus lost his reputation. Mal said, "How do you know that?"

Gus turned around and said, "I should maybe call the law. I'm thinking this guy is in some trouble we don't need to know about. One thing we need to do is be careful about not blurting out how we got those plants upriver. Last thing we need is for some hammerhead we don't know to find out about the crop."

Mal said, "It's a good thing Windshield has no memory."

They didn't think about how the camcorder still ran.

Prison Tat Pat and Windshield returned. Pat said, "That's all right. I can pull that one out of the water and get it to a mechanic and lease me another one in the meantime." He sat down and said, "Miller Lite ain't doing it for me. Do you know how to make a perfect Manhattan? You got you any cherries back there?"

Windshield said to Prison Tat Pat, "Frankie Perkins once had a girlfriend they called Cherry. I went to his funeral on Sunday, but she didn't show up there. He asked about her, though."

Pat Taft said, "You kind of remind me of Frank Sinatra, my man. One time Frank and all his boys came to Nashville, back when I lived there. Well, let me tell you, they say that Nashville cats know how to party hard, but they ain't got nothing on the old Brat Pack." Gus said nothing about the misnomer. "They was wanting to smoke some dope? And I just happened to have some with me? The next thing you know—they got Sammy Davis, Jr. to pop out his glass eye. Then old Frank took some screen and put it in the empty eye socket, you know. Then he pinched a good bowl down there. You had to hold Sammy's nose clamped and inhale from his mouth. It was the damnedest bong I ever hit in my life. Good old Sammy Davis, Jr."

Mal sat up and looked at the Winnebago. He said, "You say your ex wants to know that you can act right in front of people? I haven't ever studied up on the etiquette books, but maybe you shouldn't be telling her about smoking the marijuana." Mal looked at Gus. He gave a look that let Gus know that this was Mal's way of changing the subject.

"She was there!" Prison Tat Pat said. "Hell, man, she was there! Well, I take that back. She might've been off showing Joey Bishop and Peter Lawford Tootsie's Orchard at that point, I forget."

Gus said, "You full of shit, man. I was going to hold off, but I call bullshit on all this. You ain't much more than forty years old. Joey Bishop and Peter Lawford were long gone from the Rat Pack by the time you could've been old enough."

The bar's telephone rang. Gus stared at Prison Tat Pat. Mal said, "If that's for me, I'm not here." It rang another twenty times before stopping. "It was for me."

Pat Taft placed his right palm up. He looked back at his camcorder and said to the lens, "Tell them, honey. Tell them it's true." He drank his Manhattan—which was really only bourbon and a splash of Cheerwine mixed together—and said, "You some kind of racist? If you're some kind of racist judging me because I pinched down Sammy Davis, Jr.'s nose and intook weed from his face, then I don't want anything to do with you. It wasn't like I was kissing him."

Gus shook his head. "I'm not a racist. You might just be in the wrong place, buddy."

"Okay. As long as you ain't a racist. I handled both Charlie Pride and B.B. King at one time. Say, this is good," he said, drinking Gus's version of a Manhattan. Prison Tat Pat looked back at the camera. "Hey, I'm not slurring my speech or anything."

Mal Mardis thought, I should call up Brenda and ask her to meet me here. She could look at Prison Tat Pat and understand that living with a lottery card-scratching drunk isn't all that bad.

Pat Taft said to Gus, "You know anyone around here with a tow truck with a wench? You mind if when I pull out the RV I leave it here for a while till it dries out and I can sell it? I'll pay you rental space. I'll pay you whatever they charge at one of those RV storage places."

Gus said, "Beer's five dollars a can. The Manhattan's ten." They weren't, but they would've been in Nashville, he figured. Gus liked to memorize all the bar prices from around the nation, just in case a stranger walked in. People used to make fun of him for knowing what the going price was for a margarita in Los Angeles, a gin fizz in Detroit.

"You take credit cards?" Prison Tat Pat asked. "You got an ATM machine?"

"The answer's 'no' to all of your questions, going all the way back to the tow truck."

Gus poured a bourbon and placed it in front of Mal. He said, "Three bourbons, two beers. Your tab's six-fifty." Prison Tat Pat didn't flinch at obvious favoritism. He smiled at the bartender, then back to his camcorder.

Mal got up to go to the bathroom. Inside, he called his wife.

Windshield finally caught up with the conversation and said, "You used my head for a bong, you might get a mouthful of glass. They say I still got little chunks of glass stuck in my face."

Mal came back from the bathroom and slid his bourbon toward Prison Tat Pat. He said, "You might need this more than I do. Hey, Gus, make me some kind of vodka drink and set it in front of my seat. Brenda's on her way over and y'all need to say I didn't drink any brown liquor. I need to run over to the closest place that sells frames so it looks like at least I got that far."

Gus said, "I tell you what. Stranger from Nashville, you drinking anymore Manhattans?"

Pat Taft said, "They call me Prison Tat Pat."

"I need me either some real cherries in a jar, or a couple more bottles of Cheerwine soda, Mal. Whichever you come across first."

Mal said okay and left. He got in his pickup and made sure to keep one foot hard on the brake before getting in reverse and popping the clutch. He looked down at the bottom side of the Winnebago and thought about how it resembled a lodged metal turtle of sorts. He thought, That guy did it on purpose, so we'd all feel sorry for him.

Mal drove his truck south on Saluda Dam Road not more than two miles before coming up on a Dollar General store he'd never noticed. He went inside, brought twelve frames they had on the shelf up to the checkout, and read the cashier's nametag. It seemed misspelled. "Hey, Maime, I got a lot of pictures I need behind glass. You think y'all got any more of these things in back?"

Maime looked at Mal hard. She chewed gum. She said, "You might want buy breath mints. Cop comes in here smells you, charge for public drunk."

Mal picked some Tic Tacs off the counter. He shoved them beside his stack of frames. He said, "I know, I know. I normally don't drink this early, believe me."

"I ain't judging you none," Maime said. She picked up one frame, studied it, and yelled toward the back of the store, "Hey Rena! Rena! Go in back and see we got any more these big frames." To Mal she said, quieter, "How many you want?"

"I need another dozen."

Rena called from the back, "We got some. I know where they are."

"Fifteen more!" Maime yelled. "Not the little ones. The *noir black* ones."

Mal laughed out loud. Maime cocked her head as if to say, "I'll call the deputies on you, son." She said, "What?"

He shook his head. He stepped back and picked two sixteen-ounce bottles of Cheerwine out of the point-of-purchase soft drink cooler. He set them on the counter. Maime ran them across the electric eye and placed them in one yellow plastic Dollar General bag. Mal said, "Nothing. I'm just laughing at my own wife." He explained how she renovated rooms then put pictures up on the wall of the old room.

Maime said, "I'd like to meet her. Damn. That's a good one. Back when I lived in Rock Hill, I had me a second husband used to make a big production out of painting the bedroom about twice a year. Word was someone got shot in there before us, and Byron thought the blood still bled through. Anyways, he'd paint a different color every time he painted and always leave a little square down behind the bed to show what the last color looked like. It looked like a gotdang weird checkerboard by the time I finally had enough and moved out."

Mal tried to imagine what she talked about. Rena brought the fifteen extra frames, which he bought without correcting anyone. There would come a time, he knew, when he'd need to fill up the walk-in closet with photographs of the old walk-in closet. I'll have a head start, he thought. To Maime he said, "Where in the world is 'Raw Kill'?"

"Rock Hill's up by Charlotte. You ain't ever heard of Rock Hill?"

He shook his head. He paid in cash and said he didn't need a bag. "Raw Kill," he said on his way out of the store. "Raw Kill, Raw Kill, Raw Kill." He said, "Maim me. Maim me. Maim me. Raw Kill."

Mal was surprised to not find his wife's car parked in front of Gus. He walked in to find Rodney Sheets sitting in front of what Mal assumed was his last bourbon ordered. Mal said, "You off not do-ing chores today, Rodney?"

"Pretty much. Is this your drink? I been here ten minutes. Where'd everybody go?"

From where he sat, on the other side of the camcorder, Rod-ney couldn't see the river. Mal pointed and said, "We had a little episode earlier. This guy let his RV slip on down into the river."

Rodney got up and looked. He said, "Gus won't mind if I just keep a tally," and reached across the bar for a plastic cup. Then he walked around the bar and grabbed a quart of bourbon. He said, "No, I don't have any chores today. Wife's gone off to spend some time with her old college roommate in Chattanooga." He gri-maced to himself. Rodney didn't like to let on that his wife went to college or that he taught American literature to ESL students at one of the satellite campuses. As far as Mal or Gus knew, Rodney harvested marijuana on the banks of the Saluda in order to make ends meet, just like everyone else did.

"If you don't want strangers knowing your business," Mal said, "don't say anything in front of the camera. This old boy wants to make a film of himself for his run-off wife, or something. I might didn't catch everything he said."

Rodney walked back around the counter and turned off the camera. He said, "No problem." Then he changed barstools in order to look down at the Winnebago. Gus had his arms out-stretched. Prison Tat Pat nodded. Then they both looked down-stream before trekking uphill.

"I'm definitely going to need a tow," Pat Taft said back inside the bar. He looked at Rodney Sheets and said, "Prison Tat Pat," and stuck out his hand. "You can sit there, I guess. You won't be in the way." Pat Taft sat down to the right of Rodney. Mal thought, There are a dozen barstools here and we're sitting three together like fools.

Gus came in and said, "If it tears up my land, you're paying me some money." He handed over a cocktail napkin that he'd stolen from another bar. "Sign your name here at the bottom and I'm going to fill out an IOU if it costs me money in grass seed and whatnot," he said to Pat Taft.

"And you got it on film," Pat said, pointing his thumb to the camcorder. Mal and Rodney said nothing.

The door behind them opened, and again Mal inwardly cringed. But it was Maime. She said to Mal, "I figured you'd be here," and plopped down the two bottles of Cheerwine he'd forgotten to pick up off of the Lazy Susan plastic bag dispenser. "You forgot these. Well, I admit that I forgot them, too."

Prison Tat Pat said, "Now we're talking! Say, do you know the country superstar Jeannie C. Riley? I'm the one who talked her into changing over from bonds into goldmines. See here?" Pat showed off his knuckles.

"You off work?" Gus asked. "You want you one them rum drinks?"

Maime said, "I tell you what I want. I want me a new job. Me and Rena ain't exactly getting along so well. Me and Rena, and me and Cindy, and me and whoever the manager is today. I need me a job either waiting tables or bartending."

Mal thought, Me need some attention.

Gus said, "Well I'll keep you in mind."

"What's with the camera?" Maime said. She shook hair out of her eyes and smiled at the lens. "It ain't on, you know."

Prison Tat Pat said, "Damn. What happened?"

Rodney Sheets said, "The lights flickered in here a few minutes ago. Maybe it turned it off." No one thought about how the camera wasn't running on electricity.

"What happened to Windshield?" Mal said. "Where's Windshield? His moped's still out front."

Maime said, "Turn it on."

"Do you know that 'Harper Valley PTA' song? I'll turn it on if you sing the 'Harper Valley PTA' song," Prison Tat Pat said.

"I know that one, and I know some more," Maime said.

Mal Mardis looked out the window. He watched as Windshield emerged wet from beneath the carriage of the RV. He had a rope in his hands, and Mal knew from experience that the other end held a grappling hook Gus kept nearby in case anyone ever needed to drag the river.

When Brenda showed up, covered in grout, paint, caulk, sawdust, and glue, Maime stood in the center of Gus, her legs spread apart unnaturally, belting out "I Fall to Pieces" into Prison Tat Pat's camcorder. Mal sat at the bar smiling; he lifted his vodka tonic toward his wife. Rodney Sheets kept his back to the spectacle, and Gus looked up from behind the bar as if ready to pull out his pistol.

Windshield had looped the rope around one of the building's smooth, round pine pylons that served as supports for the back end of Gus's establishment. He tied the end to the back of his moped and revved the tiny engine, faced toward the non-submerged end of the Winnebago. Rodney Sheets said, "You might want to go downstairs and tell that old boy he's going to pull this bar off its foundation, if it works. And it *won't* work, by the way."

Gus turned around, cursed, and told Mal that he was in charge of the bar for a minute. Brenda arced around Maime and said, "I called up One-Hour Photo and the man said they haven't had problems with deliveries. He said they were open for business."

Mal got up from his barstool and went around to Gus's side. He said to his wife, "Let me fix you a little something." He raised his voice. Windshield's moped sounded like a chainsaw below.

"Okay. Fix me a triple scotch. Is that the most expensive drink there is?"

Maime finished up the song, extending the word "pieces" into a trill of about twenty syllables. She said, "I won karaoke one night doing that song."

Prison Tat Pat said, "I'mo tell you what. You stay in touch with me, and I'll get you a Nashville contract. Or at least one in Branson. I know everybody there is to know. Well, to be honest, there's one record producer we can't talk to seeing as I had him invest in a mutual fund called GUNK—they specialized in Guyana, Uganda, Nigeria, and Kenya. That didn't quite work out like some people thought it would." Prison Tat Pat turned to Brenda and said, "Well hello there."

Brenda took her triple scotch from Mal and threw it in his face. She said, "That was good. I'll have another."

They all heard Windshield yell "No!" and gathered at the counter, looked out the window. Either the rope broke or the knot untied, and Windshield rammed into the back of the half-sunken Winnebago at thirty miles an hour. Rodney Sheets said, "If this were a movie, the post would've come loose downstairs, and all of us would've fallen down to the ground. Rising action, climax, denouement. Traditional development. I guess things don't work out around this part of the South like they do in movies."

Mal poured his wife another scotch. He only poured two shots, though. "You need to pace yourself," he said, laughing. He shook booze out of his hair. Mal said, "Go ahead and throw it," but Brenda took a sip and placed the cup down. They all looked down at Windshield. He tested both arms, then felt his face. "When he comes back up here," Mal said, "let's all call him Bumper. Tailgate. I bet he won't even notice."

"Traditional development," Brenda said. "Where's the film rolls? Give me the film and I'll go get it done myself."

"I'll do it right now," Mal said. "I promise. Let me just finish this last drink and I'll do it myself." Brenda stuck out her hand. Mal fished in his pocket and handed her the rolls.

Prison Tat Pat said, "I need him here to help me get my RV out of the water."

Brenda got up. She looked at Maime and said, "You *should* go to Nashville. From what I hear, there's a lot more opportunities for karaokeists there."

Prison Tat Pat nodded. He said, "Let's all live dangerously and try to pull my RV out of the water. It'll be fun. I'll buy drinks for everyone if it works out right."

Brenda didn't respond. She walked out of the bar, got in her car, sat there a moment, then returned to Mal and his new comrades before they emerged from the bar to dislodge the Winnebago. Maime now sat at the bar next to Prison Tat Pat, the camera turned their way. Mal stood at the end of the counter, and Rodney used the bathroom. Brenda walked slowly so as not to spook her husband and said, "I might as well confess, even though I'm still mad at you for coming here."

Mal said, "What now? I'm just going to help these people, Brenda. That's it."

"Yeah, yeah, yeah. I was going to say, you didn't need to get the pictures developed anyway. I changed my mind. That gris gray grout would've stained too much. I'm going to…"

Was she going to tear up the tile and re-grout the entire project? Mal wondered. Brenda stopped in midsentence, for she overheard Prison Tat Pat's conversation. Pat was in the middle of saying, "I can't believe no herbiculturalist ain't thought of it before. But I know a man in Nashville who's right at the brink, and I'm investing all my money in him."

Brenda said, "Say all that again. Hey, man from Nashville, start your story over."

Prison Tat Pat said, "Pat Taft. They call me Prison Tat Pat." He spoke louder, obviously for the camera. "I got a good acquaintance who has developed bonsai grass. It'll grow two inches, and that's it. Never needs cutting, you know. You plant it, you water

it, it gets two inches high, and you're done. It's going to revolu-
tionize the lawn care business. Hell, once this spreads nationwide,
it'll cause enormous unemployment for people who cut grass
for a living. It'll knock out John Deere lawnmowers. Snapper.
Husqvarna. Murray push mowers. There's already a bonsai grass
out on the market, but it ain't as good as my friend's will be."

Mal Mardis sat down at the nearest barstool and dropped his
head on the linoleum. He didn't bring up how he managed the
Garden Center at Home Depot. Mal thought, It'll knock out
miniature golf courses seeing as everyone would have one on
their front yard. Eventually, it'll cause my unemployment, and
then I'll be stuck at home.

Brenda kissed him on top of his head and spit gravel out of the
parking lot, but not in an angry way, Mal understood. No, she left
excited. Already he envisioned how her next project would involve taking up entire squares of sod and replacing them. He tried
to imagine what his yard would look like with eight-by-ten photographs of the old lawn. Would Brenda nail them to the trees?
Would she balance them right on the ground? Would she obtain
and blow-up one of those satellite photographs of the housetop
and surrounding land as it is now, and maybe glue it to the front
door, the driveway, the mailbox?

When Windshield returned muddy-kneed, wet, and bruised,
Gus followed holding the grappling hook. Gus checked his bottles behind the bar and asked who'd gotten into the scotch. Mal
thought, This is how people end up making what strangers call a
rash decision. He thought, If we get that RV out of the water, I'm
getting in.

He asked for water. He said, "I need to lay off the chemicals
and sober up."

Two weeks later he'd think the same thing, once he figured
out that Prison Tat Pat viewed his own videotape, heard what Gus
and Mal had to say about their marijuana plot, then snuck back

onto the property and down the river—maybe with Maime at his side—in order to harvest their entire crop. Mal would tell Gus that maybe it was for the best. That's the way things run around here. He'd point out that if he sold off the pot, then he'd have a bunch of money. Soon thereafter he'd spend that on scratch cards, and he'd win. Winning money, as he had learned, wasn't necessarily good fortune, at least not for people like him.

WHICH ROCKS WE CHOOSE

Luckily for everyone in the family on down, the mule spoke English to my grandfather. Up until this seminal point in the development of what became Carolina Rocks, a few generations of Loopers had tried to farm worthless land that sloped from mountainside down to all branches and tributaries of the Saluda River. From what I understood, my great-great-grandfather and then his son barely grew enough corn to feed their families, much less take to market. Our land stood so desolate back then that no Looper joined the troops in the 1860s; no Looper even understood that the country underwent some type of a conflict. What I'm saying is, our stretch of sterile soil kept Loopers from needing slaves, which pretty much caused locals to label them everything from uppity to unpatriotic, from hex-ridden to slow-witted. Until the mule spoke English to my grandfather, our family crest might've portrayed a chipped plow blade, wilted sprigs, a man with a giant question mark above his head.

"Don't drown the rocks," the harnessed mule said, according to legend. It turned its head around to my teenaged grandfather, looked him in the eye just like any of the famous solid-hoofed talking equines of Hollywood. "Do not throw rocks in the river. Keep them in a pile. They shall be bought in time by those concerned with decorative landscaping, for walls and paths and flower beds."

That's what my grandfather came back from the field to tell everybody. Maybe they grew enough corn for moonshine, I don't know. My own father told me this story when I complained mightily from the age of seven on for having to work for Carolina Rocks, whether lugging, sorting, piling, or using the backhoe later. The mule's name wasn't Sisyphus, I doubt, but that's what I came to call it when I thought it necessary to explain the situation to my common law wife, Abby. I said, "If it weren't for Sisyphus, you and I would still be trying to find a crop that likes plenty of rain but no real soil to take root. We'd be experimenting every year with tobacco, rice, coffee, and cranberry farming."

Abby stared at me a good minute. She said, "What? I wasn't listening. Did you say we can't have children?"

I said, "A good mule told my grandfather to quit trying to farm, and to sell off both river rocks and field stone. That's how come we do what we do. Or at least what my grandfather and dad did what they did." This little speech occurred on the day I turned thirty-three, the day I became the same age as Jesus, the day I finally decided to go back to college. Up until this point Abby and I had lived in the Looper family house. My dad had been dead eleven years, my mom twenty. I said, "Anyway, I think the Caterpillar down on the banks is rusted up enough now for both of us to admit we're not going to continue with the business once we sell off the remaining stock."

When I took over Carolina Rocks we already had about two hundred tons of beautiful black one- to three-inch skippers dug out of the river stockpiled. I probably scooped out another few hundred tons over the next eight years. But with land developers razing both sides of the border for gated mountain golf course communities, in need of something other than mulch, there was no way I could keep up. A ton of rocks isn't the size of half a French car. Sooner or later, too, I predicted, the geniuses at the EPA would figure out that haphazardly digging out riverbeds and shorelines wouldn't be beneficial downstream. Off in other corners of our land we had giant piles of round rocks, pebbles, chunks, flagstones, and chips used for walkways, driveways, walls, and artificial spring houses. Until my thirty-third birthday, when I would make that final decision to enroll in a low-residency master's program in Southern culture studies, I would sell off what rocks we had quarried, graded, and—according to my mood—either divided into color, shape, or size.

I never really felt that the Loopers' ways of going about the river rock and field stone business incorporated what our competitors might've known in regards to supply and demand, or using time wisely.

"Can we go back to trying our chosen field?" Abby asked. She wore a pair of gray sweatpants and a Moonpie T-shirt. Both of us wore paper birthday cones on our heads. "Please say that we can send out our resumes to TV stations around the country. Hell, I'd give the news in Mississippi if it got my foot in the door."

She pronounced it "Mishishippi." She wasn't drunk. One of our professors should've taken her aside right about Journalism 101 and told her to find a new field of study, or concentrate in print media. I didn't have it in me to tell Abby that my grandfather's mule enunciated better than she did. When she wasn't helping out with the Carolina Rocks bookkeeping chores, she drove down to Greenville and led aerobics classes. I never saw her conducting a class in person, but I imagined her saying "*Shtep, shtep, shtep,*" over and over.

"It's funny that you should mention Mississippi," I said. I thought of the term "segue," from when I underwent communications studies classes as an undergraduate, usually seated right next to Abby. "I'm going to go ahead and enroll in that Southern studies program. It'll all be done by email and telephone, pretty much, and then I have to go to Mississippi for ten days in the summer and winter. Then, in a couple years, maybe I can go teach college somewhere. We can sell off this land and move to an actual city. It'll be easier for you to maybe find a job that you're interested in."

I loved my wife more than I loved finding and digging up a truckload of schist. Abby got up from the table, smiled, walked into the den and picked up a gift-wrapped box. She said, "You cannot believe how afraid I was you'd change your mind. Open it up."

I kind of hoped it was a big bottle of bourbon so we could celebrate there at the kitchen table as the sun rose. I shook it. I said, "It's as heavy as a prize-winning geode," for I compared everything to rocks. When it hailed, those ice crystals hitting the ground were either pea gravel or riprap, never golf balls like the meteorologists said.

"I'm hoping this will help you in the future. In *our* future." Abby leaned back and put her palms on the floor like some kind of contortionist. "I don't mind teaching aerobics, but I can't do that when I'm sixty. I can still report the news when I'm sixty."

Sixschtee.

I opened the box to uncover volumes one, two, and three of *The South: What Happened, How, When, and Why*. Abby said, "I don't know what else you're going to learn in a graduate course that's not already in here, but maybe it'll give you ideas."

I might've actually felt tears well up. I opened the first chapter of the third volume to find the heading "BBQ, Ticks, Cottonmouths, and Moonshine." I said, "You might be right. What's left to learn?"

———

I'm not sure how other low-residency programs in Southern culture studies work, but immediately after I sent off the online application—which only included names of references, not actual letters of recommendation—I got accepted. An hour later I paid for the first half-year with a credit card. I emailed the "registrar" asking if I needed to send copies of my undergraduate transcripts and she said that they were a trusting lot at the University of Mississippi-Taylor. She wrote back that she and the professors all believed in a person's word being his bond, and so on, and that the program probably wouldn't work out for me if I was the sort who needed everything in writing.

I called the phone number at the bottom of the pseudo letterhead but hung up when someone answered with "Taylor Grocery and Catfish." I had only wanted to say that I too ran my river rock and field stone business on promised payments, that my father and grandfather operated thusly even though the mule warned to trust nothing on two legs. And I didn't want to admit to myself or Abby that, perhaps, my low-residency degree would be on par with something like that art institute that accepts boys and girls who can draw fake pirates and cartoon deer.

A day later I received my first assignment from my lead mentor, one Dr. Theron Crowther. He asked that I buy one of his books, read the chapter on "Revising History," then set about finding people who might've remembered things differently as opposed to how the media reported the incident. He said to stick to southern themes: the assassination of Dr. Martin Luther King, for example; the sit-in at Woolworth's in Greensboro; unsuccessful and fatal attempts of unionizing cotton mills; Ole Miss's upset of Alabama. I said to Abby, "I might should stick to pulling rocks out of the river and selling them to people who like to make puzzles out of their yard. I have no clue what this guy means for me to do."

Abby looked over the email. I was to write a ten page paper and send it back within two weeks. "First off, read that chapter. It should give you some clues. That's what happened to me when I wasn't sure about a paper I wrote once on How to Interview the Criminally Insane back in college. You remember that paper? You pussied out and wrote one on How to Interview the Deaf."

I'd gotten an A on that one: I merely wrote, "To interview a deaf person, find a sign language interpreter." That was it.

Abby said, "There's this scrapbooking place next door to Feline Fitness. Come on in to work with me and I'll take you over there. Those people will have some stories to tell, I bet. Every time I go past it, these women sit around talking."

We sat on our front porch, overlooking the last three tons of river rock I'd scooped out, piled neatly as washer-dryer combos, if it matters. Below the rocks, the river surged onward, rising from thunderstorms up near Asheville. I said, "What are you talking?" I'd not heard of the new sport of scrapbooking.

"These people get together just like a quilting club, I guess. They go in the store and buy new scrapbooks, then sit there and shove pictures and mementos between the plastic pages. And they brag, from what I understand. The reason I know so much about it is, I got a couple women in my noon aerobics class who showed up early one day and went over to check out the scrapbook place. They came back saying there was a Junior Leaguer ex-Miss South Carolina in there with flipbooks of her child growing up, you know. She took a picture of her kid two or three times a day, so you can flip the pictures and see the girl grow up in about five minutes."

I got up, walked off the porch, crawled beneath the house a few feet, and pulled out a bottle of bourbon I kept there hidden away for times when I needed to think—which wasn't often in the river rock business. When I rejoined my wife she'd already gotten two jelly jars out of the cupboard. "There's a whole damn business in scrapbooks? Who thought that up? America," I said. "Forget the South being fucked up. America."

"You can buy cloth-covered ones, and puffy-covered ones, and ones with your favorite team's mascot on the cover. There are black ones for funeral pictures, and white ones for weddings. There are ones that are shaped like Santa Claus, the Easter bunny, dogs, cats, cars, and Jesus. They've even got scented scrapbooks." Abby slugged down a good shot of Jim Beam and tilted her glass my way for more. "Not that I've been in Scraphappy! very often, but they've got one that looks like skin with tattoos and everything, shaped like an hourglass, little tiny blond hairs coming off of it. It's for guys to put their bachelor party pictures inside."

I didn't ask her if it smelled like anything. I said, "I wonder if they have any bullet-riddled gray flannel scrapbooks for pictures of dead Confederate relatives." I tried to imagine other scrapbooks, but couldn't think of any. "When's your next class?"

We drove down the mountain on the next morning, a Wednesday, so Abby could lead a beginner aerobics class. Wednesdays might as well be called "little Sunday" on a Southern calendar, for small-town banks and businesses close at noon in order for employees to ready themselves for Wednesday night church services. Sunday, Monday, Tuesday, little Sunday, Thursday, Friday, Saturday—like that. My common-law wife took me into Scraphappy!, looked at a wall of stickers, then said, "I'll be back a little after noon, unless someone needs personal training." She didn't kiss me on the cheek. She looked over at six women sitting in a circle, all of whom I estimated to be in their mid to late thirties.

"Could I help you with anything?" the owner asked me. She wore a nametag that read Knox—the last name of one of the richer families in the area. In kind of a patronizing voice she said, "Did you forget to pack up your snapshots this morning?"

The other women kept turning cellophane-covered pages. One of them said, "Pretty soon I'll have to get a scrapbook dedicated to every room in the house. What a complete freak-up."

I had kind of turned my head toward the stickers displayed on the wall—blue smiling babies, pink smiling babies, a slew of elephants, Raggedy Anns and Andys, mobiles, choo-choo trains, ponies, teddy bears, prom dresses, the president's face staring vacantly—but jerked my neck back around at hearing "freak-up." I thought to myself, Remember that you're here to gather revisionist history. You want to impress your professor at Ole Miss-Taylor.

But then I started daydreaming about Frances Bavier, the actress who played Aunt Bee on *The Andy Griffith Show*. I said, "Oh. Oh, I didn't come here to play scrapbook. My name's Stet Looper and I'm enrolled in a Southern studies graduate program, and I came here to see if y'all wouldn't mind answering some questions about historical events that happened around here. Or around anywhere." I cleared my throat. The women in the circle looked at me as if I walked in wearing a seersucker suit after Labor Day.

Knox the woman said, "Southern studies? My husband has this ne'er-do-well cousin who has a daughter going to one of those all-girls schools up north. Hollins, I believe. She's majoring in women's studies." In a lower voice she said, "She appears not to like men, if you know what I mean—she snubbed us all by not coming out this last season at the Poinsett Club. Anyway, she's studying for that degree with an emphasis in women's economics, and I told her daddy that it usually didn't take four years learning how to make a proper grocery list."

I was glad I didn't say that. I'd've been shot for saying that, I figured. The same woman who almost-cursed earlier held up a photograph to her colleagues and said, "Look at that one. He said he knew how to paint the baseboard."

I said, "Anyway, I have a deadline, and I was wondering if I could ask if y'all could tell me about an event that occurred during your lifetime, something that made you view the world differently than how you had understood it before. Kind of like the Cuban Missile Crisis, but more local, you know."

"Hey, Knox, could you hand me one them calligraphy stick-ons says 'I Told You So'? I guess I need to find me a stamp that says 'Loser,'" one of the women said. To me she said, "My husband always accuses me of being a germaphobe." She held up her opened scrapbook for me to see. It looked as though she'd wiped her butt on the pages. "This is my collection of used moist tow-elettes. I put them in here to remember the nice restaurants we've gone to, and sometimes if the waitress gave me extras I put the new one in there, too. But even better, he and I one time went on a camping trip that I didn't want to go on, and as it ended up we got lost. Luckily for Wells, we only had to follow my trail of Wet-Naps back to the parking lot. I don't mind bragging that that trip was all it took for him to buy us a vacation home down on Pawleys Island."

I wished that I'd've thought to bring a tape recorder. I said, "That's a great story," even though I didn't ever see it as being a chapter in some kind of Southern culture textbook. I said, "Okay. Do any of y'all do aerobics? My wife's next door teaching aero-bics, if y'all are interested. From what I understand, she's tough, but not too tough." Inside my head I heard my inner voice going, Okay none of these women are interested in aerobics classes so shut up and get out of here before you say something more stupid and somehow get yourself in trouble.

I stood there like a fool for a few seconds. The woman who complained about her baseboard starting flipping through pages, saying, "Look at them. Every one of them." Then she went on to explain to a woman who must not've been a regular, "I keep a scrapbook of every time my husband messes up. This scrapbook's the bad home repair one—he tries to fix something, then it costs us double to get a professional in to do the job. I got another book filled with bad checks got sent back, and newspaper clippings for when he got arrested and published in the police blotter. I even got ahold of some his mug shots."

It was like standing next to a whipping post. I said, "Okay, I'm sorry to take up any of your time." The place should've been called *Strap*happy, I thought.

As I opened the door, though, I heard a different voice, a woman who'd only concentrated on her own book of humiliation up until this point. She said, "Do you mean like if you know somebody got lynched, but it all got hush-hushed even though everyone around knew the truth?"

Everyone went quiet. You could've heard an opened ink pad evaporate.

I pulled up one of those half-stepladder/half-stool things. I said, "Say that all again, slower."

Her name was Gayle Ann Gunter. Her daddy owned a car lot, and her grandfather owned it before him, and the great-grandfather started the entire operation back when selling horseshoes and tack still made up half of his business. She worked on a scrapbook that involved one-by-two-inch school pictures that grade schoolers hand over to one another, and she had them under headings like "Uglier than Me," "Poorer than Me," "Dumber than Me," as God is my witness. She said, "We're having our twentieth high school reunion in a few months and I want to make sure I have the names right. It's important in this world to greet old acquaintances properly."

I said, "I'm no genius, but it should be 'Dumber than I.' It's a long, convoluted grammar lesson I learned back in college the first time."

The other women laughed. They said "Ha ha ha ha ha" in unison, and in a weird, seemingly practiced, cadence. Knox said,

"One of the things that keeps me in business is people messing up
their scrapbooks and having to start over. I had one woman who
misspelled her new daughter-in-law throughout, the first time.
She got it right when her son got a divorce, though."

"This was up in Travelers Rest," Gayle Ann said. She kept
her scrapbook atop her lap and spoke as if addressing the air-
conditioning vent. "I couldn't have been more than eight, nine
years old. These two black brothers went missing, but no one
made a federal case out of it, you know. This was about 1970. They
hadn't integrated the schools just yet, I don't believe. I don't even
know if it made the paper, and I haven't ever seen the episode on
one of those shows about long-since missing people. Willie and
Archie Lagroon. No one thought about it much because, first off,
a lot of teenage boys ran away back then. Maybe 'cause of Vietnam, I guess. And then again, they wasn't white."

I took notes in a professional-looking memo pad. I didn't even
look up, and I didn't offer another grammar lesson involving subjects and verbs. For some reason one of the women in the circle
said, "My name's Shaw Haynesworth. Gayle Ann, I thought you
were born in 1970. My name's Shaw Haynesworth, if you need to
have footnotes and a bibliogeography."

I wrote that down, too. Gayle Ann Gunter didn't respond. She
said, "I haven't thought about this in years. It's sad. About four
years after those boys went missing, a hunter found a bunch of
bones right there about twenty feet off of Old Dacusville Road.
My daddy told me all about it. They found all these rib bones
kind of strewn around, and more than likely it was those two boys.
This was all before DNA, of course. The coroner—or someone
working for the state—finally said that they were beef and pork
ribs people had thrown out their car windows. They said that
people went to the Dacusville Smokehouse and couldn't make
it all the way back home before tearing into a rack of ribs, and
that they threw them out the window, and somehow all those

ribs landed in one big pile over the years." She made a motorboat noise with her mouth. "I'm no expert when it comes to probability or beyond a reasonable doubt, but looking back on it now, I smell lynching. Is that the kind of story you're looking for?"

Abby walked in sweating, hair pulled back, wearing an outfit that made her look like she just finished the Tour de France. She said, "Hey, Stet, I might be another hour. Phyllis wants me to fill in for her. Are you okay?"

The women scrapbookers looked up at my wife as if she zoomed in from cable television. I said, "We have a winner!" for some reason.

"You can come over and sit in the lobby if you finish up early." To the women she said, "We're having a special next door if y'all want to join an aerobics class. Twenty dollars a month." I turned to see the women all look down at their scrapbooks.

Knox said, "I believe I can say for sure that we burn up enough calories running around all day for our kids. Speaking of which, I brought some doughnuts in!"

I looked at Abby. I nodded. She kind of made a what're-you-up-to? face and backed out. I said, "Okay. Yes, Gayle Ann, that's exactly the kind of story I'm looking for—about something that happened, but people saw it differently. How sure are you that those bones were the skeletal remains of the two boys?"

A woman working on a giant scrapbook of her two Pomeranians said, "They do have good barbecue at Dacusville Smokehouse. I know I've not been able to make it home without breaking into the Styrofoam boxes. Hey, do any of y'all know why it's not good to give a dog pork bones? Is that an old wives' tale, or what? I keep forgetting to ask my vet."

And then they were off talking about everything else. I felt it necessary to purchase something from Knox, so I picked out a rubber stamp that read "Unbelievable!"

I'm not ashamed to admit that, while walking between Scrap-happy! and Feline Fitness, I envisioned not only a big A on my first Southern studies low-residency graduate-level class at Ole Miss-Taylor, but a consultant's fee when this rib-bone story got picked up by one of those TV programs specializing in wrong-doing mysteries, cold cases, and voices from the dead.

Since I wouldn't meet Dr. Theron Crowther until the entire graduate class got together for ten days in December, I didn't know if he was a liar or prankster. I'd dealt with both types before, of course, in the river rock business. Pranksters came back and said that my stones crumbled up during winter's first freeze, and liars sent checks for half-tons, saying I used cheating scales. After talking to the women of Scraphappy!, I sent Dr. Crowther an email detailing the revisionist history I'd gathered. He wrote back to me, "You fool! Have you ever encountered a little something called 'rural legend'? Let me say right now that you will not make it in the mean world of Southern culture studies if you fall for every made-up tale that rumbles down the trace. Now go out there and show me how regular people view things differently than how they probably really happened."

First off, I thought that I'd done that. I was never the kind of student who whined and complained when a professor didn't cotton to my way of thinking. Back when I was forced to un-dergo a required course called Broadcast Station Management I wrote a comparison-contrast paper about the management styles of WKRP in Cincinnati and WJM in Minneapolis. The profes-sor said that it wasn't a good idea to write about fictitious ra-dio- and television-based situation comedies. Personally, I figured the management philosophies must've been spectacular, seeing as both programs consistently won Nielsen battles, then went on into syndication. The professor—who ended up, from what

I understand, having to resign his position after getting caught filming himself having sex with a freshman boy on the made-up set for an elective course in Local Morning Shows, using a fake potted plant and microphone as props—said I needed to forget about television programs when dealing with television programs, which made no sense to me at the time. I never understood what he meant until, after graduation, running my family's business ineffectively and on a reading jag, I sat down by the river and read *The Art of War* by Sun Tzu and *Being and Nothingness* by Sartre.

I said to Abby, "My mentor at Ole Miss-Taylor says that's a made-up story about black kids and rib bones. He says it's like those vacation photos down in Jamaica with the toothbrush, or the big dog that chases a ball out the window of a high-rise in New York."

Abby came out from beneath our front porch, the half-bottle of bourbon in her grasp. She said, "Of course he says that. Now he's going to come down here and interview about a thousand people so he can publish the book himself. That's what those guys do, Stet. Hey, I got an idea—why don't you write about how you fell off a turnip truck. How you got some kind of medical problem that makes you wet behind the ears always."

I stared down at the river and tried to imagine how rocks still languished there below the roiling surface. "I guess I can run over to that barbecue shack and ask them what they know about it."

"I guess you can invest in carbon paper and slide rulers in case this computer technology phase proves to be a fad."

All good barbecue stands only open on the weekend, Thursday through Saturday at most.

I got out a regional telephone directory, found the address, got directions off the Internet, then drove around uselessly for a few hours, circling, until I happened to see a white plume of smoke different than most of the black ones caused by people burning tires in front of their trailers. I walked in—this time with one of the handheld tape recorders the bank was giving away for opening a CD, I guess so people can record their last words before committing suicide, something like "One half of one fucking percent interest?"—and dealt with all the locals turning around, staring, wondering aloud who my kin might be. I said, loudly, "Hey—how y'all doing this fine evening?" like I owned the place. Everyone turned back to their piled paper plates of minced pork and cole slaw.

At the counter a short man with pointy sideburns and a curled up felt cowboy hat said, "We out of sweet potato casserole." A fly buzzed around his cash register.

"I'll take two," I looked up at the menu board behind him, "Hog-o-Mighty sandwiches."

"Here or to go?"

"And a sweet tea. You don't serve beer by any chance, do you?"

"No, sir. Family-orientated," he said. He wore an apron that read "Cook."

I said, "I understand. I'm Stet Looper, up from around north of here."

An eavesdropper behind me said, "I tode you."

"By north of here I mean just near the state line. I'll eat them here. Anyway, my wife introduced me to a woman who told me a wild story about two young boys being missing some thirty-odd years back, and a pile of bones the state investigators said came from here. Do you know this story?" I mentioned Abby because any single male strangers are, in the sloppy dialect of the locals, "quiz."

"My name's Cook," the cook said. "Raymus Cook. Y'all hear that? Fellow wants to know if I heard about them missing boys back then. Can you believe that?" To me he said, "You the second person today to ask. Some fellow from down Mississippi called earlier asking if it was some kind of made-up story."

I thought, Goddamn parasite Theron Crowther. "I'll be doggone," I said. "What'd you tell him?"

"That'll be five and a quarter, counting tax." Raymus Cook handed over two sandwiches on a paper plate and took my money. "I told him my daddy'd be the one to talk to, but Daddy's been dead eight years. I told him what I believed—that somebody paid somebody, and that those boys' families will never rest in peace."

People from two tables got up from the seats, shot Raymus Cook mean looks, and left the premises. One of them said, "We been through this enough. I'mo take my bidness to Ola's now on."

Raymus Cook held his head back somewhat and called out, "This ain't the world it used to be. You just can't go decide to secede every other minute things don't turn out like you want them." At this precise moment I knew that, later in life, I would regale friends and colleagues alike about how I "stumbled upon" something. Raymus Cook turned his head halfway to the open kitchen and said, "Ain't that right, Ms. Hattie?"

A black woman stuck her face my way and said, "Datboutright, huh-huh," just like that, fast, as if she waited to say her lines all night long.

"You can't cook barbecue correct without the touch of a black woman's hands," Raymus said to me in not much more than a whisper. "All these chains got white people smoking out back. Won't work, I'll be the first to admit."

I thought, Fuck, this is going to turn out to be just another one of those stories that've bloated the South for 150 years. I didn't want that to happen. I said, "I'm starting a master's degree on Southern culture, and I need to write a paper on something that happened a while back that maybe ain't right. You got any stories you could help me out with?"

I sat down at the first table and unwrapped a sandwich. I got up and poured my own tea. Raymus Cook smiled. He picked up a flyswatter and nailed his prey. "Southern culture?" He laughed. "I don't know that much about Southern culture, even though I got raised right here." To a family off in the corner he yelled, "Y'all want any sweet potato casserole?" Back to me he said, "That's one big piece of flypaper hanging, Southern culture. It might be best to accidentally graze a wing to it every once in a while, but mostly buzz around."

I said, of course, "Man, that's a nice analogy." I tried to think up one to match him, something about river rocks. I couldn't.

"Wait a minute," Raymus Cook said. "I might be thinking about Southern literature. Like Faulkner. Is that what you're talking about?"

I thought, This guy's going to help me get through my thesis one day. "Hey, can I get a large rack of ribs to go? I'll get a large rack and a small rack." I looked up at the menu board. I said, "Can I get a 'Willie' and an 'Archie'?"

It took me a minute to remember those two poor black kids' names. I thought, This isn't funny, and took off out of there as soon as Raymus Cook turned around to tell Miss Hattie what he needed. I remembered that I forgot to turn on the tape recorder.

On my drive back home I wondered if there were any low-residency writing programs where I could learn how to finish a detective novel.

I told my sort-of wife the entire event and handed her half a Hog-o-Mighty sandwich. She didn't gape her mouth or shake her head. "You want to get into Southern studies, you better prepare yourself for such. There are going to be worse stories."

Wershtoreesh. I said, "I don't want to collect war stories."

"You know what I said. And I don't know why you don't ask me. Here's a true story about a true story gone false: This woman in my advanced cardio class—this involves spinning, Pilates, steps, and treadmill inside a sauna—once weighed 220 pounds. She's five-two. Now she weighs a hundred, maybe one-o-five at the most. She's twenty-eight years old and just started college at one of the tech schools. She wants to be a dental hygienist."

We sat on the porch, looking down at the river. Our bottle was empty. On the railing I had *The South: What Happened, How, When, and Why* opened to a chapter on a sect of people in eastern Tennessee called "Slopeheads," which might've been politically incorrect. I said, "She should be a dietician. They got culinary courses there now. She should become an elementary-school chef, you know, to teach kids how to quit eating pizza and pimento cheese burgers."

"Listen. Do you know what happened to her? Do you know how and why and when she lost all that weight?"

I said, "She saw one of those Before and After programs on afternoon TV. She sat there with a bowl of potato chips on her belly watching Oprah, and God spoke to her." I said, "Anorexia and bulimia, which come before and after 'arson' in some books."

"Her daddy died." Abby got up and closed my textbook for no apparent reason. "Figure it out, Stet. Her daddy died. She *said* she got so depressed that she quit eating. But in reality, she had made herself obese so he'd quit creeping into her bedroom ages of twelve and twenty-two. Her mother had left the household long before, and there she was. So she fattened up, and slept on her stomach. When her father died she didn't tell anyone what had been going on. But when all the neighbors met after the funeral to eat, she didn't touch one dish. Not even the macaroni and cheese."

I said, "I don't want to know about these kinds of things." I got up and walked down toward the river. Abby followed behind me. "Those my-daddy-loved-me stories are the ones I'm trying to stay away from. It's what people expect out of this area."

When we got to the backhoe she climbed up and reached beneath the seat. She pulled out an unopened bottle of rum I had either forgotten or didn't know about. "There were pirates in the South. You could write about pirates and their influences on the South. How pirates stole things that weren't theirs."

I picked up a nice skipper and flung it out toward an unnatural sandbar. Then I walked up to my knees into the water, reached down, and pulled two more out. An hour later, I had enough rocks piled up to cover a grave.

OPERATION

The Department of Social Services caseworker appeared at our door unannounced, like my uncle predicted. We'd already gone over what answers might work best when confronted by a government agency bureaucrat highly inured to vitamin B, C, and D deficiencies, head lice, rotten teeth, and lash marks, not to mention a child drooling while he sabotaged alphabet memorization. I was to use the term "sir" or "ma'am," though I called my uncle plain Cush all the time. When asked about my parents' whereabouts, I'd been tutored not to mention anything about how my father may have killed a racist and then absconded to one of the lesser-known islands located between Puerto Rico and Venezuela. I could choose from "They're on business trying to sell barbed wire for the business" or "They're dead." If asked about how come I got homeschooled, I'd been prompted to admit that it wasn't my parents' idea, that I had a problem way back in first-through-fifth grade beating up other kids on a whim, and that my teachers and classmates' parents worried over school violence. We did not have a name for Asperger Syndrome in the late seventies/early eighties. And, to be honest, I liked only to

punch people who said stupid things regarding race relations, caf-
eteria food, TV shows that involved characters with IQs less than
100, bad pop music, anti-union thought, people who thought pro
wrestling wasn't a hoax, gun worshipping, and another hundred
things. I didn't possess a syndrome-to-be-named-later. Something
about rattail haircuts set me off, it seemed. Mean, angry, nonplussed, committed kid—that was all—when it came to me.

"You're going to want to use some them big words like 'inured' and 'absconded' and 'nonplussed,' I know," Cush said to me
not two weeks before the caseworker showed up uninvited. "You
can't use them kinds a words around a person with a bachelor's
degree in the sociology. I mean it. You gone have to talk stupid."
He pulled his Fu Manchuu out at forty-five degree angles so that
it looked like a hirsute caret pointing toward his nostrils, as if a
copy editor wanted to delete his nose in order to add a word or
phrase like "Stop" or "Not now."

This conversation took place in the middle of the night as we
snipped somebody's perfectly good barbed wire in hopes of their
calling us up later to help them out with new fencing. After my
father and mother left, that's what we did. It came off more as an
adventure than an act of meanness. We ran Southern Barbed on
our own terms. Plus, Uncle Cush kept saying things like "You will
understand later" and "We need some money for what's going to
happen" and "Goddamn America ain't what it used to be." He
said things like "Jesus L. Christ do you know how much I miss
Fenfang Yang back in the Vietnam area, the best woman of the
universe?" and "You're only fourteen or fifteen."

I didn't answer much back at him. On one occasion I said,
"Stretching wire can become debilitating."

He nodded and said, "Hey, if a caseworker shows up, don't use
the word 'debilitating,' or that other word you keep using."

I said, "Child labor?"

"Hirsute," he said. "And don't mention child labor, either, goddamn it, unless you want me to quit buying you good used textbooks so you can learn more than anyone else your age."

The Department of Social Services woman showed up at eleven o'clock in the morning, right when I would've been taking the mandatory seventh-grade class in South Carolina history had I gone to Poke Middle. She was an albino whitish woman, as opposed to an albino African-American. It was hard not to stare at her, what with the nearly opaque skin, naturally platinum hair, and oversized sunglasses normally seen on elderly people exiting an ophthalmologist's office. In the past, Uncle Cush had made a point of introducing me to one-armed men, limpers, the overly obese, and tracheotomy victims so that I would never feel sorry for myself, but he'd forgotten to throw an albino into the mix. Fuck, I'd seen white rabbits with more suntan lines than this particular functionary.

I opened the door and didn't laugh or jump. I said, "Hello."

"Are you Saint Arthur Waddell? I'm looking for Saint Arthur Waddell. Could you tell Saint Arthur Waddell that Ms. Perkins from DSS is here to ask him a few questions?"

I said, "I had a feeling," because it all came back to me about my uncle's vision. I said slowly, "Me Saint Arthur. Me go by plain 'Start,' as in the beginning of 'Saint,' and the beginning of 'Arthur.'" I opened the door and half-fanned my arm for her to enter.

Ms. Perkins said, "Thank you, Start! My, what a grown-up looking young man you are!"

I wanted to see her pink eyes, of course. I'd read about pink-eyed albinos, who preferred to be called "Pigment Challenged." I said, "Come on in and sit down at the kitchen table," but wondered if the term "PC" came from "Pigment Challenged." It should've. That would've made sense.

Uncle Cush came stomping in from the den. Understand that this was the house where I grew up and the house where Cush and my father grew up. Up until my parents left, Cush lived on some land up the hill, behind the Quonset huts where we kept rolls of barbed wire. After my parents took off he moved in to take care of me. It didn't matter. He said, "Hey," to the DSS worker.

Ms. Perkins said, "Hello! Are you Saint Arthur's father?"

My uncle paused for what became, later, an uncomfortable, telling moment for me. He said, "No. Cush Waddell. Favorite uncle."

Ms. Perkins wrote something in her ledger. For what it's worth, she wore a paisley outfit consisting of mostly greens and purples, which—against her translucent skin—looked like amoebas on a vertical Petri dish. She said all that stuff about where she worked, then, "We been asked to come by check on some things."

My uncle nodded. He said, "I understand." He didn't look at me, but I could feel his thoughts going *This is what I was talking about that night when we clipped people's barbed wire so they'd have to order more.* I could feel him thinking *You don't want to live in a foster home, now, do you, boy?* My uncle said, "You want me in or out the room?"

"We ain't accusing no one of nothing," Ms. Perkins said. I looked at her neck and thought about a cave salamander I'd seen once time on ETV. She shuffled into the kitchen and sat down. I wondered if she normally used a cane, a walker, or had someone lift her elbow this way and that.

I was fourteen years old and had been out of the normal school system more than a couple years. My uncle had attended to me less than eighteen months, though it seemed like a lifetime what with his aphorisms, insults, predictions, demands, expectations, and tall tales about Vietnam that probably weren't true. I said, "Guilt has very quick ears to an accusation," which came from

Henry Fielding. I could've gotten thrown into a foster home, I thought, for having to read *Tom Jones*.

Uncle Cush said, "Sit down and make yourself at home. You want any sweet tea? Pulled pork sandwich with or without cole slaw on top of it?"

I sat down. I readied myself. I tried to remember everything my uncle told me to say. Ms Perkins kept her shades on and said No to my uncle, then to me said, "We're just going to go through what the average student should know at your age, at least around here. Can you tell me what six times six equals?"

Man, I didn't wait. I didn't pause. I said, "What is thirty-six!" as if I were on that game show. Ms. Perkins nodded and marked her ledger. She said, "Can you name me five colors?"

"Well," I said, "the primary colors are red, green, and blue. Then there are a bunch of secondary and tertiary colors. Orange, for example, and..."

"Five colors," she said.

"Okay, those primary ones, plus orange, yellow, azure, magenta, purple..."

"Okay," Ms. Perkins said.

My uncle opened up the refrigerator—mistake—and pulled out a can of Budweiser. He said, "My favorite color might be one y'all ain't mentioned yet." He said, "I know I'm not supposed to help out."

Ms. Perkins said, "Very good. Very good Saint Arthur! You know your math and your colors!"

"You knew ahead of time I wasn't the daddy. Was it old Matthew Foy who told y'all on me for taking over Start's upbringing?" Uncle Cush blurted out. "Was it Junie Teter? I'mo tell you one thing—ain't nobody bringing up a better boy than I'm doing right now, goddamn it."

I looked at Ms. Perkins the best I could and said, "One hundred forty-four times ninety nine equals 14,256." I said, "Give me one. Ten thousand divided by pi equals 3,183—check it out."

My uncle said, "Hey, did me and you go to school together? I used to pull down the fire alarm thing, you know, and then when everyone went off into the playground, me and this girl would screw on the teacher's desk. I'm talking like twice a week. Was that you? Did you go to Poke Elementary, third grade?"

Ms. Perkins shook her head No and smiled. I could tell that she didn't like my uncle's Fu Manchu. She said to me, "Are you taking any foreign languages? In the seventh grade you should be taking Spanish I or French I."

I said, "Here's my favorite Bush poem, from the Bush people in Zimbabwe."

I started clicking and clucking like no one's business, only because Uncle Cush taught me how to do so, seeing as how I hadn't actually taken any courses in Spanish or French. I went all "Dok dok dok dok-dok dok-dok dok dok dok/dok dok dok dok dok dok dok dok dok/dok, dok dok-dok dok dok-dok dok dok dok," with appropriate facial expressions. I said, "Not only is it Bush, but it follows the same meter as that famous Dylan Thomas poem. How about that?"

My uncle started clapping. Ms. Perkins shook her head twice and wrote down a note.

Not to brag, but when Ms. Perkins came over, according to Uncle Cush, I read on a twenty-ninth grade level. Before my parents took off, they'd attended to my reading the classics—Plato to Faulkner—but then when Cush showed up, and we rifled through the used textbooks at a number of college and university bookstores, I became proficient in the weird shit: Salinger, Cheever, Pynchon, Barth, Barthelme, Exley, Gass, Gaddis, and those others. I didn't finish everything put before me, sure, but I probably had a better grasp of, say, Carlos Fuentes, than anyone teaching

English or Spanish in Poke, South Carolina. Because I wasn't but fourteen, I never thought to ask, "Hey, Cush, how can a high school graduate and Vietnam War veteran such as yourself know so much about what direction in which to point me?" I guess I figured that every human being one generation older than I— unless they were good-hearted social workers—read four or five hours a day growing up, seeing as the sitcoms of the day offered little in regards to humanist, secular thinking and outright hilarity when it came to human suffering, except for maybe *The Andy Griffith Show* and *Gomer Pyle. Gilligan's Island. I Dream of Jeannie. The Beverly* fucking *Hillbillies.*

My parents had me listen to Beethoven, Mozart, and Shostakovich, whereas Cush turned me on to the Sex Pistols, the Clash, Patti Smith, Richard Hell and the Voidoids, plus more-normal Neil Young.

I read literature, and history, listened to music, and knew enough math to figure out my checkbook, in what should've been my seventh-grade year. I understood that one of my state's previous senators beat somebody with a cane in the Senate chambers.

But I didn't know *biology*. I didn't know science worth a shit. You'd think that I spawned from a tribe of holy-roller, anti-evolution fundamentalists.

Because my uncle foresaw questions and/or developments in advance—for all I knew he'd already predicted this particular social worker's next maneuver some years ago—he said, "Hey, let's jump right over to biology. Let me get out the Operation game."

Listen, it didn't take biology acumen to succeed in the Milton-Bradley game of skill, Operation. It took steady hands. The world's best biologist in the world—let's say Lewis Thomas, at the time— would've failed miserably at Operation, what with Dr. Thomas's probable digital shakiness. Dr. Stephen Hawking? The world's worst Operation player. High-stakes Las Vegas poker players might not know the difference between a spleen and a freckle, but by God they can play some fucking Operation.

Cush left me there with Ms. Perkins. He went looking for the game, which we'd played about nightly for a month in the upstairs room that had the most unstable flooring, which made it that much more difficult to perform a successful extraction without touching the sides and killing the patient.

Ms. Perkins whispered, "If I bring out a doll, can you show me where your uncle's touched you?"

I nodded and whispered back, "I don't need a doll. I can show you right here," and took my left index finger to point at my right palm. "Sometimes when I make him proud, he shakes my hand."

My uncle walked into the room with Cavity Sam and said, "You ain't asked, but I'll be the *fifth* person to admit I don't take care of myself. First there's good George Francis, the Lebanese liquor store owner. He'll say I partake of too much bourbon. Then that girl Patsy, or Patty, or Bonnie over at Poke Sack 'n' Go, where I buy my Winstons. You know we're in the barbed-wire fence business here, and we're up against these goddamn fancy rock fence people—and my main business enemy is this guy Looper up at Carolina Rocks who wants me to die so he can talk people from wire to rock easier. He's number three. He's always sending me moonshine and questionable baloney. Start here works as person number four, telling me to eat more vegetables and stay away from sausage. And then there's me. But by God I make sure Start doesn't drink, smoke, or eat sausage."

Ms. Perkins probably stared hard at Uncle Cush, but I couldn't tell what with her sunglasses. She said, "Are y'all from around here originally?"

My uncle set down the game. He said, "I just put in brand new triple-A batteries in this thing, so watch out. Old Cavity Sam's nose might light up just from the tweezers getting *close* to the edges."

I said, "I can sing you a bunch of body organs to the opening tune of the National Anthem, if you'd rather I do that. Listen to this: Co-lon sto-mach spleen! Lungs, heart skin kidney, brain!" I said, "Uncle Cush taught me how to list off the bones to the tune of one of those other famous songs."

Ms. Perkins rotated her head in tiny circles, looking downward to Operation. She said, "I'm not very good when it comes to eye-hand coordination. As y'all have probably noticed, I possess albinism. Did y'all recognize it right away?"

I didn't know what to say, because, probably, I was fourteen years old. By that time I'd met little people, about a dozen men who put pistols toward their heads and either shot out an eyeball or lost a lower jaw but still lived, a hydrocephalic, some microcephalics—we still called them waterheads and pinheads, even though it probably wasn't right—and a number of cross-eyed and cock-eyed people. I'd dealt with the blind, the deaf, the deaf-and-blind, and one time saw a woman at Poke's All Bowed Up archery shop who was born without elbows. No albinos, though.

"Pick up those electronic tweezers, Start, and pick you out whatever you need. This is biology in its most meaningful and basic form!"

I said to the DSS caseworker, "This isn't how it's played. Usually there are two sets of cards—Specialist cards and Doctor cards. We used to have those things, but we played outside one time and the wind blew them away." This wasn't the truth. I beat Uncle Cush one night and he took the cards and threw them into our woodstove. I said, "I think I'll go for Writer's Cramp" and successfully pulled out the pencil stuck in the middle of Cavity Sam's forearm.

My uncle said, "Good man!" and shook my hand. He said to Ms. Perkins, "Pick you whatever you want."

She had her head down close to the board—like an inch away. She had the tweezers up against her temple, nearly tangling in her orange hair. She said, "I'm going for Wish Bone!" and immediately stuck the tweezers on Sam's red nose, then scraped her way all over the board, from Adam's Apple to Broken Heart to Wrenched Ankle. She zapped Butterflies in the Stomach, and Charley Horse, and Wish Bone, and Spare Ribs. At least that's how I remember it. I know that we couldn't play anymore because the red nose flashed so many times successfully that the brand-new batteries gave out.

"I'm better at some other games," Ms. Perkins said. "I can bowl, for example, if it's at night." She said, "Look, you seem fine, Start. This was a waste of my time, and yours."

For some reason my uncle decided to say at this point, "They ought to've put a pelvic bone in this game. One time I was traveling alone over in Laos and I kind of, you know, made an impression on this little woman. Well, you know how those Asian women tend to be skinny and all. You can't barely even tell when one them's pregnant! Anyway, I was going down on her right well thinking, 'This is the hairiest quim ever,' but as it ended up, this little thing gave birth *at that very moment*, and I was licking her newborn's *head*. Goddamn. That was something."

Ms. Perkins opened up her mouth but no noise emitted from her throat. I stared hard, wondering if she might look like a cottonmouth behind her molars, incisors, and bicuspids—I might not've known anything about biology, but I knew some shit about dentistry, probably because I'd read both *Jaws* and *Marathon Man*. She said, "Mr. Waddell!" like that, all alarm and disgust.

I said, "Cush. Come on. Tell her you're kidding." To Ms. Perkins I said, "I apologize for my uncle."

"What I'm doing is this," Uncle Cush said, picking up the Operation game and standing up. "I'm showing that to know appropriate behavior, one must know inappropriate behavior. That's what I'm showing young nephew Start here. See? He'll now know not to go out into a public venue or job interview and say such egregious blasphemy."

I stuck my hand out to shake. I'd taught him both "egregious" and "blasphemy," though I sometimes didn't think he listened to me. To Ms. Perkins I said, "It's true. It's straight out of one of the either late-nineteenth-century or early-twentieth-century philosophers. It's either from Bertrand Russell or Ludwig Wittgenstein."

Ms. Perkins wrote down something on her chart. She said, "You two are a couple of japers, aren't you? Ha ha. You got me there, Mr. Waddell. Do you mind if I call you plain Cush? I'm sorry, but I should've introduced myself as Carlotte. I'm Carlotte Perkins. Please feel free to call me Carlotte."

Later on, Uncle Cush—I think we were driving to a literacy association's used-book sale so he could pick up a selection of biographies on major American industrialists—told me that it was at the moment Ms. Perkins asked if we japed people that he knew she needed a man like him. At the time, though, there at the kitchen table with the image of a newborn Asian child emerging into a war-torn country, I could think only of various members of the animal kingdom licking afterbirth.

"Like Charlotte without the H?" Cush said. "Carlotte. H is the eighth letter of the alphabet. You know what that means, don't you?"

Carlotte Perkins either nodded or trembled. She said, "Is it my denomination, or is it hot in here?"

Ms. Perkins fanned her neck with the clipboard she carried. I looked at my uncle and could tell that he wasn't going to stop. He would test this poor bureaucratic woman, fragile pigment or not. I'd seen it enough, before and after my parents "disappeared." Uncle Cush would start up a conversation with a stranger at, say, the Mighty Pump gas station somewhere in the county. He'd let out a "damn," and then a "hell." If the bystander didn't flinch

Cush would say something sacrilegious and within three sentences sound much like Lenny Bruce reciting a George Carlin routine. Before his tank filled he might say, "That motherfucker inside needs to get that goddamn muscle-bound mouse painted on his sign and replace it with a big-dicked Mickey having at it with that Minnie bitch."

And then I'd say, "We have to go," or "He doesn't get out much," or "He has that psychological problem."

"Okay, I tell you what else," Cush said to Ms. Perkins. "I feel as though I need to put it all on out there, you know, to prove how I'm the best guardian possible for young Start here. I don't know how the Department feels about having firearms in the house in general, or hunting in particular. We ain't got no firearms in this house. Search all you want. Bring in a dog, or a giant magnet. But I do hunt, nearly every day during season so's to pack the freezers we got down at the Quonset hut over there, other side of the property. I bet I'm like you, Carlotte—I don't think hunting Bambi with a .30-.30 is all that fair. Bow and arrow, maybe. Traps like I seen in Vietnam, yes."

She said, "You're on the verge of receiving a positive assessment. It's probably best that you don't say anything else."

"It's been a pleasure to make your acquaintance," I said, and stood up from the table. I tried to think of something intelligent to say in the realm of biology, and unfortunately blurted out, "They say skin is the largest organ!"

Uncle Cush went and turned the overhead light off. He said, "I should've thought to've done that earlier. I apologize. My fault. Anyway, listen—and Start here can tell you—I hunt with a *nail gun*, that's all. On a good lucky day here in the yard I can kill a deer and mount its head on the wall simultaneously, you know what I mean?"

I laughed. I let out an uncontrolled nervous laugh that came out sounding like a Tommy gun, maybe through some kind of subliminal cause-and-effect what with the artillery talk. I said, "Come on back any time," to the social worker.

My uncle put out his palm for the woman to continue sitting. "Hey, back in Vietnam one time, I was doing this USO show, because I was a champion spoon player, you know. They brought me on stage, but the lights were so harsh that they'd put sandpaper duct tape around the perimeter so people wouldn't fall off the stage. I think they got the idea from an albino guitar player of some repute. This was a real USO show, what I'm talking about, with Playboy bunnies and all that. Though none of them were pretty as you, Carlotte."

Ms. Perkins said, "It's a lifesaver, that duct tape. Sometimes I'm asked to give presentations on the social worker lecture circuit."

I didn't say, "There's a social worker lecture circuit? Are you kidding me?" though I thought it.

He said, "There's a social worker lecture circuit? Are you kidding me? Hey, is there some kind of newsletter? I'd like to attend some them talks. I'm always looking for ways to better educate my nephew."

"There *is* a newsletter!" Ms. Perkins said.

I thought, Okay, this would be a great time for her to leave with a good impression of the Waddell family as it were. But Cush said, "At that same USO show, Chuck Norris showed up. I'm talking Chuck Norris the martial arts movie star. He'd been Air Force, back before Vietnam. Anyway, he came out on stage blindfolded and did some moves, not even worried about that sandpaper duct tape. Pretty fucking amazing. Then he broke some bricks and boards and cement blocks. They brought out some kind of concrete life-size statue of a Cong, and he kicked it right in half. I was backstage and didn't have the best vantage point. It might've supposed to've been Bruce Lee he kicked in half, but it don't matter. What a man, Chuck Norris."

I'd heard this story a few times already and didn't want him to continue. First off, none of it was true, outside of Chuck Norris having been in the Air Force back in the late 1950s up until a few years before the gigantic grind of Vietnam. I said, "Stop, please."

"I know who Chuck Norris is," the social worker said. "A lot of my families—especially the white ones living in trailers—have posters of Chuck Norris in their dens and bedrooms."

"I don't want to say him and me got close," Cush said.

I grabbed his arm, which he'd sent above his head and held still, as if he had just thrown a tomahawk. "Not now."

Cush hitched his pants. "But Chuck was there a few days. I got to run into him on a basis. Soldiers in the field have urges, you know."

Ms. Perkins made a noise. Fifteen years later I would hear a woman make that same sound, which was the exact replica of a green and black poison dart frog—*Dendrobates auratus*, technically. Anyway, these days, one can go to the Internet and find that sound. Back then, Ms. Perkins's emission came out as surprising as a rubber-band ball unceasing itself.

I said, "Not now. Please stop." I looked at Ms. Perkins and said, "It's a lie."

She took off her sunglasses and said, "Tell me about lies, boy. I've heard them all." She took off the glasses, but had her eyelids shut, then balanced the glasses back on her nose.

"Damn," said Uncle Cush. "That kind of throwed me. Anyway, when Chuck Norris beats off, entire fully-formed *children* come out the end of his pecker. I'm talking one time I saw him behind a stand of bamboo and all these *white kids* shot out the end of his dick. No one believes me, but it's true."

I got up from the table. I looked down at Cavity Sam and raised my eyebrows. Would my own nose one day turn so red? Would a real surgeon look into my cavities at some point and exclaim, "Well, this explains some things."

What would happen to me if I got sent to a normal foster family? I wondered.

The caseworker stood up and didn't laugh. She said, "I don't want to say that I have the gift of soothsaying, Cush, but I'm thinking you and I might run into each other before long. Do you like martinis? You seem to be the kind of man who could make a perfect martini. After listening to the kind of shit and lies I come across daily, a perfect martini or four settles me down enough to feel like there's hope for the real world."

She took off her glasses again and opened her lids. I stared. Ms. Perkins eyes weren't pink, of course, but a pale blue on par with an abnormally bright sky, or a venerable ex-coquette's perfectly sculpted hair, or the weakest visible veins rippling across the dugs of a shirtless crone. Uncle Cush said, "Let me walk you out to your car."

I sat in the kitchen alone for an hour. I thought how, meta-phorically, the heart was an organ much bigger than skin. It's what I thought, I swear—maybe because I'd read too much Flaubert by the time I was fourteen. Maybe because I'd seen hearts still beat-ing in fish and deer, long after the skin quit twitching. I felt good about not saying, "I knew you were going to say, 'I don't want to say that I have the gift of soothsaying,'" seeing as I hailed from a tribe of con men, visionaries, hoydens, liars, quick-tempered reac-tionaries, contrarians, and hard-working near-anarchists, thus hav-ing visionary status myself. I considered looking out the window, but didn't want to see my uncle's truck bouncing up and down, or no truck at all.

BAIT

Although both of my parents insisted that he'd been my good friend—that somehow I must've forgotten him when we moved to Norfolk when I was six—I couldn't place Frankie Hassett when we went to pick him up at the bus station. I mean, I pretended that I knew the guy, but if he'd've been in a line-up with circus freaks only I wouldn't have known my supposed good friend, who was now sixteen years old.

"Shake hands with your good friend Frankie," my father had said, pushing me out of the depot's waiting room on Monticello Avenue.

I said, "Hey, Frankie," but he walked past me and shook hands with my father, saying, "Hey, Mr. Ecker. My mom says hey, and thanks for having me."

I got all caught up looking at the bus driver and his cool uniform with the greyhound on it, but thinking back on everything, I believe my mother stood off to the side, neither hugging Frankie nor shaking his hand or even acknowledging him. Maybe they greeted one another civilly after my father asked me to pick up Frankie's duffle bag.

We got in my father's Oldsmobile and drove home, which at the time was way out in the country but today, I imagine, is part of Norfolk's city limits, or at least part of the metropolitan area. We lived in Chuckatuck, some thirty miles away. Every time I met anyone *not* from Chuckatuck—Little League games, or the time I represented my school in the state spelling bee—they made fun of my hometown. It got to where I just kept saying I was from Jacksonville, down in Florida, no matter what. My father was a merchant seaman who worked mostly on oil tankers, and he probably spent six or nine months out of the year out on the water. My mother didn't work. I'm not sure what she did during the day, but she didn't go off somewhere to take shorthand, or write on a blackboard, or serve food with hush puppies on the side, I know that much.

In the back seat, Frankie said, "So I can drive a car now, Mr. Ecker. Did Mom tell you? If you want, I can drive this car."

I don't know if it was the truth or not, but my father said, "No can do, Frankie. My insurance agent won't let anyone drive this car but I." My father used "I" all the time, usually wrong. He said things like, "Between you and I," and "That goddamn boatswain pointed at I and told me to hurry up," and, "That's for I to know and for you to find out." I'm pretty sure that somewhere down the line growing up he got corrected for misuse of pronouns, and made a decision to use "I" at all times, hoping he'd end up above fifty-fifty percentage-wise.

Frankie tapped me on the arm and whispered, "When they're asleep, we'll go out for a spin, Jerry." He said, "Hey, you remember that time we went fishing down at Fernandina Beach and I caught that baby hammerhead shark? That was cool. Let's you and me go fishing every day when I'm here."

I said, "Yes," though I didn't remember fishing down there with anyone. My father turned the radio on. It might not be true, but I remember his singing along to "I Wanna Hold Your

Hand." How could he even know this song? Certainly they didn't have transistor radios that picked up Beatles' songs way out in the middle of the Atlantic Ocean and beyond. And how would I ever forget someone standing next to me with a baby hammerhead shark on the end of his fishing line? If anything, I should've been scarred for the remainder of my childhood and beyond from the nightmares that would emanate from such an experience.

Frankie reached up and touched my mother's hair. He said, "Hey, Rosalind."

My father turned into the driveway of a shingle-sided shack about ten miles from our house and said, "We're home!" like that. Then he laughed in a way that I'd only heard later in horror movies, put the car in reverse, and continued homeward.

When my father didn't work the tankers he helped out at a Texaco gas station owned by a cousin of his named Marvin. I had come to believe that we moved from Jacksonville because Cousin Marvin needed some help, but now understand that, perhaps, Frankie's mother began making some demands, my own mother made some ultimatums, and so on. No matter the truth, in the summer of 1967, when Frankie Hassett stayed with us, my father left the house each morning in order to change oil in customers' cars, or fill them up with gas, or sit around and eat Lance brand cheese crackers while drinking Coca-Colas. My mother said things like, "You guys get out of the house and leave me alone," so Frankie and I walked over to a nearby pond and fished for bream and crappie.

"I know the perfect way to kill someone and get away with it," he said that first week. He lit an L&M cigarette that he'd either stolen from my father or somehow gotten at the service station that was on our way to fish. "Here's what you do. You kill the bitch, and then you take the body over to some other bastard's house. Maybe it's somebody you already hate. So you get in the house, and you put her dead body in the bed. Then you go over to a pay phone and call the cops. See? You tell the cops, 'I heard a gunshot last night,' and give them the address. Cops go there, and the next thing you know, the guy you didn't like is getting arrested for murder."

I think I said, "Cool," or "Uh-huh," or "A lot of people think there are cottonmouths around here, but really they're just water snakes." In my mind I tried to think about how to use curse words correctly, so that it sounded realistic.

Frankie wore Brylcreem or Vitalis in his hair, which wasn't really what anyone else still did, even in Chuckatuck, outside of my father and his cousin Marvin. Most people my age or older let their hair grow out, and dreamed of the day when they'd be a conscientious objector. I spent most of my time raising my eyebrows in order to feel my bangs near my eyeballs. We stood there staring at our bobbers. I said, "How long are you staying with us?"

"There aren't any jobs back in Jacksonville. Fuckers. I told my mom that I wanted to go get a job. Seeing as I can drive and all, I figured I could get a job working construction or goddamn something. You wouldn't believe how big Jacksonville is now. It's about doubled since you were there. But Mom said there were no jobs for me and said I had to come visit y'all for the entire summer."

The *entire summer*, I thought. Even then, as a little kid, I understood the concept of *Are You Kidding Me*? I had this friend who lived down the road named Charles, and I didn't want Charles to ever meet Frankie. Frankie cursed too much, and I didn't want to be considered guilty by association. Charles's family went to church, we didn't, and I was already on edge about lying to my friend about where we went on Sunday mornings—I made up a place in downtown Norfolk, a church where no one else in my neighborhood or school would go. Again, I was eight, and Frankie sixteen. I said, "We start school here like the first week of August. I'm going into third grade."

Frankie pulled on his cigarette and flicked the butt into the pond. "Fish like fucking cigarettes. They dig cigarettes. One time I was fishing down at St. Augustine and I put a cigarette butt on my hook. You know what I caught? A goddamn crab. I took that thing home and my mom boiled it up for supper. We had boiled crab and French fries for supper. I didn't tell her that I caught the thing with a cigarette, which happened to be a non-filter Camel, what I normally smoke when I'm home."

Maybe his littering inadvertently turned me into majoring in Environmental Studies, which got me the job at the Department of Health and Environmental Control down in South Carolina, which gave me enough time to stand around while well water got tested to think about my mother and father's strange relationship.

I said, "Really?"

He said, "Ask your mom if she'll take us down to the beach."

I had always had two single beds in my room, for some reason. What only child had two beds? Sometimes I slept in one, sometimes the other. My mother urged me to so she wouldn't have to wash the linens but every other week. In retrospect, it's not all that bad of an idea. Maybe my parents planned on having a second child. If they had a third, maybe we could have bunk beds, plus a single cot, I don't know. I imagine the two beds came as a set, and that particular set was the only thing on sale at whatever store they found them. My father—again, gone for at least half the year—had this thing about not getting ripped off. At Christmas time he wouldn't string lights out on our gutters until the week before the twenty-fifth, because he didn't want to give the electric company extra money. On top of that, he made me help him out in the front yard, in the cold, one of us hunched down by the outlet and the other standing at the end of the driveway. We lived on a curve. He left the Christmas lights unplugged until, say, I saw a car approaching. I'd yell out, "Now!" and he'd stick the business end of the extension cord in, lighting us up. When a car's tail lights disappeared around the bend, I'd say, "Okay!" and he'd unplug the things again. Or we'd switch positions, and he'd use nautical terms like "fore" and "aft," which made no sense, instead of "now" and "okay."

When my father got back on his ships, my mother kept just about every light on in the house. She said it would keep burglars and rapists away. But she always went and opened the drapes wide open, for some reason, which seemed to work against anyone trying to dissuade all drifters passing through Chuckatuck.

"I don't think there are any fish in this goddamn pond," Frankie said about five minutes after throwing our hooks in. "I know one thing: These sons-of-bitches don't know the bait they're supposed to bite. Down in Florida, the fish will go for anything. Fatback. Crickets. Bread balls. Bacon. Baloney. Hell, I've caught more fish down in Florida using a bare hook than I have here using y'all's nasty-tasting worms. Cigarette butts, like I've said before."

It would take about five more years before I would learn to say to people like Frankie, "Who invited you here in the first place? Go on back home and go fishing with your stupid hoop cheese."

"I guess you're cool enough to know about this," he said, putting down his rod. Frankie walked over to some brush twenty feet from the lake's edge, and uncovered a plastic bag. In the bag he had a *Playboy* magazine that hadn't survived humidity very well. The pages had fanned out somewhat, making it look thicker than a dictionary. "I didn't want your mom finding this in our bedroom, so I snuck out one night and hid it out here." He opened the pages and showed me a fold-out and the parts of a woman I'd never seen before. Well, he showed me pages that *once held* photographs of women's parts I'd never seen before. Frankie placed the magazine down, stood up, pulled out his wallet, and said, "I tore out their nipples and keep them in here. Watch this." He took a piece of glossy paper, the size of a quarter, and put it on his hook. "Down in Florida, all the fish are attracted to pictures of girls' nipples. Especially snapper."

I said, "Goddamn."

He said, "Don't you go tell your mommy about this."

I said, "Goddamn."

"In starts and fits come farts and shits," Frankie said for no reason I could figure. He laughed. He cast his hook, caught nothing, and deemed my hometown's fish blind.

I had never wanted a school year to begin again as much as I did between second and third grades. We'd go fishing, catch nothing, then return home. Frankie and I would stop at Marvin's Texaco on the way back, always, and sit around. Or my father, Frankie, and Marvin sat around. I usually found myself attracted to the service bay, which was a giant hole in the ground with a metal ladder attached to its wall. It was my job to go down there, spread plain old sand on the oil spills, then sweep it up. I have never understood acoustics, but somehow everyone's voices upstairs resonated down to me. I guess Marvin and my father thought Frankie old enough to hear dirty jokes, and look at those racy calendars, and so on. For most of that particular summer, those three guys talked about neighborhood cats.

We'd finally walk home, my father drinking a can of Schlitz along the way, and then sit down to eat Hungarian goulash, which seemed to be my mother's specialty. Or we cooked hot dogs outside in a fire pit. Sometimes we went out in the back yard and threw a baseball around. Looking back, I felt pretty sure that Frankie threw the ball way over my father's head on purpose, and while my father trotted off to retrieve the thing Frankie would wander over to me and say, "Have you asked your mom about the beach yet?"

Almost every night I pretended to be tired and went to my single bed and stared at the ceiling until Frankie came in. I feigned sleep, and he said things to me like, "You want to see the hair on my balls?" or "Wake up and look at my extra finger." If I ever need to go to a psychiatrist today, I can pretty much direct him or her back to those days in my life to prove why it's important that I be untrusting and paranoid.

Frankie would get in the bed, I would keep my eyes shut tight, and then it would sound like a small fan rotated against his sheets. I was eight years old, in 1968, understand. No one in Chuck-atuck had ever clued me in to the nuances of masturbation. I only peeped my eyes open once, that I remember, when Frankie kind of groaned out "Rosalind" one night and I thought my mom was in the room.

Maybe my on-again, off-again depression stems from poor Frankie's story. Of course I said to him that summer, "What does your father do?" and "Where does your father live?" and so on, even though my parents had told me not to ask about him. They said he'd died before Frankie could even know who the guy was. But it took about one-too-many times of Frankie saying, "The reason why we never catch fish is because they see your ugly face, Pisspants," before I reeled in my line and said, "So did your dad take one look at you and then run away?"

"My father died in Korea. He died on the very last day of the Korean War," Frankie said. "That's why you never see me eating with chopsticks."

I left it at that. I didn't know much, but I understood that a father dying in a war was not a good thing to ask about. And because I didn't remember our life in Florida, I thought that maybe people down there perhaps ate with chopsticks often. Maybe they used chopsticks to pick apart all the hammerhead sharks they'd caught on such things as string, grass blades, and magnolia blossoms.

I felt so bad about asking—and now I understand that Frankie was smart enough to use this opportunity to work on my guilt— that I said, "I'll find a way to get Mom to take us to Virginia Beach."

To be honest, I never wanted to admit to Frankie that my mother didn't know how to drive. I'm sure there were a number of mothers in America back in the sixties who never learned. At the time I never thought about how perhaps it wasn't such a smart idea to live way out in the country with a child alone, not knowing how to drive, while one's husband spent most of his life at sea.

"I'm beginning to wonder if I fucking packed my bathing suit for nothing," Frankie said. He slapped my back a few times, which kind of hurt. "You might not be all that bad, little bastard."

So we went home, and I said, "Mom, why can't we drive to the beach? Frankie can drive. We don't have to tell Dad about it. He won't know."

I thought I was going to get some long-winded explanation as to why we weren't allowed out of the town limits. This oc- curred while Frankie and my father nailed a two-by-four across two pine trees in the back yard, ten feet up, so they could kick field goals. I expected my mother to say, "We can't afford the gas," or "There are hitchhikers out on the back roads waiting for people like us," or "You'll get sunburned, and then the next thing you know you're flaking skin everywhere and I'll have to change your sheets more often."

She said, "Okay. Just don't tell your father. Seeing as he doesn't ever come home for lunch, there's no way he'll ever know."

Why didn't he come home for lunch? I wondered years later. Why did he even work for his cousin Marvin, seeing as merchant seamen made some money, and my father bragged about how he usually doubled his salary in poker games aboard the ship.

That particular night we ate Hungarian goulash, and sat together without saying much. We watched *Gunsmoke*, as I recall. It was the one where Festus explained why he never learned how to read, and he told a long-winded story about how a guy named Mose in the Bible wanted to get across a river to the other side, which ended up being about Moses and the Red Sea. During a commercial my father said, "Hey, Jerry. Amy Vanderbilt's parents gave her a carton of expensive, embossed stationery for her birthday. Who's the first person she wrote and why?"

I thought for a while—I thought perhaps this had something to do with Festus not being able to read—and then I blurted out, "A thank-you note to her parents, because she was into etiquette and all that stuff," after the commercial had ended and the program restarted.

My father said, "It took you long enough. Thanks for making I miss what the Marshall just said." See about that passive-aggressive thing?

Frankie said, "What a bitch."

"I got another way to kill someone," Frankie said while we drove down to Virginia Beach. I sat in the back seat. We had to drive ten miles in the opposite direction so as not to pass Marvin's Texaco. My mother sat on the front bench seat in the spot where she sat when my father drove, which, in retrospect, might've been a little too close to the middle. She sat so close to Frankie that my friend Charles and I could've also sat in the front seat, probably without touching elbows. With all that bragging Frankie did, he wasn't much of a driver. I kind of expected him to hit eighty miles an hour, but he pretty much drove about forty, jerking the steering wheel left and right an inch or two every second. The only time he spoke—my mother gave directions—was when he said he was used to driving a manual four-speed. He said that his mother had a Fairlane, but he'd be getting a Mustang once he got back to Jacksonville, and found a job, et cetera.

"I got another way," Frankie said. "I'll tell it later."

I looked over at the space beside me. We'd brought a picnic lunch of ham sandwiches, and my pair of fins and mask and snorkel. We brought towels, and suntan lotion that smelled like coconut, and one of those cheap Styrofoam ice chests filled with ginger ale, Coca-Cola in six-and-a-half-ounce bottles, and six cans of Schlitz my mom more or less stole from my father's cache out in the garage.

When I tell this entire story—I've probably told it to my wife a dozen times, a couple of my coworkers once or twice, and my mother's second husband once—every one of them says, "I see what's coming. Frankie gets drunk and y'all have a bad wreck on the way back home."

And I always hold my hand up and say, "Nope."

I don't know if Freud or Darwin ever wrote about human beings who're drawn back to the water, but I seem to have been one of those people. Whereas most animals, complying to evolutionary urges, want to be on land, I always wanted to go deeper into the water. We got to the beach, and I jumped out of the car without even asking if anyone needed or wanted help with the ice chest. I ran barefoot down the hot, hot sand, got my feet into the tide, and sat down on wet sand in order to get my flippers on. I wet the mask's rubbery gasket for a better grip, put it on, and shoved the snorkel in my mouth. I took in a deep breath and dove in. I paddled my feet better than any amphibian ever invented, and stayed down close to the sand. I would tell people later that I saw starfish and sand dollars, a horseshoe crab or two, and other things.

I found an old asphalt road that must've been covered by one of the hurricanes years back, and barbed-wire fences, and the very tip of a mast that might've been from one of the pirates' ships. I saw the ghosts of drowning victims, schools of jellyfish, scattered gold and silver coins, sea glass that had congregated into SOS formations, globs of oil that may or may not've leaked from my father's tankers, and the skeleton of President Kennedy, though I knew this couldn't have been true. I mean, I knew that none of it could've been true, outside of maybe the mast tip. Maybe I held my breath too long, to the point of hallucination.

No matter what, I surfaced, faced seaward. I came up out of the water—probably not that far from the shore, but at the time it seemed as though I'd swum a good quarter-mile—and looked out, I imagine, in the direction of Bermuda. There were ships out there, though I saw none. There were dolphins or porpoises—I still don't know the difference—writing cursive loops atop the swells.

And then I turned around.

Maybe, because of the distance, I couldn't tell how close people sat next to my mother and Frankie Hassett. Maybe he had a secret to tell her, and that's why he leaned in toward her ear. My mother seemed to giggle, from my vantage point in the ocean, or maybe she had eaten one of the ham sandwiches and gotten some white bread stuck to the roof of her mouth. I could see his right index finger pulling away the fabric of her two-piece top, in order to see what body part he thought made the best bait down in Florida.

Maybe the slap I saw my mother plant across Frankie's face wasn't really as hard as it looked while I bobbed offshore.

"What you do, see, is you kill a goddamn bastard, and you stuff his or her body in a duffle bag. Then you go over to one of those motels that aren't but one story high, you know. You go ahead and park in the parking lot in a way that none of the maids can see your license plate. Then when they leave one of the doors open—they leave the doors open all the time, going from one room to the next—you take the body in, and lay it out in the bed, and pull the covers over it. Then you drive away real fast, you know. That maid will go back in and say, 'I forgot to make the bed!' And then she'll find the body. And then the motel manager will call the cops, and they'll spend a ton of time trying to see who was in the room the night before, and then that guy will end up getting charged."

Frankie said all of this from the back seat. My mother drove. I'll give her this: She drove faster than he did, and she didn't shake her hands back and forth on the steering wheel as if she shook Jiffy Pop.

My mother looked into the rearview mirror and said, "Does your mother let you curse like that around the house all the time?"

I opened up the glove compartment. My father always threw his spare change in there. No one paid attention, so I took out two quarters and a dime. Frankie said, "Oh, give me a break. Don't act like you've never heard anything like that. Rosalind. Ros." He reached up to touch her hair. She leaned forward. I turned in my seat and slapped his hand away. He said, "Brother, I believe I'd think twice before I did anything like that."

I said, "It's a proven fact that only stupid people curse, 'cause they can't think up any other words!" In between I kind of hyperventilated. I said it all as quickly as possible, and it kind of came out in a high voice that I wouldn't be proud of. My second-grade teacher, Mrs. Breland, used to say this kind of thing all the time to a poor kid named Ricky Cogburn who probably suffered from Tourette's Syndrome. Later on in life I would realize that some prude made that little dictum up, because I have met, over the years, cursing geniuses. I said, "And fish aren't attracted to nipples, either, for your information."

My mother stepped on the accelerator. When we got to Marvin's Texaco, she told Frankie and me to stay in the car. My father came and stood outside the service bay. He nodded more than a few times, shook his head sideways, shrugged his shoulders. He handed over a newly opened bottle of Coca-Cola to my mother, and she drank from it, then handed it back. In the car, Frankie said, "Your parents are square, man. This whole place sucks. This entire situation sucks."

I learned not to hold my thumb inside my fist when punching someone in the nose. He yelled out "Fucker!" but held his bleeding nose and started crying. And he was gone that night. My mother and I watched *Daktari* together and ate popcorn. My mother snapped off half a pain pill and gave it to me for my broken thumb. When my father returned, he said he had dropped by the union hall after taking Frankie to the bus station, and that he'd be boarding a tanker in the morning. My mother pointed at the television and said, "Look, a trained chimpanzee."

Maybe she pointed to my father. We never saw him again.

TONGUE

I can't speak for all car rental agencies, but where I work there's more to it than having your flight canceled, getting pissed off, deciding to drive from Charlotte to Atlanta or Baltimore or Cincinnati or Nashville or Memphis, then coming down by Baggage Claim to talk to either good-looking Norleen or Frankie, showing a valid driver's license and getting the keys to an Economy or Compact car that you later complain about being too small, or not having any acceleration, even though that's what you ordered as opposed to a van or Buick. I can only make assumptions and predictions. I've been here six years plus—which, as far as I'm concerned, is the exact amount of time it takes at almost all jobs before the Assumption and Prediction phase can kick in. I've got a five-year service pin I've worn for fourteen months and two days. I have five-year pins from a few other places, too, none of which are car rental agencies. But they were places where I got to see how people acted. They were places where I noticed how we, as humans, don't have much in the areas of truth, patience, cleanliness, or forgiveness. Before inspecting rental cars before they went out and came back, I'd worked in insurance, and then in retail, and then in hardware. Five years, five years, five years. Before that I went to college. Growing up, my father made me sell encyclopedias door-to-door like he had done back when people actually bought encyclopedias. I can only make an assumption—I have no proof—but I guess that my overall view and distrust of people started during the encyclopedia days. You wouldn't believe how many people stopped buying right after volume D, just because they didn't like the way Jefferson Davis got portrayed. They said they didn't want to get all the way to volume L just to find some lies about how great a man Abraham Lincoln was according to the biased encyclopedia writers and researchers. A B C D, A B C D, A B C D—I'd like to know how many households in South Carolina have only those World Books up on their shelves above the television.

And tolerance. We, as humans, don't have much in the area of truth, patience, cleanliness, forgiveness, or tolerance. There are more. I'll add on some others, I'd be willing to bet, long before I come close to my ten-year pin.

Another prediction: There will be no ten-year pin.

But this isn't about longevity. It's not about how the company makes me wear a work shirt that doesn't have my real name across the pocket, even though that's kind of interesting and a lesson in paranoia—since 9/11 the company's been forced by the Homeland Security people to worry about renting out cars to possible terrorists and suicide car bomb drivers. Norleen and Frankie—at least in our Charlotte office—have a lot of responsibility in this regard. They're the ones making the first decisions. I mean, Butch, Mike, Lou, and I have the authority to raise our hands and say something like, "This guy's luggage is ticking and maybe we should send him back over to Hertz or Budget or Avis," but Norleen and Frankie went through *three training sessions* that included being able to identify eye color, judge height and weight, and so on. Some guy with government connections came down and showed off a bunch of fake IDs and taught our customer service reps how to spot them. Back when I grew up, people used fake IDs to get liquor, or maybe to rent a car if they were running away and had a lot of money. It's different now. I don't need to tell anyone that it's different now. That's a given. It's going to last this way until everyone in the world gets along.

The company says that men with one-syllable names come across as handy with their fists and can possibly scare off possible car-renting terrorists who always have six or eight syllables. You get a guy with some kind of family name for a first name and by the time he introduces himself a car-renting terrorist can pull out a dirk, saber, machete, or switchblade and disembowel the guy like they do in Middle Eastern countries, past and present. That's what the company handed down to us, in those words.

They let us pick our own tough-names. I'm Chuck. I like it because it's not only a name, but a verb. I got used to it early, and even introduce myself as Chuck after work, when I go off to one of the bars, or to the bookstore to see if there are any terrorist women poring over *How to Rig a Rental Car Bomb* books, which I've never actually seen on the shelves but wouldn't be surprised to find, what with the First Amendment and a stretched view of the Second Amendment.

People always want to know what I find inside rental cars after they've been returned. People say to me both at the bars and book store, "Chuck, you ought to write a book about what you've come across."

Mike and I have an ongoing game we play to find the best things. That's why I'm talking here, I guess. At the end of our shift we gather up everything, and we don't tell each other our finds until the very end. It builds some suspense and makes the day go by faster. Most of the time we have to meet up in the parking lot of either Fatz Cafe or Applebee's or TGI Friday's or Mulligan's or Ruby Tuesday's or Monterrey's before we can pull things out of our respective boxes, one at a time, saving the best find for last.

You can imagine the usual—CDs, hair brushes, spare change, a million cell phone chargers, house keys, dirty magazines, business cards, cell phones jammed into the passenger seats—which meant a man picked up a hooker and she sat down and then he got all paranoid that she stole his phone so he never called up the number again—packs of cigarettes even though we tell people they're not supposed to smoke in the rental cars and so on. I'd say that Mike and I have about tied, over the years, on weird things. One time I found an eight-ball of cocaine. One time Mike found a quarter pound of weed left in a scooped-out Gideon's Bible. One time I found a signed copy of a novel by that guy William Faulkner, but Mike didn't believe me and said I'd only found a book and forged the signature. So the next day he found a non-scooped-out Gideon's Bible and wrote on the first page, "Hope you like my caracters—God." I told him that God would probably know how to spell.

Anyway, we go over what we've found, and we try to be objective, and whoever has the best thing doesn't have to buy the first beer. Well, when I find the best thing I always order a beer, but Mike's one of those guys who sits up at the bar and orders something fancy and expensive, like a salty dog in the summer months, and a single malt scotch when it's below forty degrees outside. He's one of those guys. You know those guys.

I should mention that, in the beginning, when it came to rings and watches and other good jewelry, we actually turned them in to Lost and Found. We thought people would come back to the rental agency looking for things like that. The rest—I would be willing to bet that years ago there was a Lost and Found for everything, but evolution took care of people like Mike and me—the rest, we knew it would just sit in a box in a room far away from the actual place where you sign up to rent a car. It's one of those things. For the last few years, though, we didn't turn anything in. I don't know how it works in other car rental agencies, but for ours it went like this:

People came to where they turned their rental cars in and said, "I lost my cell phone."

I would say, "Our Lost and Found is not here. It's way out on Independence Boulevard."

If the person went ahead and drove out there, the person working the office would say, "No cell phones have been returned in the last six months," or whenever. She'd say, "You know, maybe you left it at your last hotel where you stayed."

Then the person would say, "No, I called the hotel."

Then our person would say, barely audible, "You know, those cleaning ladies don't usually report what they find."

Look back through all of the history of travel, and I'm betting that the blame ends up with the cleaning lady.

So somehow Mike and I learned about this little ploy, and we quit turning things in too. What's more, I'll go ahead and admit that Mike and I both do a little something in order to get people to leave things accidentally. We talk. We're supposed to walk around the car and give it an eight-point inspection: dings, scrapes, excessive bird droppings, cigarette butts put out on the dashboard, cigarette burns from a driver trying to throw out his butt and it flying into the back seat area, excessive mud on the floor mats, odometer reading, and gas gauge. There's always going to be some kind of ding, and that's what the drivers worry over. Me, I start talking like crazy, asking questions about politics, weather, baseball, gas prices, the gestation period of rats, lactose-intolerant people, drought, the next solar eclipse, poisons that most people don't know about, merit badges I never earned, my ex-wife DeLaura's new Professor of Leadership husband at a community college, the stench of a dog that rolled on roadkill—*anything*—and the next thing you know the guy's getting his suitcase out of the trunk and trying to run off, leaving something in the glove compartment, console, side-door pockets, or above the visor. One time I almost won Best Find of the Day with Mike when I came to the bar with a Swiss Army knife, but he'd found a machete. Another time I got a snubnose .38, and he had a shotgun.

We've never found blueprints of federal buildings, train stations, airports, bus stations, college campuses, or any other place the company has told us to keep a lookout for. Mike and I have never found any notebooks filled with Arabic scrawl, though I got all excited one time after finding what ended up being a takeout menu written entirely in Chinese. On that particular day, Mike found a remote-control helicopter with two sticks of dynamite attached to its runners. At the bar he ordered a kamikaze right away.

We've found money and canes and a couple scooped-out Korans, but there was nothing inside them. I guess in that religion you're not supposed to drink, so they finished off the booze. I can only speculate, which is a close cousin to Assume and Predict.

Sometimes I vacuum, but more often than not I only use a whisk brush. Sometimes I get down on the asphalt and check out the undercarriage, but most of the time I look in the driver's eyes and make an educated guess.

So it came to this. Right here is what it's all about. I'm going to repeat it word for word.

Mike and I had a big haul because it was the Sunday after Christmas. That's when people needed to return their Hyundai Sonatas, Kia Rondos, Dodge Calibers, and whatnot. Sometimes Mike and I sit around in the bars making up names for future car models. When the Rondo came out we had to look up what it even meant. It's a poem. Sonata's a long-winded song. The Dodge Caliber might not be the best car on the rental lot, but at least it's not named for a song or poem. Who gets hired out to come up with these names? How much money does the Vice President of Car Names get? In my notebook of future models, I have written these options for the Asian car market: Villanelle, Haiku, Quatrain, Rhyme, Couplet, Sestina, Spondee, Terza Rima, Tanaga, Aubade, and Iamb. I had to look them all up, understand. It's not like I ever knew anything about poetry, outside of what would make a good name for a car model of the future. It's not like I have a five-year pin from some kind of English or Music department. I have written down Chant, Madrigal, Sea Shanty, and Yodel. "Blues" won't work, obviously. "Punk" won't work either. I'm pretty sure there's already a car called the "Anthem." Personally, I think that the Hyundai *Yodel* has a ring to it, but I'm betting with myself that my first winner will be the Daewoo Dirge.

Listen, I've written down all these names, sealed them in an envelope, and sent them to myself in case one day I can sue Toyota or Honda or any of the new Japanese or Korean or Chinese auto manufacturers-to-come for copyright infringement. Then maybe I could be considered a real "leader" in this sector, which is more to say than my ex-wife DeLaura's new husband the Leadership professor.

Anyway, we had a big haul. I had two filled liquor-bottle boxes, and Mike had a Rubbermaid garbage can. There were a slew of hardback books, and I'd be betting that they were Christmas gifts that the respective receivers took and thought, I ain't going to make my suitcase heavier with this thing packed inside. Then they said to the givers, "I'm going to keep this out so I have something to read on the plane." Here's what I've learned about people who give visiting relatives books: They want the receivers to change their ways. These books are almost always nonfiction, and they're either written by left-wing politicians or right-wing radio commentators. Let's say I go visit my ex-wife's father. He'd load me down with books by or about Rush Limbaugh, Newt Gingrich, Ronald

Reagan, Richard Nixon, George Bush's daughters, and that dude on TV who says we not only need a fence around America but also some kind of burp-top lid. My ex-father-in-law would say something like, "Here. Read this right here I got for you about the flat-tax rate, then tell me again how come you think everyone deserves to have medical attention when they need or want it." He's one of those guys. You know those guys.

So I had a bunch of books, and so did Mike. We could've opened up a used book store with just far-right and far-left walls of shelves. We took out the books to see which ones were signed—none during this particular holiday season—and set them back aside. I save up all my books and donate them to the literacy society once a year. Mike drops his off at the library's book drop just to confuse librarians in the morning when they look all over for a bar code or that little pocket in the back like in the old days.

We placed our books in our respective cars—we both drive ex-rental cars seeing as we get a deal after 37,000 miles—and then Mike borrowed one of my empty boxes so he wouldn't have to lug a Rubbermaid into Mulligan's. We walked in and Mike said to the hostess, "We need a booth."

We never needed booths. I didn't even like booths. Two grown men in a booth looks funny, if you ask me. If they're not having an affair, it looks like they're planning something illegal, or know some things to talk about that they shouldn't know.

Which brings me to here. Mike and I showed off our Finds of the Day, working up to the big one. My best find was a bamboo fly rod. I could already see myself selling this thing on eBay. Mike had a beautiful red-and-white silk scarf that he tied up on his head like a do-rag, and then a turkey call on his next-to-last find, so it looked like I'd win and he'd buy my first beer. I even said, "I might order me one of those special Christmas beers they got—those bock beers."

Mike leaned across the table. He said in a voice that I once heard a desperado use in one of those Mexican-American War movies, "Hold on, amigo. There's no way. I'm thinking that you and me ought to've found us a flight attendant inside the airport to get us a couple airsick bags before I do what I'm about to do."

The waitress came up wearing one of those Christmas hats with the fuzzy ball on the end, hanging down to her shoulder. She said, "What'll you fellows have? Would you like to look at a menu?" She had a glint sparkling around in her mouth from a tongue ring.

Mike said, "Oh, this is just too perfect." He said, "I'm so glad that you're our waitress. Y'all got eggnog on sale seeing as it's no longer Christmas? If you got it on sale, I'll have eggnog. If not, brandy. In a snifter. What we're about to do is a cause for celebration."

I said, "No menu. I'll have a draft and a shot of bourbon. Whatever draft you got that's not light or the color of root beer, I'll take. And a shot of bourbon."

She nodded and said "Okay," and kept standing there for some reason until Mike said, "Now would be a good time to go get it."

He leaned over and said, "I want to make it clear that what I have here came exactly as I'm going to present it. It came in this box."

He pulled out an old wooden pine box. The seams were dovetailed, and it looked like it maybe was made to hold a junior scientist's microscope. I said, "My bamboo fly rod bests a wooden box."

"I want to go on record as saying that I didn't have anything to do with this. Something highly violent and illegal took place somewhere along the line not too long ago, and I had nothing to do with it. This ain't like the time when I brought in that engraved Zippo from Vietnam and said I found it when really it was my Uncle Billy's."

The waitress brought our drinks. She said they wouldn't have eggnog for another 350 days or thereabouts, but she had the brandy. Mike swirled his glass like I'm sure he saw somewhere. I tried to remember the Zippo. I said, "If you cheated on a Find of the Day, then I call foul. You owe me two days of drinks no matter what."

He nodded. He smiled. Mike used to sell mobile homes before he got a job at the agency. He told me once that he had a nervous breakdown and a possible conversation with God one evening during tornado season, and he never went back in to the trailer lot. Mike said, "After this, we might have no urge to ever play again." He looked around to make sure no one could see him. He opened the box slowly, lifting its lid my way.

At first I thought it was only another of his Uncle Billy's keepsakes from the war. I thought this only because he'd admitted to the Zippo. Then I thought it was a big piece of beef jerky, or maybe a smallish over-fried piece of calf's liver. I said, "What the hell."

It kind of let off an odor. I leaned back in my booth.

Mike took a fork from the table and turned it over in the box. He said, "Human tongue." He clicked tines to a tongue-bob not that much different than our waitress's. "The driver'd flipped up the backseat and shoved it down there next to the flat tire tools."

I said, "Goddamn," in kind of a whisper. I took another look at the thing to make sure it wasn't some kind of special, "thick 'n' wide" beef jerky. I said, "You can't just keep this thing. Did you tell anyone? Did you tell Lou, Kurt, Curt, Kent, Jim, Bill, Len, Dan, Abe, Zeke, Bob, Wes, Ted, Ned, Pete, Frank, Glenn, Gene, or Slick? You have to tell someone. You have to go *above* and *beyond* the office and tell the authorities."

Mike stared at me hard in a way I'd only seen him do once before—when he found a blowgun and two poison darts. He said, "This is going to be my ticket out of here. This is so big, I'm going to buy *your* drinks, even though I obviously won Best Find of the Day."

Our waitress appeared and Mike closed the lid. He said to her, "You ever see any of those *City Confidential*, or *America's Most Wanted*, or *True Crime* TV shows? I'm going to be on one of them pretty soon."

She said, "You are, huh?" She stuck out her tongue. I tried to imagine it living outside of her body, in a box.

I said, "Could we get another round?" even though we weren't ready. I wanted to veer the conversation somewhere else.

"You going to be on those TV shows because of something you did?" the waitress asked.

"Well, you never know, do you? Maybe it was for something I found, though. Something I discovered," Mike said. He pulled that do-rag scarf down lower on his forehead.

"Well what'd you find? One time me and my boyfriend were walking through the woods and we came across a whole village of little snail-back trailers being used for meth labs. It smelled like cat pee from a long ways off, until we saw the trailers."

I slid in my booth back up to the wall. "I've changed my mind. I need double bourbons, no beer."

"Anyone can find a meth lab these days," Mike said. "You might find this interesting, what with your tongue and all." He reached for the box.

I said, "No, no, no. You don't need to open that thing up and show her."

"What is it?" she asked, drawling out the words with little squeals in between. "Show me. Come on, show me."

I took the box off the tabletop and placed it next to me on the bench seat. I said, "Maybe later."

"Okay. I'mo remind you that you promised," she said, swishing away.

"You can't go show this to anyone," I said to Mike, "outside of maybe Bud or Buck or Sid in management."

"I got it all figured out," he said. "That's how my mind works.

Listen. What happened was, one them really religious cult people—like the Fundamentalist Church of Jesus Christ of Latter Day Saints, or the Amish, or Jehovah's Witnesses, or maybe the Baptists—one them really religious cults where they don't let women wear make-up or dance or become preachers? Well, this tongue came out of a woman who rebelled against standard operating procedure, you know. She went into a town somehow, and got her tongue pierced. I'd be willing to bet that there's a box somewhere in another rental car with a hank of tattooed flesh inside. Anyway, she went and got all rebellious, and came home, and stuck her tongue out at her husband or father—or maybe her husband was her father—and the next thing you know he's got a big old butcher knife out."

Mike couldn't keep his hands still. I picked up the box and slid it across the table. He tapped on its lid. I said, "Why would the guy rent a car? Some of those religious cults have laws against renting cars. He wasn't Amish, that's for sure."

Mike said, "When I first saw the thing, I thought it was a gigantic belly button cord. You ever seen a kid's belly button cord?"

I didn't answer him. I wanted to call up DeLaura and get her to ask her new husband what he might do in a situation like this, his knowing about leadership and all. A few minutes later I said, "I wonder what happened to our waitress."

Maybe chain restaurant managers have to undergo training that involves being able to predict and assume who's a likely terrorist, I don't know. They must go to yearly workshops down in some place like Myrtle Beach, then pass on their knowledge to waitstaff, bartenders, cooks, and dishwashers. I've never earned any kind of five-year pin at Hooter's or Longhorn Steakhouse, so I wouldn't know. I had had enough to drink with an extracted tongue in a box across from me to understand only that the manager of this particular Mulligan's had undergone a good leadership training program that taught managers to identify regular customers and find ways to keep them happy. Our waitress finally came back all smiles and said, "Sam says that your money's no good in here. Sam's our manager. He says that y'all have been such good customers, that the rest of the night's on us. He even said if y'all want to drink till closing, Mulligan's will pay for the cab. Sam says your money's no good in here. It's our new policy for regulars."

Looking back, I should've understood that something was awry. The waitress—her nametag had read Elizabeth at the beginning of the evening, but changed to Liz somewhere along the line—wouldn't make eye contact with us. She looked at the box, then looked away at one of those triangular stand-up tubes that advertised Mulligan's Favorites: Fairway Fries, Hole-in-One Jalapeño Poppers, five Bogey Burgers, three Birdie Chicken Strips, and the Putter Platter.

I didn't have time to think, Sam and Liz are one-syllable names.

Mike said, "I knew that it was my lucky day before I even went to work. I knew it! I love it when you have a feeling and it ends up being true. This might have to be the last night of us doing what we do, Chuck. You need to know to stop when it won't get any better. I wouldn't be surprised if a bunch of virgins showed up in our lives about right now."

Hell, I ordered a brandy just like Mike had started off with. I said, "I'll have a brandy. Does this go for food, too?" I turned the advertisement. "If we can have food, too, then I would like a couple hot dogs in the rough."

"Make that four," Mike said. "Four hot dogs in the rough."

Liz said, "I'll get that order right in. We're a little backed up, but I'll tell the chef to get them as fast as possible."

She took off away from our table as if she'd been stung by bees. Mike said, "'In the rough' means it comes with cole slaw. I wish I'd've thought that up. Me and you ought to think up possible food names for these theme restaurants we always go to. Like when we think up car names, you know."

Then we sat there like idiots, I suppose trying to think up golf-themed foods that the Mulligan's people hadn't already figured out. I finally said, "Nine-Iron Nachos," but couldn't think of nine ingredients that made sense. I thought of six, but Six-Iron Nachos didn't have a ring to it.

Mike said, "I bet they don't have Chi Chi's chili named after Chi Chi Rodgriquez because there's already a chain called Chi Chi's and I bet there's a copyright."

We waited another fifteen minutes for Liz to come back with our drinks or our hot dogs. I leaned toward Mike and said, "Did you look around the car any more? Did you slip that box in your Rubbermaid can and wait to look at it, or did you open it up right away?"

Mike said, "Uh-huh. Uh-huh. I opened it up right away and knew what it was, seeing as my uncle fought in Vietnam, and I used to have a girlfriend way back when from either Syria or Lebanon or Saudi Arabia, depending on how things were going between us and them. So I looked at it, then closed it up, then looked all around—I'm talking about even beneath the emergency brake handle—thinking I'd come up with at least a finger with a ring on it. Nothing more, though."

I looked at my wristwatch—a pretty nice old-fashioned Timex that needed winding about every thirty-six hours. I'd gotten it out of a Ford Taurus. It had a metal, accordion-style band that pulled on my arm hairs but—indirectly, I'm convinced—got me to quit smoking. Because of the Timex's powers, I never chose to wear a woman's Bulova I found in a Subaru on the day after Valentine's Day, or a Citizen Eco-Drive I found in a Geo on Arbor Day. I *saved* them, understand. One day I might try to sell everything off and put the money in a CD, for retirement, you know.

At nine o'clock the bar looked desolate. As a matter of fact, no one sat within eyeshot of Mike and me. Outside of some bad 1980s songs overhead, and a man giving sand wedge tips on six TV screens—that's something Mike's found once, a bent set of golf clubs—there was no longer any crowd noise, but I'd not been paying attention or taking on-the-minute notes per usual seeing as a booth isn't the best place to scope out what's going on inside a bar that caters to golfers, women attracted to golfers, female golfers, and women attracted to female golfers. And drunks who work menial jobs somehow proud to receive five- or ten-year pins.

That's right, I said it: "On-the-minute notes per usual." It's what's expected of a good car rental agency employee, according to management. It's what'll get you noticed, promoted to a leadership capacity, and inevitably trained to fight the war on terror.

Mike said, "Goddamn. Maybe she turned lez somewhere between taking our orders and going to the bar. She was checking us out, my man. That's the way it is with women around here. You tell them you're about to be famous on TV, and they won't leave you alone. Show up every night by seven o'clock with a day's pay and something found in a rental car worth keeping, women won't even make eye contact. At least that's how my first two wives operated."

I'd never brought up to Mike that he had what they call "a misogyny tendency." I learned all about it in a signed first-edition book by a woman named Camille. Unfortunately, the book entered my life about a month after my wife left me for the professor. If only I'd read the thing, memorized some nice sensitive passages, and recited them during lovemaking, then maybe I wouldn't be hanging out with Mike and not even be concerned with whatever my Timex says.

Mike stood up from the booth and took about three steps toward the empty bar. He said real loud, "Hey! Hey! We're ready!"

Let me tell you about the training and precision of the North

Carolina Law Enforcement Department, the FBI, special Homeland Security agents, and even some of Charlotte's everyday police officers. Maybe not all of them were there, but it seemed
like it. I couldn't say for certain, seeing as they stormed in from
all directions wearing riot gear. It looked like the Grambling or
Southern University marching bands spilling inside Mulligan's is
what I'm saying—that kind of precision.

Two men had Mike pinned against the bar in such a way that
his head, beneath the countertop, made him look like an Allen
wrench. Don't ask me why I started laughing at his situation for
about one second until I got pulled out of the booth and flattened
on the floor.

A lot of men said, "Freeze," and "Don't move," and "Don't
you fucking think about blowing this place up, raghead," among
some other things. They had it down. Let me tell you, our tax-
payer money is going to a good and worthwhile cause. Personally,
I would've thought that if they indeed suspected a bomb in that
tongue box, they'd've sent in a robot. Maybe these guys were just
braver than most bomb experts. Or more expendable, either one.

Without ever taking off a stitch of my work clothes those men
gave Mike and me strip searches. They did! I hear that regular strip
searches can be painful, but let me tell you about strip searches that
include cotton underwear and Dickie's work pants getting shoved
up there, too. Any later colon cancer procedures I might decide to
undertake in the future won't feel like anything, I'm betting.

Sam the manager and Liz the waitress came out of a back room
as we were escorted out the front door of Mulligan's. Liz pointed
and screamed, "That's them! That's them right there!" I don't want
to judge her or anything, but she'll need some faster synapses to get
beyond waitress in the fast-paced world of food service.

Later on, in separate interrogation rooms housed in some kind
of mobile step van, then later on at the regular jail, I guess Mike
and I convinced everyone that it was only a found tongue in the

box. Like I said before, our waitress had more than likely been trained and motivated to pinpoint possible anti-American, terrorist activities. All of Mike's bragging about "You will see me on the news real soon," coupled with the old-fashioned dovetailed wooden box alerted her. His wearing a turban probably didn't help, either. Without us even noticing, she and the manager got everyone out of the bar and restaurant areas—even in the Smoking Allowed section, which is a difficult thing to do without much noise—and contacted the authorities who lined up in their strategic ways.

I don't want to say that my ex-coworker's a prophet but, sure enough, we were on television for about a half-day of CNN reports, every hour. Mike couldn't take it. He got all paranoid. Seeing as no one can figure out the owner of the tongue, or the renter of the car, Mike figures he's got a hit planned on him in the same way that Salman Rushdie—I have that first edition, too, but the signature's a fake; I did it myself—underwent from all those old-timey extremists. Mike went back directly to selling mobile homes, saying he hoped that only terrorists *and* FBI agents bought from him, and that they all got involved with a tornado.

I believe it's either the FBI or Homeland Security that owns the tongue now. I imagine they'll hand it over to some other government agency in order to do some DNA testing. Word is, if steroids are detected, Congress might get involved.

I don't care. I have other things to think about—namely, the lecture tour some kind of publicist guy set up for me to tell my story. The company's letting me take a sabbatical—just like if I taught at a regular college. So far I haven't been contacted by my ex-wife's new husband's place. I hope it happens, though. I'd like for her to see how she should've hung around the marriage a little longer. I'm flying to some places, driving to others in one of the competition's rental cars. Everywhere I'm going, I bet, I'll either get frisked, or questioned about excessive mud and dings.

BETWEEN WRECKS

The kid's mother stole my pallet of river rocks stacked out by the driveway, she said, to complete the thousand arrowheads on order from Cheap Chief Charlie's roadside attraction down near Myrtle Beach, among other places. The woman introduced herself as Sally Renfrew and claimed that the chalcedony vein below Andrew Jackson Prep—her son Stan's school—finally "ored out." Sally Renfrew said that she had run a fake arrowhead business for fifteen years; that she now understood Malthaus's notion of supply and demand; that it wasn't easy being a single mother anywhere on the planet but seemed particularly difficult off Scenic Highway 11, some twenty miles from at least an Auto Zone, Staples, public library, grocery store chain, GNC, or hardware store that specialized in durable chisels; that she couldn't return what flat rocks she'd already slowly stolen (and I never noticed, seeing as I'd allowed the family river rock business to fail while I hopelessly worked on my low-residency master's degree in Southern culture studies) over the past month; that she was worried miserably that her boy wasn't going to follow through with college once he graduated from high school in the next year. She rattled on. I thought that maybe she feared I would tie her up, throw her into a secret back room, and torture her for the unspeakable crimes she performed upon a man, namely me, whose pregnant wife took off on him in order to raise their child far from South Carolina. Then I felt so guilty about standing there on my own land on the banks of the Unknown Branch of the Saluda River, blocking Sally Renfrew's exit strategy, that somewhere during her manic monologue I agreed not only to help her load rocks, but also to be a "big brother" of sorts. She chattered on and on about how Stan recently met his biological father, how the father died in a motorcycle accident, and how the kid had it in his mind that he could skip college and become a stand-up comedian. I looked down at the river. I wondered if my father or grandfather ever had poachers of this sort, and tried to think of how they might handle the situation.

I said, "Shut up. Get all the rocks you want. I tell you what— make your arrowheads, and give me ten percent of your gross profit. I know all about the arrowhead market," which wasn't a lie seeing as my mother had manufactured fake arrowheads long ago. I looked at Sally Renfrew—if she had a seventeen-year-old son she must've had the kid at age sixteen, I thought, for she appeared to be my age—and stuck my hand out.

"We live about two miles away. I promise that I haven't stolen from you before this past month. I didn't steal back when your dad pulled river rocks out and sold them to landscapers, or even those couple years when your father kind of slacked off after your mother's death, or when you gave up altogether in order to go back to studying full time. Or when Abby took off for Minnesota."

I kept eye contact. "You certainly seem to know enough about what goes on around here." I wondered if she *knew* that I was trying to complete a low-residency master's degree program in Southern culture studies from Ole Miss-Taylor, and that I waited daily for some kind of omen to send me in the right direction in regards to a new and daring thesis.

Sally Renfrew shrugged. She placed a nice flat piece of slate that might've been part of my house's roof some sixty years earlier. She said, "I'll tell Stan to come over here tomorrow. He's not much into sports. But he eats. Maybe y'all could go hang out and eat breakfast. Tell him how important it was for you to study all those things you studied before you came back here with Abby and gave up. How many bachelor's degrees do you have anyway? And as for the Southern culture studies thing—good God, man, there's a term paper a minute going on around you."

I said, "Hey, wait," but then forgot what I was going to ask her. It had to do with scams, the South, and people, maybe.

When she left I think she might've called out the open truck window, "Five percent."

Stan Renfrew said that he now pronounced his name "Stain," and that it was his biological father's idea. He said it would get him more attention on the comedy circuit. We sat inside Laurinda's, the closest diner from my house, in a square brick building that over the years had housed an auto body repairman, florist, office supplier, biker leather goods, bait shop, lawn mower repairman, and a number of other people running their money-laundering, drug-selling, slave-trading fronts. There was no valid or business-rational reason for a florist to set up shop in an area where houses stood about three per square mile on a two-lane road that only connected ridges, hilltops, and valleys. I hadn't yet figured out what Laurinda did illegally, and my visits to her good diner went from twice a month to about daily after Abby took off to birth and raise our child in the upper Midwest without my help.

Because I didn't want this Stan kid snooping around my property, I drove over to Sally Renfrew's place and found him waiting for me at the end of their quarter-mile driveway. He leaned against the mailbox, tall and skinny, but not with the ubiquitous ennui-ridden look on his face that most seventeen-year-old kids perfected from watching bad situation comedies. Stan got in my truck, said, "I hope you're Stet Looper," and stuck out his hand to shake.

I said, "Your mother must be the top saleswoman in all the world. I realize that you probably don't want to hang out with an old guy."

He nodded, apologized. Stan said, "I just spent ten days with my father. He died on me. But he was seventy-seven years old. So I'm kind of used to old people."

I U-turned and headed toward the diner, trying to do math in my head. "Your father was *seventy-seven*? Good God, man, how old is your mom?"

"It's a long story that involves a famous visiting professor named Stanley Dabbs and a starry-eyed college senior who wanted to be an art critic. I'm what came out of all that."

I grinded my gears and didn't look at the road. I knew Stanley Dabbs's name. I thought about how I might have had a book or two the man had written, from back when I was either a philosophy or history or anthropology major. Dabbs was the last of the great social critics and commentators. "Stanley Dabbs is your father?"

"Was," Stan said. "Are we going to Laurinda's place? I used to go there when it was a driving range. There used to be a tree farm with migrant workers back behind the place, and everyone yelled out 'Quatro!' after hitting tee shots."

I didn't remember it being a driving range, but that sounded about right. I said, "Do you play golf?" I tried to think of all the correct and relevant golf terminology I'd amassed over the years. I said, "What's your handicap?"

I drove past my own long driveway. A vee of geese flew over-head. Stan said, "That was all just a joke. Quatro! I made that up. Hey—if the Special Olympics had a golf tournament, would it be all right to ask competitors what their handicap was?"

I stepped off the accelerator and looked at Stan. He didn't smile. This is a different kind of boy, I thought. "So your mother wants you to go to college, huh? She told me that you wanted to forego college and be a comedian." I pulled over into Laurinda's, which seemed to have more cars in the lot than usual. "I have a feeling your momma isn't going to like my advice."

Before Laurinda—she worked as cook and waitress, somehow—got to our booth, I looked outside and saw a man who, I thought at first, suffered from an inner ear problem. I'm that way mostly, I swear. I ignore people's vices. I told Stan, "That guy either has an inner-ear problem or a gimpy leg." The man weaved around the newspaper rack outside, then looked east up Highway 11. He took four mini-steps to turn around and look uphill in the other direction.

Stan said, "I've been thinking about going to the vocational school to study construction. Then I'm going to build a wooden house entirely out of yardsticks for the exterior. I figure it'll make it easier to prove the square footage when it's time to sell." He didn't laugh.

The man came inside, doffed his stained cap that advertised Celeste Figs, then sat down at the counter. "Chicken truck turned over three mile thataway, and a three-car wreck the other," he said loudly to no one in particular. Laurinda flipped a round mold of hash browns over on the stove.

She said, "Coffee?"

"Well, two cars and a van of illegal aliens, you know."

I said to Stan, "Order whatever you want. Except the sausage or bacon. I don't want you clogging your arteries. Or the chicken, seeing as I guess we can drive down the road and get chicken for free."

Laurinda came around the counter and said, "Stuck, too?" I didn't nod or shake my head. I must've stared blanker than corn-fed trout. "Are y'all stuck between the two wrecks, too?" she said.

Stan Renfrew said, "No, ma'am," like a regular gentleman. He said, "We're out looking for our trained cadaver dogs that got out of their pens. Is there a cemetery nearby, by any chance?"

Laurinda said, "Oh my God." She set her coffee pot down on our table. "You mean those dogs go round pointing out dead beneath the rubble?" When she held her mouth open I noticed that she chewed two separate pieces of gum.

"I've heard both of those jokes, Stain," I said. "The one about cadaver dogs. The one about yardsticks. Just order. There's no snare drum inside here for rim shots."

Laurinda stared at me. She closed her mouth and, with a look of impatience, shook her head. "Okay. You boys ready to order?"

The man with the inner-ear problem folded his cell phone in half, swiveled our way and said, I thought, "Ford ate." Maybe he talked about himself in third person, I thought. Maybe he left a buddy named Ford at home, seeing as Ford had already eaten breakfast.

Laurinda turned over our coffee mugs without asking what we wanted to drink. She poured both cups to their rims without asking if we wanted milk. To the man at the counter she said, "Hours?"

"Yeah."

I said, "What's he saying?"

"Drunk say ford ate hours before the roads get cleared."

Four to eight, I thought. "He's drunk all ready?" I kind of whispered. And I felt like a hypocrite, seeing as I'd been known to partake of bourbon shortly after sunrise. Laurinda nodded and looked out the window. Stan Renfrew asked if she served muffins, and I waited for some kind of off-color joke that he never delivered, even after she said, "Haven't yet. Mostly serve hungry people, honey."

"I've been to your house before," Stan said. Laurinda brought him two pieces of toasted white bread cut into circles, scrambled eggs, and a hot dog. "Before and after you moved back there."

"Did you know my father?" I asked. Abby and I moved back to my childhood home after I'd finished my fifth bachelor's degree, and after Abby—who had a lisp—realized that she wasted her time trying to get an on-air reporter job at a TV station. My father had promised to let me "study myself out," as long as I promised to return home to operate our family business.

Laurinda brought me a plate with six over-well fried eggs stacked atop each other. I had ordered pancakes. Stan said to me, "I never met your father, no."

I said to Laurinda, "This isn't mine."

She checked her order pad, then looked at the booth parallel to ours. A family of four bowed their heads in prayer. Laurinda swapped eggs for pancakes, quietly, right beneath the praying woman's nose. Six fried eggs! I thought. Who eats a half-dozen fried eggs at one time?

Laurinda placed her finger on her lips and asked us to keep the secret. Stan said, "That is so cool." He leaned over and whispered, "Second Comers," which were members of a religious cult that chose northern South Carolina to bombard with believers, thus taking control of the area after running for various councils. As far as I'd heard, only one family ever emigrated, and here they were stuck between scenic-highway wrecks. Stan got up, grabbed both of their syrups, and placed them next to my plate. He reached over again and took the man's fork, then smiled at me. I wondered what a proper, responsible Big Brother or mentor would do in this situation. I probably should've said, "That's not appropriate behavior," or quoted something about having and having not. Instead, I nodded and smiled, and took a glass of water from their table. Stan said, "I know all about these people."

I said, "Go ahead and finish the joke."

Stan said, "No joke. But to answer your question: Nope. Never met your father. But I helped your wife move out, sort of."

I looked across at him. The drunk guy at the counter got up and saluted two men who walked in. He said, "Ford ate hour. Y'all hear? Y'all scared check point, too? *Got*-damn. Can't get to the red dot store now."

Stan said, "I really *smoked* a sex education course I had to take. I made a 69. I think it was the oral exam that put me over the top."

More people walked into the diner. Laurinda came by and said, "Either y'all ever cooked, washed dishes, or waited tables before? I need me some help. I should order up some wrecks more often. Or a rock slide."

I said to Stan, "Whoa, whoa, whoa—you met Abby? You came onto my property and met my wife at some time?"

Stan said to Laurinda, "You ever hear the one about the popular blind waitress who spent most of her time shaking up bottles of ketchup? I got to work on that one. Something about how they're not really bottles of ketchup, but men with their pants down."

Laurinda went off saying, "I'll comp your meal if you pitch in." She turned around to the Second Comers and said, "Y'all's food's getting cold. My booths aren't rented by the day."

I didn't have time to think about theories of synchronicity; or why we're all put on this planet; or the plays of Samuel Beckett,

Harold Pinter, or Jean-Paul Sartre wherein characters are stuck endlessly against their wills; or Martin Luther King's "Letter from a Birmingham Jail"; or how the best way to kill yellow jackets is to let them all get in their underground nest at dusk, then pour gasoline into the hive hole and light it; or how sharp fronds prevented fish from swimming out of baskets used by prehistoric Native Americans, thus trapping them; or the history of alienation in regards to psychology; or how helpless, distraught, confused, frightened, and relentless squirrels can be, once caged.

Well, no, I did have time to think about that last part, because the man at the counter announced to everybody, "I got enough squirrels in my cage. I don't need none of *that*."

I said to Stan, "I'd be willing to bet that that guy's just as irrational sober as he is drunk."

The Second Comers remained bowed. I reached over and grabbed the father's bacon. Stan leaned over and said, "I didn't know she was leaving you. If I'd've known you back then, I wouldn't've helped your wife move out. She didn't seem to know how to use bungee cords, and luggage wouldn't stay up on the roof rack, you know. I was walking down the road picking up aluminum cans, 'cause it's free money, and the more I save the easier it is for me to buy gold, and then I'll turn in the gold bullion later in order to fly to Illinois and get a cell phone with a valid area code so my mother thinks I'm truly at the University of Chicago, and then I'll still have enough money to pay for my apartment up in New York while I'm doing the comedy circuit and telling my mother and dead biological father that I'm attending and passing all of my American studies, philosophy, art history, linguistics, classic rhetoric, and interpretive dance classes. Anyway, there I was with my burlap bag of crushed Budweiser cans—you know it only takes about twenty-five cans to make up a pound, and aluminum's going for fifty cents a pound—and your wife was hunched over the hood of her car half-crying. I said, 'Hey, you got any beer cans in the back seat?' and she said she didn't. I tied up her trunk and couple suitcases, she handed me two dollars, and I walked back home realizing that I probably wasn't going to find another two hundred cans on that particular afternoon. It'll get worse if more of these Second Comers show up, seeing as they don't tend to drink a lot of beer and throw their cans out moving car windows like the rest of us."

Stan finished off his sausage biscuit. I said, of course, "You selfish little bastard. I knew you'd turn on me sooner or later. Sometimes you really scald my testes. Ingrate!" for I felt sure that it's what a regular father might say. Then I got up to help Laurinda with the dishes.

The drunk said, "Ford ate hour" as I passed him. I listened to Stan slide out of the booth and follow me.

I leaned over the man, smelled plain beer, and said, "Bush ate whole years." I thought, What hour did you awake in order to get this intoxicated?

My protégée Stan called out, "Wait up."

Here's what I thought, perhaps. Here's what I thought up elbow deep in dish water, without a Hobart machine in the kitchen of Laurinda's diner: If I were a father, I would want my son to know manual labor. I thought, If my son were a stand-up comedian, I would want him to know that there's not much funny in working for minimum wages, which in turn, somehow, made it all that more comedic. Why would anyone choose to wash dishes for a living unless he either had lost hope altogether or never knew that there were self-satisfying vocations out there, like digging holes in the ground and filling them back up. Stan worked beside me with large white towels draped over both shoulders and one in his hand. I said, "This is not how I planned to spend my day. But we must pitch in and help the community. We're not doing a bad thing, understand. If there's a heaven, maybe we'll be remembered for helping out Laurinda. Even if there's not, we can feel sure that by helping her out, she won't later go nuts from being inundated and go off on a shooting spree. Shooting sprees aren't good things."

I wished that some of this was on tape, so I could show both my rational side and my stern side to Abby up in Minnesota. Then maybe she'd return, give birth to our child, and believe me when I said that this place was the best of all possible areas to raise a child, four- to eight-hour road congestion or not.

Stan smiled. He handed a plate back to me and pointed at some egg yolk. "You don't officially have to do all this," he said. "You can ask my mom out on a date if you want. Ya'll've been watching too much TV. In the real world I don't think prospective boyfriends really have to hang out with the mother's kids and act all cool and normal."

I handed Stan the rewashed plate. I looked through the kitchen porthole and noticed that the Second Comers finally began their meals. Laurinda cooked and talked loudly over her shoulder to the customers. A state trooper walked into the door and took off his Smoky Bear hat. I said to Stan, "What? What're you talking, man?"

"It's a great idea if you ask me—my mom has the arrowhead business, and you have the rock business. You're single and she's single. Even if y'all end up not liking each other—and you will, because you're both smart and stuck in a place where brains isn't exactly the first organ mentioned when people ask to list them out—it's a smart idea business-wise. Economically speaking, you know. Like a family that owns the Pepsi distributorship and another that owns the bottling company."

"Maybe you can get a job running one of those Meet Singles agencies if you don't go to college or end up making it as a stand-up comedian, Stan." I pronounced his name "Stain," like he wanted.

"That's 'Pimp Daddy Stan' to you, my man." *Pimp Daddy Stain* didn't sound very hygienic.

I unstoppered the sink. I said, "I'm still married. I'm not looking for a girlfriend, I'm sorry to say."

Stan smiled at me. He loaded a caddy of clean silverware. "I'm thinking about joining a Hermits Anonymous group, but I have a feeling that no one will ever show up to the meetings." He looked at me. "Would it sound better as 'Hermits Anonymous,' or 'Misanthropes Anonymous'?"

I said, "I used to be a member of Cannibals Anonymous. Great buffet."

This might be selfish on my part, but I enjoyed spending time with Stan Renfrew not for the right reasons: To be honest I didn't give a crap about his self-esteem, or the so-called weighty decision before him involving whether to forgo college to make people pay money in order to laugh. As far as I could tell—and I wasn't but some sixteen years older than Stan—no children made less than a B in high school or college anymore, and then they graduated and found high-paying jobs without ever having to know the discomfort of blisters. I had read an article somewhere about a group of college graduates who *didn't* get high-paying jobs and successfully sued their alma mater. Pissants.

We caught Laurinda up with clean dishes, pots, and silverware, then took to reloading spring-action napkin holders, checked on the salt and pepper shakers, gathered up wet dishrags and tossed them in a take-home hamper. Stan and I walked around with coffee pots, topping off people's mugs. I didn't have time to think about my low-residency master's degree projects that I would probably never finish, about the prospective theses that I didn't

want to undertake. And I didn't have time to think about my confused, determined, wayward, pregnant, and estranged wife.

"Y'all sit down and have some pie," Laurinda said. "I wonder if I'll have everyone here for dinner, too, what with the road
blocked."

"Ford ate hour," the drunk man said, though his eyes looked
much clearer.

I hadn't paid much attention to the Second Comers, who had
finished their praying somewhere along the line and eaten their
meals—I assumed—without complaint. I said, "I'm still full," to
Laurinda.

Stan said nothing, but turned to look at the patriarch of this
particular religious cult family. The father stood up and held both
hands up high. To me Stan said, "Here it comes. Here's the reason
why they have to pray so long." I waited for him to finish up a
joke of some sort. He didn't.

"While y'all are all trapped here I guess it's as good a time as
ever to make you an offer."

"They're grave robbers," Stan whispered to me. We leaned
against two stools adjacent to the drunk man. "I've followed them
around before. They're grave robbers."

The man must've only stood five-five at the most, which I
couldn't tell when he kept his head bowed. His blue jeans showed
patches of red clay at the knees. I leaned forward to see both of
his children staring down at their empty plates, appearing embarrassed. The wife looked up at her husband in that beautiful,
hopeful, dreamy way that only women can pull off. Abby once
looked at me that way when I added transmission fluid to her car,
I remembered.

"As y'all may or may not know, the price of gold has sky-
rocketed what with our being in a war and amid high fuel costs
and on the brink of upcoming inflation. Not to mention the end
of the world as we know it, praise Jesus."

I started to laugh. Stan said to me, "Hallelujah."

"Anyways, gold's now upwards of six hunnert dollar a ounce, and I'm talking the good kind of gold the dentist puts in your teeth. Anyways," he reached into his pocket, "I got here with me a nice collection of gold teeth I'd be willing to sell right at half the price of what they got it going for up in New York and down in Hong Kong."

I looked at Stan and craned forward to look at what the man held in the palm of his hands. Stan turned to me and said, "I told you so. That's why they pray for so long—in case grave robbing's frowned upon by God. And of course it won't be, seeing as God told them to chisel gold out of dead people's heads."

"Sister Rebecca?" the man said. She stood up—her pants held mud stains, too—opened her purse, and pulled out a set of scales best known to small-time drug dealers.

I said, "Damn. What's the world coming to?"

The drunkard blurted out, "Why'd anyone want to buy gold if it's the end of the world like y'all're saying? I thought you couldn't take it with you, end of the world and whatnot." He stood up, and for a second I thought he was going to attack the family of grave robbers. He said loudly, "Does *any*body have a *got*-damn bottle of *booze* stashed in your car outside?" and banged his right fist against his thigh.

The grave robber, of course, said, "We have some communal wine out in the van we'd be willing to sell."

Stan smiled. He said, "Man, I'm going to get a whole mother lode of jokes out of this place. Get it?"

I kind of wanted some booze, too, at this point. I wasn't proud to say that since Abby had taken her "necessary sabbatical," I had gone from stealing a shot or two of bourbon a week—maybe a can of beer if I was interviewing prospective Southern culture

studies subjects worthy of a thesis—to a good near-fifth a day.
I had gone from telling myself I wouldn't drink until dusk, and
then that went backwards to happy hour, and then that went
backwards to as soon as the sun was one degree past its zenith. I
had made a point not to've slugged down a sixteen-ounce plastic
cup of bourbon and Pepsi before going to pick up Stan. I rum-
maged around the cupboards until I found a pint of boysenberry-
flavored vodka—Abby's—and glug-glugged a couple shots into
my coffee. I learned that if I ever lived in the Land of Only Boy-
senberry-flavored Vodka, I would be a sober man.

"You ever had a drink, Stain?" The grave-robbing Christian
and the drunk had left for the parking lot. "Maybe you and I
could get in on some of that wine action. I think it's my duty as
a big brother to make sure you know how to handle your inebri-
ants, or whatever. Your beers, wines, and liquors." Let me say now
that I felt like an idiot saying all this. I understood that Stan was
smart enough to figure out my ulterior motive.

Stan said, "I spent ten days with my biological father. Then he
died."

I took that answer as meaning that he'd been drunk, and he'd
done some drinking afterwards in order to ease his guilt, pain,
wonder, misery, flashbacks, Oedipus complex, no sense of worth,
anxiety toward college, and/or panic attacks about jokes that
don't get laughs. I said, "Let's you and me go meet Mr. Gold and
see what kind of deals he has, seeing as we're stuck here."

We aren't stuck, I thought as I was shaking the Second Comer's
hand. *Stain and I can drive right back home between the two wrecks.* The
drunk man said, "Ford ate hours. I can't wait that long. This is my
idea of Hell."

The Second Comer man said, "I could tell by the look on
your face that you didn't believe my gold to be gold. I promise on
a stack of Bibles that I ain't done no alchemy tricks."

Stan said, quietly, "Double negative." I wanted him to be my younger brother. I wanted him to be my son. He looked at me and said, "I know what you could go investigate." Understand that he shouldn't have known about my life whatsoever without doing some detective work. "There's a man who buys fake arrowheads from my mother. He walks from North Carolina to Oklahoma throwing them down on the ground. Part of what he's doing's political, and part of it's plain crazy. He says that he's filling the Earth back up for what we've extracted. He says that he's also making sure we never forget the Trail of Tears. He calls himself Johnny Arrowhead."

I said to the Christian, "I believe you got gold. I'm more interested in the wine."

He handed me an unlabeled bottle and said, "Muscadine. It's good. It's what Jesus drank. Five dollars."

Stan took the bottle, took the cork out with his teeth, and tipped the bottle up like a professional. I said, "Hey." I said, "Hey, hand that to me." I gave the Second Comer a ten-dollar bill, and he handed me over another bottle from the trunk of his car. I looked inside and saw two shovels, eight muddy boots, a crowbar, a pair of pliers, and a map with highlighted yellow circles. The drunk went back inside with one bottle.

Stan's mother, of all people, drove into the parking lot of Laurinda's diner. Stan said, "My mom. Damn."

He handed me his bottle. She got out of her car wearing heavy leather gloves. She looked at her son, then at me. She smiled. "I just heard on the news about some big wrecks. Thank God y'all are here. Oh my word the whole drive over here I thought it would be y'all." She wore some tight blue jeans, that's all I have to say. I don't know if it was on purpose or anything, but she had these scuff marks on her thighs that pointed straight up like arrowhead points, toward her zipper.

The Second Comer man knew enough to close his trunk. His wife and children came out of Laurinda's diner and got in the car. He took off, and I assumed that he either squatted on nearby land, or he would sit in a traffic jam, waiting. Stan stuck out his hand to shake his mother's. He said, "Ford ate hour, Mom. Ford ate hour."

She said, "Are you drunk?" She looked at me. She said, "Are you not the man of whom I thought?"

Stan said, "Now *that's* some good English."

I looked toward Laurinda's front windows. Inside there were people feasting on good bad food. I said to Sally Renfrew, "I'm just trying to do the best I can. I'm just trying. I didn't sign up for this particular mission, you know."

Sally said, "Go on inside, Stanley."

I said, "Stay, buddy."

She kind of sidled around, as best I could figure. I think I'd seen my wife Abby sidle, maybe near the beginning of our marriage. Sally Renfrew ebbed and flowed left and right, shifting her weight. She said, "Go inside and see if they have any toothpicks. I need some toothpicks."

Stan said, "Yes, ma'am."

I said, "Don't you do it, Stain. It's a trick."

What the hell? I laughed, and looked off in the distance in the same direction as to where the Second Comer drove off with his family. Stan said, "Ford ate hour, ford ate hour, ford ate hour," and walked back into the diner. To his mother I said, "Well. Here we are. How long have we been neighbors?"

She said, "I've lived off Highway 11 for sixteen years. I moved here right about the time you went off to college the first time. I'm older than you are, Stet. Not by much, but I'm older than you are."

I offered her my bottle of wine. "It ain't bad, really. It's good. It's not bad. It's different. It's bottled by a Christian of sorts. It's not bad. It's good."

Sally took the bottle and turned it up in the same manner as her son. She wiped her mouth with the back of her hand. Overhead, some ducks flew by. Way above, a jet flew north, or toward the Midwest. Or West. It didn't fly south. Sally said, "Well. Here we are."

I didn't say, "Yes." I didn't say, "I get along well with your son, and maybe we can all move in together." I didn't say, "Hoo-whee ain't it weird all these cars piled up and we're stuck at a diner?"

I said, "You don't look older than I am."

Sally nodded. She looked at me in the same way that women always looked at me—as if I'd said something about the correct way to boil Brussels sprouts wrong—and said, "Right." From inside Laurinda's Diner I heard someone say, "It doesn't matter," and wondered if that person talked about his eggs not being sunny-side up. Did he say it didn't matter about hash browns, or grits, or toast? Sally said, "Yeah, people tell me I look too young to be Stan's mother. But I am. I think they're being nice. Like you're being nice. Well, you have to be nice for letting him drink wine."

I was officially married. I didn't need complications or temptation. I noticed how I too began shifting my weight involuntarily. I held my right elbow with my left hand, and swung my right forearm back and forth. Sally Renfrew said that she wanted me to write about her. She wanted me to write my low-residency master's thesis in Southern culture studies on the way she invented a prosperous fake arrowhead empire, and how she had finished an unpublished scholarly treatise on the philosophy of craft.

Stan came out of the diner smiling and holding something up to the sky. The Second Comer grave-robbing Christian had dropped one of his gold teeth on the linoleum. Stan said, "Would this be bad luck or good luck?"

I said, "I think it's good."

Stan's mother said, "Bad."

Stan got behind the wheel of his mother's car, and I opened the door to my truck. I told Sally I would go get my tape recorder and notepad, then come over to see how she manufactured fake arrowheads. It seemed like a good idea at the time—I couldn't imagine anyone else writing such a thesis. Stan put his mother's car in reverse by accident and backed into my truck. He said it was a joke. Sally told me to bring my own protective eyewear.

VULTURE

A couple months later, with everything going right in our marriage, my wife pulled out a photo album I'd never seen. She blushed, and for some reason I thought she was going to show me some near-professional nude photographs she'd posed for and taken herself. I think one night when I couldn't sleep I might've punched the channel changer until it hit those movies shown in the 500s, and witnessed a woman who, for her husband's birthday, wanted to give him some 8 x 10 glossies of her wearing, I don't know, the half-peels of a kiwi fruit hanging off her nipples. I knew that Patricia had the top shelf of a hall closet stacked with photo albums, new and used. The ones from back when she was in high school and college tended to have butterflies or kittens on the covers. The one from our wedding looked like the yearbook cover of an all-women's Catholic college—all in white, with raised gothic lettering that spelled out Marriage. Patricia had inherited her parents' photo albums, and they had inherited theirs—ones that were filled with what appeared to be daguerreotypes, you know, with stiff subjects staring mean-eyed at the camera, as if they faced a firing squad. Patricia pulled all those photo albums down about twice a month and turned the pages backwards. She looked at magazines backwards, too, if it matters. If it says anything about her as a person. Maybe in a previous life she lived in China, or Arabia, or wherever it is people read right to left, and back to front. You'd think that that's how they'd read south of the Equator, like in Australia.

Anyway, Patricia pulled down the new photo album, which ended up being two inches thick and had a picture—I'm not making this up—of an electric chair taped to the front of it. I'm not sure where she found the picture, but it had been torn out of a book with thickish, beige paper. It looked like it might have come out of one of those old Funk and Wagnall's encyclopedias. I didn't have my micrometer nearby, but I would estimate that the paper ranged in the 10/1000ths of an inch range—the same as a lottery scratch card, the same as that black paper used in the old photo albums that held blank glares of Patricia's ancestors straddling slaughtered hogs or favorite mules.

Patricia said, "I don't want you to get mad at me, but I need to show you something. And I want you to know that what I'm about to show you should let you know how much more I love you." We sat at the kitchen table. I knew something was up, because Patricia reached in the back of the pantry and extracted a bottle of Old Crow she'd hidden from me some time back. I was pretty sure that Patricia did this on a regular basis—not as often as she daydreamed over photographs of her sorority sisters and her having a pillow fight, or holding shots of beer aloft before chugging them, but more often than most men have their whiskey hidden.

That's right, I said *shots* of beer. I'd met some of her sorority sisters. They had all gone on to become either corporate attorneys or do-gooders just this side of being nuns. Notice how my wife's named Patricia, and not Tricia, Trish, or Patty? Her sorority sisters went by Cynthia, Christina, Suzanne, Melinda, and

Dorothy, never Cindy, Kit, Tina, Christy, Sue, Suzy, Mel, Linda, or Dot. Patricia was a do-gooder who worked for a non-profit called Light the Way, which had something to do with trying to get solar-powered lamps shoved down into the yards of poorer neighborhoods across America so that, at night, people would feel safer. Light the Way had all kinds of questionable statistics that concerned darkness and burglary, darkness and domestic violence, darkness and sexual assaults, darkness and illiteracy. A splinter group of Light the Way, whose members held an interest in more environmental concerns, promoted the need for more fireflies in both urban and rural areas.

Me, I called her organization "Light the *Wayward*," usually behind her back. I said to her, during tough economic times when no corporations donated money, that she and her cohorts needed to contact arsonists.

I unscrewed the top of the bourbon. I said, "What's this all about?" and tapped the electric chair.

Patricia continued to blush. Her eyes zigzagged. She said, "You'll see."

I opened the album and saw a slightly out of focus picture of Patricia and me in the Publix, with me pushing the shopping cart, from behind. I wore my favorite pair of Bermuda shorts that I only wore on summer Saturdays either grocery shopping, or out in the back yard reading the Faulkner stories and novels I kept saying I'd finish before I turned forty. I wore rubber Nike flip-flops. Patricia held, of all things, a giant can of V8.

I said, "Who took this picture?"

I poured some bourbon—maybe three fingers—into an old Welch's grape jelly jar that I liked to drink straight bourbon in because my father did so, and his father did so. Mine had a picture of an Asian elephant on it from the Welch's "Endangered Species" collection, which I liked to drink from so I wouldn't forget. We didn't have photo albums in my childhood household, but by God we had some jelly jars. I looked on the recto side of the album and saw a photograph of Patricia and me sitting in my Jeep at a red light.

Patricia said, "I'm so sorry that I ever doubted you."

I said, "Do we have any Pepsi, or did you hide that from me, too?" I got up and looked in the back of the refrigerator to find a sixteen-ounce bottle of ginger ale. It wasn't my favorite chaser, but it wasn't the worst.

My wife got up, went into the garage, and came back with an eight-pack of tiny Pepsis. She said, "I had a feeling that this was going to happen. I looked ahead! I got these yesterday at the store. I knew it was going to happen!"

Grapefruit juice is the worst chaser, if it matters, when it comes to bourbon. The tie for second place goes to Squirt, buttermilk, Fanta orange soda, soy milk, cranberry juice, and Mr. Pibb.

I turned the page. I turned the page again and again: photographs of my wife and me sitting in the car, entering the automatic carwash down the road, of us walking in a park, of us dropping mail into a drop box. I went to the very back page—maybe Patricia had affected me—to see if there was some kind of plot. The last photograph showed my wife and me sitting inside a vegetarian café that I despised but frequented with her when she craved hummus. On a side note, if you ask me, Patricia and her cohorts should get a group of people to eat hummus, then stand around with matches in poor neighborhoods to keep itinerant and haphazard flames going.

There I was cutting the front yard with Patricia watching me, and there I was opening the door to a convenience store for an old man, and there I with her picking up litter down the road from where we lived. More photographs with Patricia: inside a theatre at one of those goddamn movies wherein three or four women talk about the past, destroy men, and drink shots of beer; inside a yoga paraphernalia outlet; in a music store, standing between the goddamn Show Tunes and Folk Music sections; in the parking lot of the Humane Society before we went inside and ended up with a mixed breed we named Mule who looked like a bird dog with the face of one of those actresses who always show up in movies that Patricia made me attend with her.

There were others. Some of them had a windshield wiper, or steering wheel, in the foreground. The only photographs of me alone—or at least not with Patricia—showed me at Skeeter's bar in town, sitting on the first bar stool by the door, reading one of those goddamn classic books I'd promised to finish. There were a dozen of those pictures, and in each one I wore my favorite going-to-a-bar shirt with two pockets.

I finished off the jelly jar and poured some more. I said, "Okay. I guess that this is going to either be about satellite imagery, or about my not really going to a book club on Tuesdays and Thursdays when you do those night classes."

Patricia taught Sociology 101 at the community college part-time to a number of unemployed, aimless drifters who never took the SAT and could go to college for free as part of the state's unemployment package. She came home crying at least twelve times a semester, mostly because some kind of self-important ex-doffer from the cotton mill insisted that "mores" were eels. For some reason there had always been a man in attendance named Norm who would blurt out, "Here!" or "Present!" when Patricia used his name, and "norm" might be mentioned, oh, six thousand times in a Sociology 101 class.

My wife pulled the jelly jar her way and took a sip—Patricia!—winced, coughed twice, and said, "I hired a detective to follow you around. Sorry. As it ends up, our marriage was fine all along!"

I sat there trying to grasp the situation, and tried to look both pensive and slightly confused, much like the actors and actresses looked in those goddamn movies Patricia made me endure. I said,

"Fine all along, huh? Well that's good to know. Maybe we should celebrate by spelling out 'OK' in the front yard with some of your Colonial-style LED solar-powered landscape lights."

I learned that my wife had been watching too many of those after-the-evening-news programs that deal with famous acting people and their infidelities. One of the "psychiatrists" had mentioned that adultery was contagious, as was divorce, and that it wouldn't be surprising statistically to find out that the only monogamous people in America were, oddly, polygamists. Patricia'd gone off and hired a local detective who specialized in cheating mates—a man named Vonnie Coggins, who had billboards advertising his services, plus a whole back cover of the telephone book where lawyers usually buy space. I always thought "Vonnie" was a woman's name, but evidently it can be a nickname for someone of Italian heritage named "Giovanni." Maybe "Coggins" is a shortened form of an Italian family name. I don't remember ever hearing about a normal Italian named Coggins.

Within twenty-four hours of watching *Entertainment Tonight* or *Celebrities in Action!* or *Hollywood Today*, Patricia got in touch with this detective via the dreadful, civilization-killing Internet. Here's how it worked: Patricia got on the computer and found Vonnie's website. He wrote back to her, "Send me a photo of your husband, and your address." She did. He wrote, "Send me your Visa card number, I won't steal from you, I'm bonded." She did. Vonnie wrote, "I'll follow around your husband, take some photos, and send them to you. Go rent a post office box so your husband doesn't get the mail." Oddly enough, I had, in the past, drank with Vonnie on Thursdays at Skeeter's, across from the bookstore where I told my wife I met weekly with other literary enthusiasts. Patricia wasn't a reader, among other things. I would come home from the bar with a copy of anything that wasn't a tabloid and she'd say, "I don't know why you read that stuff. It's not true! It's all made up. Why would you want to know anything that's made up and spend time with other fools who did the same thing?"

We had to get married, if it matters. If it explains anything. She was pregnant—she said, though I learned later that she made it up—we got married, and then she wasn't pregnant. She didn't have a miscarriage or abortion. She just wasn't pregnant anymore. It's not like I was the first man who ever fell for this ploy. I mean, in the history of marriage, I wasn't the first to fall—I don't think Patricia ever told another man, "I'm pregnant, marry me, don't read books," and so on.

Vonnie followed me around for a while. He took photographs of me with "another woman," who happened to be my wife. Vonnie must've thought that I was up to no good in Skeeter's, seeing as I used an alias there: My real name's Buddy, but in bars I go by Franklin. It's not that odd. I don't like turning my head nonstop whenever somebody says, "Hey, buddy," inside a bar. People say "Hey, buddy" inside a bar more often than you'd think. My middle name's Franklin. And I'm not an adulterous individual.

As a side note, people use the term "buddy" a lot at the Humane Society, too. When Patricia and I were in there selecting Mule to be our dog—which ended up being more *my* dog, and I'm glad—all the other prospective adopters were in there bent down looking into cages saying, "Hey buddy, hey buddy, hey buddy," which made me turn my head about as much as inside a bar. Could you imagine having the name Buddy and being a stray? That would be one skinny dog, always running up to people.

Occasionally Vonnie sat two stools down from me—now I know it's because he liked having the light behind him for better surveillance photographs. I read *The Sound and the Fury*, or *Sanctuary*, or *As I Lay Dying*—all meaningful titles, looking back on things. We watched reruns of the World Cup soccer matches that Skeeter had recorded and played over and over—from something like 1990 to the present because his family came from either England or the Netherlands. No one in the bar cared about soccer, but the hum of all those European chanting spectators, right on up to those vuvuzelas in South Africa, made us—I'm making an assumption here—feel safe. It made all of us drowsy. I didn't want to tell Skeeter how to run a bar, but sleepy drinkers didn't seem like such a great plan.

The one time I actually spoke to the detective who followed me around, I said to him, "Scotch and whole milk, huh? I've read about that somewhere. It's because of having an ulcer, right?"

Vonnie wasn't the most likeable bar patron. He said, "It's because my family owns a dairy and I don't want to see them go out of business." That might've been the time he took a photo of me from his secret hidden camera gizmo. He said, "You worry about your drink, and I'll worry about mine."

I didn't say it out loud, but I thought "Dickhead." After Patricia explained the photo album, and showed me Vonnie's picture on the back of the telephone book, I wish I'd've said "Dickhead" and more to the guy. First off, if I'd've known everything, I might've said, "How smart is it to have your picture on the back of a telephone book? If you're tailing someone, don't you think he might've seen your face and say to himself, 'Uh-oh, there's that detective Vonnie Coggins with his weird non-Italian last name. I hope he ain't following me around'?"

I'd been back to Skeeter's just about every Tuesday and Thursday night since that time, and not seen Vonnie again. Skeeter even said to me a couple times, "Hey, don't scare off my customers anymore." I thought he meant it because I had big hands that looked strangle-worthy.

I sat there with Patricia. I understood that, subconsciously, maybe she wanted me to fool around on her so she could get out of the marriage. I wasn't much of a do-gooder, and do-gooders who believe in an afterlife don't want to be alone, more than likely.

If they believe in Heaven and Hell, like Patricia did—wrongly, I believe—then they don't want to consider living on a cloud with a harp, consumed with wondering how their non-do-gooder spouses are getting along with the fire and brimstone. I have no evidence to back this up. None of those Snopes characters ever brooded about it.

I said, "What's with the electric chair?"

She got up from the table, opened the pantry door, dug around, and pulled out a tiny square bottle of expensive Cointreau I'd bought a few years earlier and thought I had finished off. Patricia went to the cabinet, pulled out a fancy hand-blown snifter of sorts, then dropped it accidentally on the granite countertop. She said, "Damn! It's your fault, you know."

That's what I do for a living, and what my father and grandfather did. I make and install granite countertops, and believe me when I say that—if I wanted to—I could have affairs with a number of unhappy housewives whose husbands try to assuage the daily matrimonial tensions with overpriced and unneeded kitchen accessories. I think that the wives believe that because I have big hands, maybe I have a gigantic pecker, like they say. Again—no scientific proof here—but the gigantic hands of granite countertop workers is a direct result of banging and smushing every finger, over and over daily.

I said, "Use one of my jelly jars. And put an ice cube in the bottom of it first."

Patricia said, "The electric chair was supposed to be symbolic." She came back to the table and sat down. She pulled the picture off the cover and said, "I guess I need to replace it with a dove, or a penguin. Those are animals that're monogamous."

I didn't say, "Black vultures." Black vultures mate for life. I'd gotten all obsessed with vultures while reading one of those novels, and done some research.

I said, "Black vulture."

Patricia stared at me and then shook her head. "You're disgusting." She thought I'd said something about vulva during this, our unplanned reconciliation I didn't even know about.

As anyone who'd ever watched an afternoon talk show might imagine, our marriage didn't last much longer. Maybe I wasn't paying attention. Sometimes Mule looks at me an hour after I'm supposed to feed her, and the look on her face says, "You're not paying attention." The look on her face says, "There's a program on the Animal Planet I've been watching when you go off to work, and it's about people who call in the cops on people who aren't taking care of their animals."

Maybe Patricia met someone at the community college who planned to work for UNICEF, or Habitat for Humanity, or the United Way. Maybe the college hired someone to teach geography part time because of his experience in the Peace Corps. She woke up hungover the day after we looked at her clandestine photo album, said she was sorry, said she couldn't spiral downward with my addiction and self-destructive streaks, said she couldn't live with a man who never planned to go to college after dropping out after three and a half years even if he did so in order to get married and take over his father's business, said that we were fortunate to never have had children.

I got up out of bed with my thumbs hurting, as usual. I said, "What?" I said, "I didn't cheat on you, Patricia. What the fuck more do you want out of me?"

Mule didn't get out of bed. Mule lay there like she always did, as if she wanted me to pick her up and take her outside.

Call me irresponsible and inattentive and unobservant, but I'd not noticed that Patricia had already packed up her car the day before. As I figured it out later, she wanted me to throw a tantrum. She wanted me to look over those photographs of us together all the time, and say, "You didn't trust me, bitch?!" like that. She wanted me to raise a hand in anger, to go burn somebody's barn, to speak to her as if she were simple-minded, to threaten her with a corn cob, to take up wing-walking as a pastime and die. She wanted me to get a slight lobotomy and think that our world could be cured with no darkness available.

"I appreciate your being patient with me" were her last words, which didn't make a lot of sense, if you ask me.

I had no other option but to call up Liz Pembroke—who was a nice, sane woman who didn't go by Elizabeth or Eliza or Lizbeth—and say that, although I prided myself, as my grandfather and father had done, on being punctual and trustworthy, I couldn't possibly make it to her kitchen for two days. I lied. I said, "I've been asked to send all my scrap granite down to the Gulf of Mexico in order to help with that oil spill."

Where did that come from? I even thought to myself.

Liz Pembroke said, "I completely understand. What a nice thing you're doing! Are they going to plug that leak with your granite? Will crushed granite stop the force of oil coming up to the surface? I guess it will, seeing as granite holds back oil everywhere else on the planet. I've been thinking about getting some one-of-a-kind sculptures in the back yard—not like garden gnomes, you know. Do you ever make one-of-a-kind sculptures for people, kind of like Stonehenge?"

I said, "I have no clue." I said, "I have no clue" about six times, like an idiot. My mind wandered over to Patricia having an affair with Vonnie Coggins, for some reason. I said, "I'll take some money off y'all's price, for my being late."

Mule got out of bed. She walked up to me and wagged her tail twice. I asked her if she wanted to go outside. She ambled toward the sliding-glass door. I watched her trot to the middle of the back yard, and then I thought—what the hell?—I can have some of that Cointreau seeing as I'm not going to work.

When I walked back out to the sun room I saw my dog looking straight up into the air. Did she smell something dead on the horizon? Was she looking for birds of prey to swoop down? Was she merely stretching her neck in a way to relieve some tension?

I looked down at my disfigured, ugly hands. They looked like talons, I thought. What woman, in the future, would ever want me to touch her kindly?

THE SINKHOLES OF DUVAL COUNTY

It's not like I didn't understand how we preyed on octogenarians, the shell-shocked, paint-fume addicts, and the superstitious in order to gain something for future use, though I couldn't imagine the long causal progression at the time. This little scam and trek occurred in 1987 and would be considered the germ of what happened in 2008 when Uncle Cush, according to him, single-handedly maneuvered North Carolina's electoral votes in the presidential election. Because my uncle could sew, and because he had access to free parachute-like material that he recovered from a questionably locked storage room behind the defunct Poke Cotton Mill—and because we'd both read Machiavelli and Jeremy Bentham and John Stuart Mill—there seemed to be no other option but to pack up a step van and visit the faulty limestone foundations of Florida, two states south of us. I had turned eighteen a month prior. This would have been some kind of slightly aberrant graduation present had I actually not been homeschooled since seventh grade and never undergone a traditional convocation.

"I might've picked a bigger state to visit had you done gone to Poke High like every other goddamn linthead's child wrongly hoping to be all valedictory in his or her wants," Cush said right about the time we crossed the St. John's River via ferry boat—my first time—and then pulled into a VFW lounge he'd researched. "I might've picked us Texas. But your momma was all worried about the violence in the schools."

This VFW took up the bottom floor of an ex-department store that appeared to be three stories high. It will matter.

Anyway, I didn't contradict him. He'd only been back from Vietnam for five years after choosing to stay there after the pull-out to hike Southeast Asia alone and mesmerize villagers with his spoon-playing repertoire. Uncle Cush's softest visage compared to that of a trailer hitch, his normal eye contact that of two balls of barbed wire. On more than one occasion over the years we'd walked into convenience stores only to have the assistant managers raise their arms up in the air. One time when he was looking at new trucks over at Forty-Five Motors the lot manager went inside and called two deputies. People often took him for the actor Jack Palance's crazed brother, if Jack Palance's brother ever slicked back his black hair with shellac and let a Fu Manchu grow down below his clavicles.

I didn't say, "Mom wasn't so concerned with the violence in elementary and middle school as all the other parents were, seeing as I beat the shit out of all those kids every day. The violence came from me." I didn't say, "I enjoyed being homeschooled without a Bible portion of the curriculum, seeing as I could be President of the Solitaire Club and captain the tetherball team."

We got out of the step van, there in a paved lot on St. Augustine Road, and my uncle—because he was a visionary and mind reader—said, "And you loved it when your daddy took you down in the basement to teach you how to beat off for sex ed while your momma stood upstairs with no girls to counsel or inculcate." Uncle Cush looked at himself in the side mirror. "Now. We get in here, you say you my son so's not to cause suspicion, understand? If you say you're nothing but a nephew, everyone's going to be asking questions about where your daddy is, or how come your daddy let me take you on a joyride. Right now we're just going to water the testosterone, as they say."

I said, "I shouldn't mention the parachutes," and nodded.

"No. You shouldn't mention parachutes. Don't mention that goddamn Jean-Paul Sartre you been reading, either. Don't mention how you ain't never had no pussy I ain't set up for you. How you love long-distance running over football or baseball? Don't bring that up. Your ideas that we shouldn't've invaded Grenada? I'll kill you if I even think I hear you starting up a word that starts with *Gr*. Don't bring up how in twenty years there will be nothing but life one pubic hair away from being American anarchy because of Second Amendment arguments, or how corporations will flourish on the backs of workers stuck with part-time minimum wage jobs without insurance benefits, or how I'm the only man living who has figured out a way to stop it."

Sometimes my uncle veered into crazy talk, and I assumed that there in the hot northern Florida sun he'd succumbed to such nonsensical diatribes. I said, "Last semester I studied up on the filmography of Charlie Chaplin, Harold Lloyd, Buster Keaton, and Lillian Gish. I know how to be mute."

"Watch and learn," my uncle said. Then—and understand that we'd been in the loaded step van for six and a half hours, taking back roads—he said, "By the way, we'll be gone for at least ten days."

He pointed out into the Gulf of Mexico, I assumed, but then waved his arm that could've meant somewhere south of the Equator.

———

There on the western edge of the Gulf, my uncle said, "Hey there, comrades, anyone here from ASA Radio Research?" which I later learned was some kind of battalion or platoon of soldiers who scored high on military intelligence tests. "Anybody here spend time in Bing Bang Ding Dong?" At least that's what it sounded like to me.

Everyone nodded. They didn't nod as in, Yes I Was in Your Platoon, but more like You Are in the Right Place. A jukebox in the corner played a song that skipped right in the middle of a yodel. "Name's Cush Waddell," my uncle said loudly. "This here's my boy, Start. Just graduated first in his class up in South Carolina, so I'm taking him out on a little celebratory vacation, show him how his old man's about to save the lives of veterans down in Florida."

The bartender wore a decorated garrison cap that somehow balanced on the right side of his head. "We could use some saving, long's it ain't the born-again kind, you know what I mean."

I said, "I'd like a Budweiser, please."

"Nah, nothing like that," Uncle Cush bellowed out. He couldn't've have been louder with a megaphone. "One thing I was reading near a year ago was how all our brothers who made it out of 'Nam came back home to unemployment, demons, post-traumatic stress, suicidal tendencies, and freak accidents that lead to death and maiment."

I didn't say, "'Maiment' is not a word." I looked at the bartender. He wore a military name tape over his pocket that read WARREN. I didn't say anything to my uncle about how that could be a sign—that this bartender might warn others about the hoax that Cush had in the works, the hoax I'd not been privy to at this point. I said, "Or whatever you have on special, bottle or can, Admiral Warren."

"I read that same article," a man at the bar said, nodding. "Got all these old boys like us dodged bullets and landmines, come back here and get shot in the head minding our own business in line at the Snack 'n Gas. Them's the kind of maiment I can't figure out."

I wanted to go kick the jukebox. Why didn't anyone bring up the skip? The more I listened to it, the more it sounded like a troop of howler monkeys I'd seen when Cush took me to a zoo for another one of his celebratory side trips.

Cush pointed over at the man and said, "There you go. What I have in mind here for y'all, and you boys look like you might could use the money, are mini parachutes to be worn at all times. I read another article—I bet you read it, too—about all the sinkholes in Florida. You think the government's going to stop everything, come down here and build a stronger manmade foundation for Florida? They ain't. It's every man–woman–child for hisself. Sinkhole drops out from under your feet twelve or twenty stories deep, you gone need one these parachutes to slow down the descent. Just like the little emergency chute everyone knowed about in Airborne. I tell you what—it's a lot better landing fifteen miles an hour into the limestone and dolomite pits of Florida than at forty miles an hour, don't that make sense?"

Warren reached down and slid two cans of Dixie toward my uncle. "So what you're saying is, you get people to go around wearing these things all the time. Kind of like protection, should the ground give way."

My uncle took both cans of beer in his left hand, reached in his right-hand pants pocket and pulled out a five-dollar bill. He said, "We come down with a truckload of them. What I was hoping to do was, I was hoping to sell the things wholesale, let my brothers from 'Nam go 'round making a profit for theyselves. A normal parachute for jumping out of planes might go for over two thousand dollars. Of course I ain't offering all the extra doo-dads, so these emergency chutes shouldn't retail for more than two hundred. I'm willing to sell what we got for a hundred dollars each to anyone wants to go out and sell them for whatever. We already sold a whole shipment to some veterans up in Tennessee. They got them some sinkholes south of Knoxville you wouldn't believe. One them things goes 250 feet deep and spans three-plus miles. Look it up."

My uncle had been sneaking out textbooks I'd bought used from college bookstores, for I had come across a story about Big Sink in White County, Tennessee, and another about Grassy Cove—one of which was indeed 250 feet deep and the other three-plus miles across, but not the same place altogether. I said, "Hey, tell the story about your brother who had to move away because he might've killed a man," so that Uncle Cush would hand over the beer in order to quiet me down.

"Let's take a look at one," Warren said to my uncle. To me he said, "I wasn't an admiral. Hell, I spent most of my time in the brig, to be honest, when I wasn't on a sub. Call me Shorty."

I said, "Aye-aye."

I figured out later that the parachute material from Poke Mills was free, and the nylon backpacks my uncle ordered in bulk only came out to $1.22 each. I never learned, over the ensuing years, how Cush became a champion seamstress—sometimes he told me that a woman named Cu taught him how to taxidermy water buffaloes in Vietnam, sometimes he told me that he worked in a sweatshop while hiding from the FBI on non-nefarious charges—and wondered when he had the time to construct miniature pseudo parachutes for sinkhole possibilities. For some reason I doubted that he hadn't slept since 1971, though he always held his hand up and dared me to go find a lie detector test.

Warren and my uncle left for the truck. No one talked to me. The man on the stool got up, rounded the bar, extracted two more cans of Dixie, and slid one my way. He said, "I still owe you for tying that tourniquet on my leg, back in the jungle. Man, that was an emergency, wasn't it, until the helicopters showed up."

"We have a little left over in our emergency fund for occasions like this," Warren said when he came back wearing a neon orange child-sized backpack, a ripcord slung over his right shoulder. He yelled out, "Hey, boys, I know some y'all wish to die, but how many y'all want to die in a sinkhole? How many want you and yours to disappear into the hollowed-out caverns of Duval County?"

No one raised a hand. Uncle Cush shifted his weight from one foot to the other. I could tell that he wanted out of there before one of the ex-Air Force guys asked a number of pertinent questions, as ex-Air Force retirees are wont to do, especially the ones who couldn't qualify for astronaut training. Cush said, "How many of y'all want to have a tombstone that reads 'Dropped Into the Earth and Was Never Found'?"

Again, no one raised a hand. The yodeler still skipped in such a way that made me envision a sack of cats dealing with a professional wrestler adept at the infamous "pile driver" maneuver. I finished that second beer and blurted out, "I want my tombstone to say 'Born 1969,' and then just an en-dash after it, meaning that I never died."

A man wearing blue jeans that someone had ironed flat-wise stood up and said, "I got mine picked out. It'll say, 'First There Was Seoul, Now This Hole.' I'm a Korean War vet, see."

It was on. Another man stood up and saluted the television mounted on the wall, which had the sound turned low and showed *The Price Is Right*. He said, "Mine gone be First a Pain, Then an Itch. Here Lies One Mean Son-of-a-Bitch."

"Someone Send Down Some Water! That's mine," a man yelled out, not turning to look at us. Then he pointed toward the screen and said, "I got me a Kawasaki jet ski just like that one.

Goddamn it, if I was on the show like I was supposed to be, I'd say $6,999 and be up there on the stage with Bob Barker."

My uncle held up his arms and said, "Whoa, whoa, whoa." He looked at Warren and said, "Help me out here."

Warren said, "This man has some chutes for sale that we all need. Now, I believe it's my job to advise everyone in attendance to line up and buy one these anti-sinkhole devices. And I advise that we go out in the field just like we did on foreign soil and teach the savages what they need to do in order to survive. Get on up here and buy you a chute, Tonto. Skidmark. Finger Man. Gutter." He went on and on. When each veteran's nickname got called up, he stood at attention and marched to the bar counter. Me, I got all caught up wondering what I would have to do in life to acquire "Finger Man" for a moniker.

Uncle Cush said, "Don't be afraid to buy as many as possible. You can sell them twice they worth, easy."

I reached over and got my third Dixie beer. At the time—at age eighteen—I only knew Pabst, Budweiser, and Miller. Later on in my life I would understand Dixie to be a beer drunk mostly because of its provenance, but at the time, to me, it was as exotic as Camembert or hashish. I said, "When this gets done you better tell me what you meant about Dad and Mom moving," and my uncle glared at me. He concentrated hard, I could tell, until he gathered up the "cold blue polished steel" glower. I said, "I mean Uncle and Aunt."

I stared at the beer can for a moment before looking up to find every man inside the VFW lounge sporting a miniature lifesaving sinkhole parachute. Each man had his right hand clenched around the ripcord. Uncle Cush said, "You know what might get us all into Heaven, is if y'all get on the phone and call loved ones to come on down here to pick one or two up. You know what I mean? Any y'all go to church, you might want to call up the pastor. I'm sure he wouldn't want any his congregation falling down so close to Hades should the earth give way."

I excused myself to the men's room where, at the urinal, I aimed at a plastic roulette wheel of sorts and watched the arrow spin until it ended up Big Shot.

Big Shots would've known better. In retrospect, Uncle Cush and I agreed that we should've sold six or eight faux parachutes and then driven off to the next VFW. We should've parked at a busy intersection and hung a banner like those people who sell name-brand tennis shoes or mattresses on the roadside. But Warren got on the phone and called his people, who called their people, and so on. Within the hour the VFW parking lot filled with the hopeful, the hopeless, the discombobulated. It was the preachers who bought multiple chutes—and I overheard one say to the other, "All's it gone take is saying God tode me to tell everyone they needed one these things at two hundred a pop. Next thing you know, I got me a new Cadillac to drive around in, show people how good God is to those who live a Christ-like life."

Uncle Cush and I stood back, the back doors to the step van swung wide open. He said to me, "This is working out a lot better than the grocery store trick I miscalculated. Way better."

Uncle Cush had gone into a Winn-Dixie a month earlier with a specific grocery list: Sunbeam Old-Fashioned bread, 32-ounce Jif Crunchy, Wheaties, Oscar Meyer Beef Bologna thick-cut, large curd Breakstone's-brand cottage cheese, a gallon of whole Pet milk, that sort of thing. He bought it all, took it to his pickup truck, and set down the bags. Then he extracted the receipt and walked back in the store. Me, I sat in the truck reading a book called *A Theory of Justice* by John Rawls, a chapter on civil disobedience, because that's what I'd been trained to do. My parents—

and Uncle Cush, for that matter—hoped that I'd be able to get out of Poke, South Carolina, and fix the world.

I wasn't smart enough to understand how much pressure they put on me, if it matters. I couldn't comprehend how much of my learning process at home depended on figuring out what *not* to do, how *not* to act in public, how it was important to learn the *opposite* of Good in order to appreciate and discern what was right. My father spanked me once and used a variety of lashes—a rolled magazine, a thin peach branch, his belt—so that I grasped what a cut-off piece of barbed wire felt like on the back of my thighs.

Anyway, at the grocery store, I plodded through a chapter called "Classical Utilitarianism," then skipped ahead to "Principles for Individuals: the Natural Duties," and didn't even think about how the milk might spoil back in the bed of the truck, how cottage cheese shouldn't sit out in the sun. I might have been absorbed and befuddled for an hour before I thought, I wonder if Cush got lost, had a heart attack, got caught for shoplifting, came back into the parking lot and got in the wrong truck, underwent flashbacks in the noodle aisle.

I walked into the store to find him standing there by a Buy One/Get One Free bin of damaged cans. He yelled out, "Where you been, goddamn it?"

I shrugged. He held onto the handle of his filled shopping cart. I said, "What?"

His whole plan was to buy foodstuffs, take his receipt back in, get the same items, and then if he got asked about his grocery shopping peculiarities he could pull out the first receipt and say, "Check it out, manager." Then there would be the same items. The time printed out wouldn't be but five minutes' difference, as if he dallied by the fifty-cent claw machine trying to garner a stuffed animal. "Go back out to the truck and get me them bags from the first order. This ain't gonna work like I thought unless I can get my groceries in *bags*."

I don't know if my reading on civil disobedience helped me out at this point, or if it was a previous book on logic, but I said, "In the future you need to bring your own bags. It wouldn't kill you to go green, you know, like those people west of the Colorado River."

He left his filled cart there and, out in the lot, said, "Well, I still did a good thing. Somebody inside will have to go place all those items back on the shelves. So I kept them a job. Listen here, Start—it's all about making sure people keep their jobs. If there weren't people like me going around like that, that Winn-Dixie manager might have to lay off people, saying 'Hey, we don't need nobody to restock shelves.' Job well done!"

"Job well done!" Uncle Cush said there in the VFW parking lot to a preacher who bought a sinkhole parachute for every member of his choir.

I said, "I want to call home."

Cush shook his head. "Listen, I can't blame you for not understanding everything, but we have to finish what we started here. You know how much land I can buy up in the North Carolina mountains for $200,000? It's a bunch. There's a man in trouble up there wants to get rid of his holding for a hundred dollars an acre. Do the math. We get that much land, we can set down teepees eight to an acre, easy. Four people per teepee, thirty-two per acre, all that times two hundred. Do the math. We get the right people from out in California who ain't needed in that state, that's enough to change the voting landscape. Sixty-four thousand new voters can change a place like North Carolina, what with the liberals living in the Research Triangle."

Twenty years later I would convince myself that I came up with the idea—that finding a way for America to vote out the incumbent party was what my parents long ago trained me to do—and Uncle Cush would never deny me my pride. He'd go along with the gently forced mass migration and offer his congratulations.

I said, "I want to drink eighteen cans of beer. Would that be a record for an eighteen-year-old?"

He twisted one strand of his Fu Manchu and put his arm around my shoulder. "Don't try it. I drank twenty-two beers in 'Nam on my birthday. You know how come you never see me with my shoes off? It's because I'm missing a toe. It happened on that same day."

Warren yelled out, "We ain't had a day like this since that Girl Scout cookie truck broke down here a couple years ago!" People bought parachutes, donned them like lucky capes, then wandered into the VFW as if they belonged, as if they once fought the mighty Hun, the mighty Cong, the mighty Grenadians.

Uncle Cush took folded-up twenty-dollar bills and shoved them into his pockets until he bulged like a multi-goitered Freemason. Then he pointed to me when buyers strapped on their emergency vests. I took in proceeds and—because of my age—thought about ways to steal from my own uncle, about a new stereo I could buy, about all the books I could buy new or used. I thought about how maybe I could drive into downtown Poke waving money around until a young woman I knew in elementary school agreed to accompany me to the nearby Forty-Five for a movie and special celebratory flounder dinner. I thought about how I could use the money for an airline or cruise ship ticket to visit my runaway parents, how I could acquire the best defense lawyers in the country. Then I got to daydreaming about booze, and how I might need that money compounding interest daily in a CD so I could afford rehab lessons at some point when my wife had had enough.

"Most people I ever meet need to have a tombstone that reads 'Well That Wasn't Worth the Time,'" Cush said. "Mock it down:

Everyone who buys a sinkhole-saving parachute here—or where we'll be going later—should probably die from a fatal unexpected fall into the depths of Duval County. Or, fuck, any county, any state."

More people drove into the parking lot, people who must've gotten a celebratory and exhortatory warning, men wearing grease-smudged khakis and women in worn cotton-print dresses. Mothers showed up yelling, "Will it work for my bay-bay?" and men asked, "It ain't gone blow up like a airbag, is it? I don't want to be down there with the ancient coral alive but burned up like a bad wick."

This particular scheme wasn't failing like the free groceries hoax. I would've pondered about it more, but well-meaning and hopeful derelicts stretched their hands my way as if I owned Fountain of Youth water best known down forty miles south of where we stood. I felt surrounded by zombies. I had witnessed late-night evangelical channels with similar desperate dawdlers hopping up to the stage in hopes of having that missing leg reappear.

I yelled out, "Step right up! Step right up! Step right up!" like any obnoxiously buzzed eighteen-year-old might do after realizing that he'd never see these people again. I didn't notice two things: First off, somebody had worried about their drug-addicted children who showed up after huffing fluorescent pink paint from paper bags. These kids—six of them, about my age—leaned down to idling car headlights, then stood erect to show off their glowing alimentary canal entrances. In the dusk, as they wandered around, it looked as if frosted strawberry doughnuts hung in the air, or like the little blips that live inside one's eyelids had taken steroids and threatened to run away. If they stood in a line according to height it looked like O O O o o o standing between our truck and the entrance to the bar. I got mesmerized for thirty seconds or so, and listened to these boys wearing my uncle's parachutes end every sentence with "dude." I didn't notice, too, that said

pink-encircled-mouth huffers found a way to ascend to the roof
of the VFW lounge soon thereafter—again, three stories high—
and yell down to us those words that never offer good news, viz.,
"Hey! Dude! Hey! Are y'all watching us? Get out of the way!"

"Get out of the way," Uncle Cush said to someone as he got in
the step van and turned the ignition. To me he said, "Close those
goddamn back doors and jump in fast."

I said, of course, "I think I'm going to regurgitate." I reached
into my pocket and pulled out what ended up being $900. What
were all these people doing with a hundred dollars to spare? I
thought. Or at least I thought it later. I thought about it twenty
years later, too, when people made the news for falling into sinkholes every other day. From the way we were parked in front of
the VFW, I was on the side closest to the door. People slammed
their palms against the step van's panels like zombies looking for
living meat. Like groupies hoping that the lead guitarist would
emerge from the venue's back door with his pecker hanging out.
Like Southerners wanting milk and bread at the grocery store
when the temperature dipped below forty.

Uncle Cush turned the ignition and palmed the horn. In retrospect, I think he kept the horn going so as not to hear the sound
of six deranged teenagers hitting the ground from thirty or forty
feet up.

I grabbed Cush's arm and made the horn stop. And then I
heard "Geronimo" and watched as one fluorescent pink circle fell
from the sky, first quickly, and then slowed down. The five other
circles followed with the same result. Cush backed up the step van
and aimed his headlights toward where the boys had landed, all
of them standing upright, their miniature parachutes unfurled on
the ground like spent condoms thrown out of a moving vehicle.

Uncle Cush said, "I'll be goddamned," and looked at me. He said, "The bridle pulled the D-bag out, the bridle pulled the D-bag out!" though at the time I thought he referred to the assortment of huffers as douchebags. He'd not gone into details about the technical terminology of a parachute, hand-crafted or not.

I said, "They're alive," but not with much enthusiasm, for I still felt as though all those cans of Dixie beer might leave my body in an undesirable way.

Cush put the step van back in park. "Get out and let's get back to work," he said to me. To Warren he yelled out, "If that ain't a commercial for how to survive a sinkhole attack, I don't know what is," and Warren said, "Shit, man, let me go back inside and open the safe. I'mo buy me another dozen them things for resale."

This was a time before cell phones. No one got on the World Wide Web and advertised how a Fu Manchu-ed Vietnam War veteran and his "son" brought lifesaving technology to the largest city area-wise in the United States of America. The paint huffers descended, landed safely, and somebody made another call from a pay phone in the parking lot of the VFW. Then the callee called some people, and they called some people, and so on—just like Malthus pointed out in *An Essay on the Principle of Population*, which I read in the fourth grade at the urging of my parents after I wouldn't finish the Catfish Surprise that my mother baked for supper, and which I think shouldn't have been called an "essay" seeing as it plodded on somewhere into the 42,000 word range.

"Sober up, son," Uncle Cush said to me. "I don't mind a man drinking, but you need to know how to act sober on the spot, with no warning, when it comes to high finance. We get back home? I got some films of Wall Street tycoons testifying before Congress. They know how to do it better than anyone."

We didn't sell out of the parachutes there in the VFW parking lot, but the huffers' questionable feats of daring helped us, I would bet, sell another sixty or eighty units over the next few hours. The crowd dwindled. The original nicknamed veterans had gone home to undergo their personal nightmares. Warren locked up the front door to his bar and told us he didn't mind if we stayed in the parking lot overnight to sleep, just like people did at Wal-Marts in their recreational vehicles. My uncle thanked the man, waited for his taillights to disappear, then got in the step van and said to me, "I pride myself on not making mistakes with the Singer machine, but I can't promise nobody's going to go jump off a bridge tonight and have a failed chute. No need to sit here like a radioman tattooed with bull's eyes, knowing snipers are everywhere, aiming for us."

Cush drove and I unfolded a road map provided by a Texaco station down in south Georgia. I said, "Daytona Beach looks like the next best place for a VFW, if you want to get out of Duval County entirely." I directed him toward Highway 1.

"Daytona Beach," my uncle said. "That's the kind of place where people would want to live a long time, not fall victim to the earth's frail decisions. That's a type of place to grasp and decipher the truth."

We didn't get two miles down the road when, up ahead, the headlights showed the round flourescent mouths of those daredevil huffers, turning around to hitchhike. I knew already what would happen. My uncle didn't say, "Hey, do you think I should pick these boys up and take them down to Daytona?" He didn't say, "What these boys need is a good role model, like me, so that they get off the paint fumes and quit acting like shell-shocked soldiers in a way that won't allow them to become comfortably superstitious octegenarians." I read his mind though. He felt as though he could offer some of his hourly advice and turn them around, at least after they proved his mini-parachutes' worth when leaping from a Holiday Inn's tar-and-gravel roof, to the shock and amazement of local onlookers who—whether they admitted it or not—had long feared being swallowed up inside the bowels of a relentless state not known for moderation on any level.

I closed my eyes and felt my uncle ease up the accelerator, then tap his brakes. In my mind I imagined his losing control when he pulled off to the gravel berm, maybe accidentally wrecking into the guardrail, scaring the boys we would ask to join us. I looked way into the future and thought about how we would measure our lives between such wrecks, and that there would never be a time when we could feel safe or content about the next one looming.

UNFORTUNATELY, THE WOMAN OPENED HER BAG AND SIGHED

Rodney Sheets couldn't stop thinking about deforestation. He'd seen three separate documentaries on three different networks, and thus concluded that there must be a connection between innumerable acres burning on two continents and the reason why the temperature outside hovered at 100 for three weeks straight. He thought, Those narrators and scientists and actors are right—I can change my daily habits and help save the planet. He'd finished his fourth gin and tonic.

No one else populated Gus Bingham's bar on the Saluda River. Gus said he had to go check out a smell in the crawl space. He set two bottles in front of Rodney, along with a cut-up lemon, a pen, and cocktail napkin. He said, "Hatch off your tally. Anyone else comes in, bang the bar stool for me. I got to get some lime, and not for your drink."

Rodney nodded. He marked four lines at the top of the napkin, then a fifth. He unfolded it and wrote, "Plant trees in yard. Buy recycled products. Promote constipation—save TP." Then he stalled.

The door opened and a woman limped in. She carried a filled canvas satchel. Her matted hair reached past her shoulders, and not in the I'm-a-white-hipster way that Rodney saw on a whole other documentary about the unfulfilled lives of ex-Deadheads. The woman plopped down indelicately two stools away and placed her heavy bag between Rodney and herself.

She emitted an odor of week-old perspiration and moldy Roman Meal bread. Rodney said, "Hey. Gus'll be right back." He didn't get off his stool and bang it on the floor. Gus wouldn't be happy to emerge from a fouled crawl space only to have a homeless drifter woman plead for alms.

The woman said, "Buy me a drink." She looked at the bottle.

Rodney said, "What you got in the bag?"

"I have money. Damn, man. Whatever happened to men buying women drinks in bars? In New York and L.A., there're still men buying."

She reached in her back pocket and pulled out twenty one-dollar bills. Rodney said, "You turn in some aluminum at the recycling place down the road? Good. I was just sitting here making a list of ways I could recycle paper products."

The woman reached below the counter and grabbed a plastic cup. She said, "You could write on your hand, instead of cocktail napkins." She sneered at Rodney. She shook her lice-likely head. "Write that on down, Bozo. For your information, I have better, higher-calling things to do than collect cans off the roadside." She leaned in Rodney's direction and took the bottle from him. She didn't slide it back.

Beneath them, Gus bellowed out, "Oh, hell," and wretched audibly in great, measured wails. "This one's bad."

Rodney said, "That seems like an appropriate segue. So. If you don't clean up the environment...You're not from around these parts, are you?"

The woman opened her bag and sighed. She pulled out a number of advance reader's copies. She stacked them up and balanced her cup atop the uncorrected proofs. "I'm a reviewer for Kirkus Reviews," she said. "I don't expect you to know the journal. I don't expect you to understand anything about anonymous criticism." She downed a shot of straight gin and poured another.

Like Gus below, Rodney didn't cotton to sighing, eye-rolling, melodramatic people in the bar. He said, "You need to take a bath. How's a little of that for not being anonymous? If you're as smart and haughty as you're trying to come off, you should know about the secret life of bacteria. What'd you do, get a merit badge in Alternative Lifestyles, then quit the Girl Scouts?"

Then he wrote on his cocktail napkin, "Eradicate anonymous critics." Who are you to be so presumptuous? he started to say, but didn't. He thought to ask her if she'd ever read Salinger, Yates, Carver, O'Connor, or Hannah, like he did daily. But his thoughts strayed.

Gus came in through the back door, clapping lime dust from his hands, smiling.

JAYNE MANSFIELD

Some kind of manhunt kept me locked inside Crosby's while SWAT teams scoured the area looking for two supposed bank robbery suspects. Looking up at the bar's normally irresponsible TV set, I sat there watching the action taking place outside, almost making out exactly where I sat from News Four's rarely used helicopter's shots, and when the reporter paused to catch her breath back in the studio, in between her mispronouncing words and stumbling over teleprompter sentences, I heard the rotors overhead. Crosby had left me and the one other patron alone so he could carry a St. Patrick's Day banner up on the tar-and-gravel roof in hopes of gaining free advertising for the green draft beer he planned to sell cheap in two weeks.

"Y'all look for me, Warner," Crosby had said. "They say the camera puts some weight on you. If y'all see me, notice if I look normal." Crosby stood six feet tall and weighed 130. He had owned and operated his bar for a decade, since he was forced to retire early as a supervisor at Central Yarn. Crosby might've been married to the only woman who ever said to her husband that he should buy a bar, drink nightly, and try to put on some pounds.

I nodded. How could I even expect to be either alive or free from jail on St. Patrick's Day?

"This is like living in Los Angeles," the other man said. "I used to live in Los Angeles. I bet I couldn't count the days I heard a helicopter over my house. Or turned on the news and seen a car chase on a street I'd traveled earlier in the day." Then he said, "I'm Mike."

I lifted what had been a straight triple bourbon. I said, "Good to meet you, Mike. I'm Warner." Mike lied, I knew, for no one said "Los Angeles" who'd ever really spent time there. My first real girlfriend in college went west for a month to get on a game show, and she called it "L.A.," as if she'd been a mayoral candidate. And my current girlfriend Justine had lived there for her first eighteen years and called it "L.A." Justine had also lived in San Francisco and Nashville before we met up, places she referred to as "Frisco" and "Nash Vegas." Since my trouble began a month earlier, she'd been talking of moving to "Chi-town," or "The City," or "Big D."

I sat in Crosby's thinking about these women who abbreviated their homes and destinations. It wasn't the first time.

"Happy February thirtieth," Mike said. He stood up, his feet on the bottom rungs of his bar stool, leaned over the countertop, and poured a draft. "You probably don't think there's ever thirty days in February, am I right? Twenty-nine every four years—that's called a 'leap year'—but mostly twenty-eight. Am I right?"

I looked at the television screen. The local manhunt had cut to a commercial for Advance America payday loans. I said, "Yeah. I don't know. Are you going to tell me about one of those pre-Julian calendars?" I thought, Jesus fucking Christ, man, talk about sports, weather, or pussy like everyone else inside a dark wood-paneled bar.

Mike shook his head. He kept eye contact, descended from his stool, and reached for his wallet. He said, "I'm the only man in America born on February thirtieth. It's my birthday! Look at this."

Mike pulled what proved to be a worn birth certificate from his wallet, unfolded it, and held it by two corners. I first read "Unknown" beneath the father's name, then scanned upward to, sure enough, "02-30-45." I said, "I'll be damned.You didn't get that made up at one of those places down in Myrtle Beach, did you— those places that make fake newspapers with fake headlines?"

"You didn't believe me, did you? I celebrate my birthday on March second, you know, or sometimes March first. You didn't believe me, did you?"

"It's like a bar trick," I said. I looked at the TV and said, "Is that Crosby?" The helicopter cameraman had zoomed in and focused on a parking meter.

"It ain't no trick," Mike said. "Shit, man, you wouldn't believe what kind of trouble this birthday has caused me."

"I'm sorry. Happy birthday. I should've wished you a happy birthday right away. Get a pint and put it on my tab," I said, pointing to the draft beer dispenser. "It's already March? Fuck. I think I forgot somebody's birthday"— which wasn't true. I knew the date. At this moment my lawyer supposedly was meeting with another lawyer, and by the end of the day I would know what decisions I'd have to make—as in, move out of town, get ready for jail, or kill myself.

"I'd been in the air force already, you know, bombing the hell out of Indochina on a secret mission, and then when I come up to apply for being an astronaut they look at my birth certificate and say, 'This ain't right, Bubba. They might be thirty days in February in Russia or China or Cuba, but not in the United States.' I got reneged from NASA only because some nurse got all confused back in 1945 because her brother or husband was returning from Iwo Jima or Dunkirk. Ain't that the something, how things work out?"

I'm not sure why I thought it appropriate and necessary to say, "I was born in 1983. I guess the war in Grenada hadn't gotten to the point where nurses got confused back home from people dying." This wasn't true, but I couldn't think of any kind of known war going on in 1981.

"I've died twice, unofficially," Mike said. He held his mouth open in a way that astronomers who discover new planets, or microbiologists who discover new viruses, might. He reached over for another beer. "Twice officially, and I don't know how many times unofficially. A bunch, unofficially. Like twelve. Or fifty."

I didn't listen closely as Mike listed off times when an EMT, nurse, doctor, or unlucky passerby was present to witness what could have been regarded as unnoticed death. No, I looked back behind the bar and watched a common American cockroach— *Periplaneta americana*—skitter its way between stacks of beer mugs. I thought, How in the world can they accuse me of not being qualified to teach children the ins and outs of the insect world? How can they accuse me of endangering the lives of others just because I don't have a PhD?

I got up and served myself at least another three fingers.

"Shit, man, I was *born* dead," Mike said.

I became fascinated with the insect world at an early age, collected specimens, went to college, and in my junior year veered away from the agriculture and life sciences department with an emphasis on entomology in order to study philosophy. My father—a tobacco farmer, among other things—didn't actually say, "You're disinherited," but when he had to sell off the land later he made a point of telling me, "It's your fault," and "You'll remember this day when I die and you see my will."

I went to graduate school to concentrate in medical ethics, of all things, but halfway through my second year a professor said to me, "Hey, you're a farm boy. My daughter, Beauvoir, has a class project to finish up that involves bugs. She's scared to death of the things. Is there any way you could help her? I'm not exactly enthralled by the insect world, *a priori*, or *a posteriori*, either. I mean, could you come talk to her, and maybe hold some crickets and worms so she can see that they're not deadly?"

Who the fuck talks like that? I thought right off. And I thought, Why would I want to spend my time with people who throw in stupid Latin terms rightly or wrongly every day, much like lawyers did?

Not only did I come over and handle the crickets and worms—plus explain the benefits of their droppings in regards to fertilizer—but I volunteered to escort the girl to her sixth-grade class, pretended to be an expert, and taught her classmates all about why they should never kill honeybees, wasps, spiders, wooly bears, ants, beetles, and so on. Beauvoir's teacher—who had lived in L.A. for the first eighteen years of her life and became my second real girlfriend—thought so much of my expertise that she said, "I am going to make a few calls. We can get you some grant money. We've had people come in here with injured birds of prey and snakes to teach or scare the children, but nobody's ever been so funny and qualified and comforting."

Maybe I didn't have enough courses in *regular* ethics, for I didn't say anything like, "I'm not really an entomologist," or "Because I'm more interested in medical ethics it might be more beneficial for me to teach your sixth graders about how God gave us the gift of life, and if it's a true gift then we, as humans, should be able to return the gift whenever we feel necessary, i.e., commit suicide." No, I said, "I would be honored. You want to go get a drink after you're done today?"

And then I got hired on to visit other middle schools regularly, and elementary schools, and the occasional vocational school where students arrived in short buses, so I dropped out of my graduate program. I got asked to talk to scout troops, retirement centers, the Optimist Club, Big Brothers Big Sisters of the

Upstate, and so on. Understand that after helping out Beauvoir—who names a kid that? Did she have a brother named Jean-Paul and cousins named Nietzsche?—and getting Justine's backing, I had to go out and collect worthwhile venomous and parasitic insect specimens, which, here in the South, took upwards of two hours. And then four inconsequential years later a goddamn kid named Jacob, afflicted with OCD, and ADD, and ADHD—born to a mother who drank tequila and smoked crack during her pregnancy—supposedly stuck his hand in an ex-pickle jar filled with black widow spiders, got bitten, went home and told his white-trash mother, and she made some phone calls to the police, the school district, an attorney, and so on.

Listen, I'd been doing well as a fake non-bonded entomologist with no credentials for all this time. When my situation became newsworthy—Jacob's mother had called various local media outlets, including the station with the helicopter that flew above Crosby's bar—reporters went out to ask "regular" citizens their views on the situation, as was their wont. The spider bite was the least of their worries. Everyone believed that I had infiltrated the schools with Buddhism, what with all this talk about not harming insects.

For thirty-six hours, unemployment, two wars, a Gulf of Mexico oil spill, droughts, a heat wave, serial killers, border conflicts, global warming, tainted food, car recalls, and Bank of America bailout scams took a back seat on the local news to my supposed "ulterior motives."

Like I said, there at Crosby's bar, sitting with Mike the Liar, I thought about two things: leaving town and killing him.

When my cell phone rang I looked down and saw that it was Townes Bannister IV, a man Justine had told me to hire on. Mike the Liar said, "Your phone's ringing. I remember when my phone rang one time and it was Jayne Mansfield asking me to come over, play some strip poker with her because she'd missed my birthday and she was in town. Back when I found myself living in Biloxi."

I answered. Townes Bannister IV said, "Where are you, my man? We need to go celebrate somewhere. I got to the bottom of everything."

I said, "I don't know that I can leave, because of the manhunt."

Mike the Liar said, "I don't even know of a bank nearby. I think it's something else going on. Maybe it's finally come to us turning into two planets." He grabbed my arm hard as Townes Bannister IV said something about "long story short" and "charges dropped" and "foster family." Mike pulled the cell phone away from my ear. "See, the Gulf Stream and whatnot's going east to west, but below the equator the water's moving the other way in the opposite direction. Eventually all that erosion's going to turn the Earth into looking like an hourglass. And then it'll finally pinch itself into two orbs, you know. I'm of the belief that they've been hiding it from us for a while, that we're about to be pinched in half because once they decided that Pluto wasn't a planet official-like, they needed to add another planet to keep things in balance. We needed a ninth. There were nine, then Pluto wasn't one so there were eight, and now we need to split apart so there are nine again. Because nine is three threes. And threes is important on Earth, what with the Father, Son, and Holy Ghost."

I pulled back my arm and said to the lawyer, "Sorry."

Townes Bannister IV said, "You might not be able to go around showing bugs to kids anymore, but it's come out that the kid probably got bitten at home a long time ago. I called some bluffs is what I'm talking! It's like the first thing you learn in Trial Lawyering 101. *Ipso facto!*"

Either Townes hung up or the call was lost due to heavy helicopter turbulence in the surrounding area. I said, "I got the next round!"

"Exactly," Mike said. "We can probably leave, but why would we want to?" He held out both hands and touched the beer taps.

"Roadblocks mean breathalyzers, and I don't need to call a lawyer again," I said.

"Anyway, where was I? I couldn't become an astronaut, so I went to college on the GI Bill and almost got my doctorate in chemistry, what with what I know about chemicals. But my advisor didn't like that I knew more than he did, and he wouldn't pass me."

It sounded like two helicopters hovered above the bar. I looked at the TV, took the remote, flipped to the other local channel, and sure enough they had a pilot in the air too. Then I saw Crosby, running atop his establishment, trying to gather the banner that flapped and blew across the roof. I said, "He's going to fall off, not paying attention. Or get himself shot by a cop thinking he's a bank robber."

Mike said, "I been shot six, seven times. That's on the unofficially dead list."

There's a good chance I'm going to kill you, I thought. There's a more than likely chance that, when you stand back up to steal a beer while Crosby's up on the roof, I'm going to kick the legs of the bar stool beneath you and crush your skull atop the bar counter right about the time your chin hits it. I envisioned everything, the murder of near-astronaut Mike the Liar, in the same way I saw myself in night dreams: pissing on a politician's shoes; putting a favorite, though feeble, dog to sleep; taking the stage to sing along with Jason and the Scorchers; or co-starring in a movie with Bill Murray. I said, "I need to get out of here, really. I need to call up my wife before she takes off on me."

Hippocrates gets all the glory, but in my studies of medical ethics I found that the Oath of Maimonides often helped me get through the day when dealing with living organisms. Like a mantra, I repeated to myself, "May I never see in the patient anything but a fellow creature in pain." I bet I repeated that part of Maimonides' oath about ten times a day, especially when bitten by an uncooperative insect, or when dealing with a kid who said I was creepy.

Mike got up from his seat and wandered behind the bar. He picked up a bottle of Jim Beam, set it on the bar, and slid it my way. He said, "Not on my birthday, you're not." He said, "First off, you ain't married. If you was married, you'd wear a ring. Two, I haven't even told you how I got all my money through the lawsuit. I can tell from listening that that was your lawyer calling you, and you got good news. I recognize you from there," Mike said, pointing at the television. "Bug man."

I didn't say "yes" or "no" to him. I needed to call Justine and let her know that she shouldn't be moving back to L.A. or wherever she planned to go right in the middle of her school year. I pulled out my cell phone but couldn't get a call through. I stood up to use Crosby's land line and Mike said, "I was in Chicago to throw the first pitch at a Cubs game, and the hotel where they put me up had some kind of elevator problem. I'm talking I was on the fourteenth floor. Don't tell nobody, but maybe I'd been doing some drinking. Anyway, next thing you know, I thought the door was open and I stepped in. Fourteen floors later, I understood that both the Otis elevator corporation and the Hyatt had made a mistake. You ever fallen fourteen floors down an elevator shaft?"

I picked up the receiver behind the bar and turned to look at the TV screen. The reporter back in the studio was saying that eyewitnesses described the bank robbers as white men, between twenty and seventy, between five-two and six-seven, between 130 and 240, with tattoos on both their inner forearms.

The description matched me exactly, seeing as I had a cicada tattooed on one arm and its vacant shell on the other. It had always been a high point of my presentation to elementary school kids, the way I could press my arms together and show the cicada emerging from its husk. I made a high-pitched drone when I performed the little trick, too, in order to sound like cicadas stuck to the sweet gums they're prone to use for nighttime tarmacs.

I said to Mike the Liar, "Don't call me 'Shaft.'" I said, "I've never fallen down an elevator, no. You haven't either. While you're up, grab some of those peanuts Crosby keeps back there."

Mike bowed up and said, "Okay, fucker. You don't believe me? Okay, fucker. You calling me a liar? You saying you don't believe me?"

I started laughing. I looked behind Mike and noticed a moth fluttering toward the ceiling—an army worm moth—probably in need of foliage. I said, "Yeah, you're a liar. You're not even close. If you want to lie, tell lies that can't be traced back on the Internet, my man. I mean, it's easy to look up who threw the first pitch at every Cubs game in history. Or who used to bomb Indochina. I tell you what—I'll believe the February thirtieth birthday, but that's about it."

"It's my birthday right now!" Mike yelled out. He came around the bar my way, his mouth held open, his fists clinched. "Warner! One who warns! I better warn you about what's about to happen, man."

May I never see in the patient anything but a fellow creature in pain.

I said, "I'm not looking for trouble, buddy. Sorry. I mean, yeah, I think you're a world-class bullshitter, but so am I. It doesn't matter when it comes down to everything." I pointed at the newscast. "Let's you and me sit down here and look for Crosby."

I should mention that all of this took place in mid-afternoon, when it wasn't unusual for Crosby to have fewer than three patrons inside the bar. I dropped in most days after school let out, after I'd taught students the importance of pollen and/or antennae. On other days I continued reading all about medical ethics, just in case I wanted to return to school. Or I daydreamed of learning how to play guitar. Or I daydreamed of writing a crime novel wherein the bad guy carries a satchel of bedbugs around with him and stays in the classiest hotels for free. Or I tried to antagonize my collection of live rhino beetles into warfare.

Mike took a wild swing at me, missed, fell to the floor, and began to cry. The only thing sadder than a sixty-five-year-old drunken liar crying on an unclean bar floor is, of course, a seventy-year-old drunken liar, et cetera. Or a woman of any age, I imagine, at least for me. Mike reached his arm up for help. I didn't respond, for I knew the trick—certain members of the insect world do the same thing, namely hornets. They'll be all buzzing on their backs, twirling in circles, acting as if they're about to expire, and then when something comes by to flip them over, they sting. Mike said, "I promised myself I wouldn't cry on my birthday. Damn! I promised not to fall down, and not to cry. The last time this happened was down in Biloxi, right after playing strip poker with Jayne Mansfield. I don't need to tell you what happened to her later that night, down in Slidell."

I thought of Maimonides again: "May neither avarice nor miserliness, nor thirst for glory or for a great reputation engage my mind," and reached out and helped Mike up. He patted down his backside, cleared his throat, and sat back down. He quit crying, sniffled, and I could tell that he hoped I'd soon forget the occasion of his frailties revealed and observed. I pointed at the television screen. I said, "Maybe I should go see if Crosby's okay up there."

Mike said, "I never knew for sure, but I think Jayne wanted to be naked. I think she folded her cards even when she had, you know, a full house or a flush. And then she'd take off a glove, or her bra. You should've seen her! Those were the days."

The bar's land line rang, so I got up and answered "Crosby's Bar," like that, like a professional. Justine said, "What're you doing?"

I said, "Hey."

She said, "Did Mr. Bannister get you?"

Mike the Liar began making some dry-heave noises. I said, "All is well, evidently. Are you home?"

Justine said, "All is not well, Warner, as I think you know."

"Okay. Well, okay. Do what you think you have to do. From what I understand, I'm stuck here because the cops have cordoned off a few blocks in order to look for a couple bank robbers. I guess now would be the perfect time for you to pack up and go. I ain't leaving. I mean, I'm innocent—I don't need to pack up and go."

Justine remained silent on the other end. I thought about how she kind of looked like Jayne Mansfield, minus the blond hair and unnaturally large breasts. I thought about how it would be nice for me to get out of the bar, go home, and play some strip poker with her. She could tell me about her day, and I could tell her about Mike. Justine said, "What's that noise?"

I said, "It's either helicopters overhead or Mike the Liar about to throw up." I said, "Hey, turn on channel four, and I'll run outside and wave. You can see me on television."

"I've seen you on television enough," she said.

Crosby came back in and said, "Did I look normal?" He dragged the banner behind him and limped visibly. He said, "I got yelled at by a cop on the roof of the Christian Science Reading Room. I thought Christian Scientists were all pacifists, or whatever they're called. I bet y'all can't say you got yelled at by a cop standing on a roof." He looked at Mike and said, "What's up with you? Have you fixed the toilet yet?"

I said, "You were supposed to be fixing the bathroom?"

Mike said to Crosby, "This guy is that pedophile they keep talking about on the news who goes around making spiders bite little boys."

Crosby dropped the end of his banner. "Fuck, man, you mean to say I can't leave my bar for an hour without this happening?

How long was I gone? I wasn't even gone an hour. Y'all kiss and make up. I can tell that something happened."

Crosby took his skinny self back behind the bar. He said to me, "You want another bourbon?"

"Crosby knows all about my predicament, Mike, you asshole." To Crosby I said, "I got a call from my lawyer and all the charges were dropped. Those parents confessed that they made up everything, or at least some kind of truth came out about it." I held my left hand up, as if taking an oath. "What's the story going on outside?"

I looked at the TV set and noticed that regular programming had resumed. Like I said, there was unemployment, two wars, a Gulf oil spill, droughts, a heat wave, serial killers, border conflicts, global warming, tainted food, car recalls, and Bank of America bailout scams going on, but the local mid-afternoon programming involved a talk show wherein a questionable judge listened to a newly married bride plaintiff complain that the defendant, a florist, hadn't offered the best arrangements for her recent wedding. The plaintiff argued that because the roses weren't but half-bloomed, she shouldn't have to pay but half of the bill.

"Maybe some of them flowers had some of your bugs inside the petals," Crosby said to me.

Mike the Liar laughed. He said, "Maybe that florist had a thing for convicts and that's why he was watching you," which, of course, didn't make any sense.

Crosby said, "Goddamn it to hell, Mike, go fix my commode." To me he said, "I'd be willing to bet that the bank wasn't really robbed. I'm thinking that someone wanted a distraction while he did something else illegal, but that's just a theory."

I said, "You looked good up on the roof, Crosby. You almost looked lifelike." Mike the Liar shuffled off to the back hallway, mumbling. I said, "I ought to kill you for leaving me with that guy. Where'd he come from?"

Crosby left his banner on the floor. He got behind the bar and tested the taps. "You know his real story, don't you? Man. I hired him on because I felt so sorry for him."

I went through war hero, almost-astronaut, winner of a strip poker game with Jayne Mansfield. Crosby said, "I don't know about all that. I haven't heard any of those stories. No. What happened was, back about ten or fifteen years ago he was falsely accused of murder-for-hire. I'm talking about the business end of murder-for-hire."

Crosby pulled a draft PBR and handed it to me. I said, "The business end of murder-for-hire would be the guy who got killed, wouldn't it? What do you mean?"

Crosby looked back toward the restrooms and leaned my way. He whispered, "He'd been accused of getting hired out to kill someone. As it ended up, somebody couldn't stand Mike so much that he went to the cops and said, 'I hired a guy to murder my wife, and he agreed to do it.' By the time everything got to the court stage, the man confessed. Mike was totally blindsided, of course. He'd not been asked to kill anyone, for one. The man who made up the entire lie ended up going to prison. I think he's out now, though. That's one expensive practical joke, if you ask me."

I didn't need to hear any of this. What if some parents got together and hired somebody to murder me just because I wasn't officially certified to show off insects to their children? What if an *exterminator* didn't like me going around espousing the symbiotic relationship between cockroaches and crumb-spilling husbands? What if Justine decided that she didn't want to move out of our rented house, that it would be easier to kill me off than to pack her own boxes? This medical ethics thing I had been so obsessed with at one time, to the point of memorizing various oaths— what if people around here thought it best to kill people who believed in euthanasia? I said, "Fuck, Crosby. Fuck. It might be best if I move to another state. I can't see anything but trouble ahead for me around here."

"I told Mike to do the same thing way back when, but he wouldn't listen. Here he is, you know. Here he is." Crosby laughed. "In case you don't own a mirror, go back there and look at Mike in the face and maybe you can see yourself in twenty or thirty years. Or tomorrow."

A police officer opened the door to Crosby's bar and yelled, "Everything okay in here, Crosby?"

"Good as it'll ever be," Crosby said. "Was there really a holdup, or were y'all just playing cops and robbers?"

The police officer stared at *me*, I swear. He talked to Crosby, but he kept looking at me. He said, "They surrendered peacefully. As it ended up they lifted a manhole cover and got in to wait it out."

I don't know why I thought it necessary to say, "Maybe News Four needs a submarine instead of a helicopter," but I did. The policeman stared at me a good five seconds, didn't respond, and closed the door.

Mike the Liar came out of the restroom carrying a plumber's helper in one hand and a crescent wrench in the other. He said, "All is well. All is well. Both toilets are now flushing fine, and neither's running water. This reminds me of the time I got hired out to fix every goddamn clogged toilet at Madison Square Garden in 1971 when Joe Frazier beat Muhammad Ali. Frank Sinatra ended up helping me for a little while."

I looked at Crosby as if to say, "See?" but Crosby nodded. He said, "Fifteen rounds and a unanimous decision. Those were the days."

Mike sat back at the bar, two stools away. He smiled to himself. Crosby gave him a draft. I thought, That cop's waiting for me outside. I thought, If I leave this bar, I'll end up riding to jail for some reason.

Crosby said, "I'm glad they found out the truth about you, Warner. Listen, is it true what they say about a female praying mantis?"

I said, "Yes. Bites the head off her mate."

Mike drank his beer in two gulps and set the glass down. He said it wasn't true about Jayne Mansfield being decapitated. Crosby said something about how he needed a good St. Patrick's Day in order to keep his bar afloat financially. Mike said that Jayne Mansfield's breasts looked like cocoons, waiting to erupt with the most beautiful butterflies ever.

LEACH FIELDS

This story isn't about me, though it took place during my wilder days, in a small town where I spent time in the county jail. This particular anecdote—which got me to thinking about how everyone's out to fuck with everyone else, how there's no defense against a well-obsessed man, how no sane person should even try to settle down in a marriage and expect it to work—*this* particular story, which I believe fully, came out of the crooked mouth of a fellow petty criminal named Sarly Fink. If you ask me, Sarly Fink's parents tabbed him with two options only in life: petty criminal or septic system cleaner, what with the name. Oddly enough, he turned out to be both, plus a real talker.

I had agreed to not pay bail and do my thirty days, because I knew no one in town yet and had zero money. I'd been charged with littering, burning without a permit, destruction of private property, stealing, public drunk, resisting arrest, and assault on an officer of the law, in that order. Actually the public drunkenness charge came last, but it wasn't much true. I couldn't walk a straight line during the roadside test because I'd hurt my ankle. I sprained it while running from the deputy, who—unless I'd not stuck my foot in the underground yellow jackets nest—would've never caught me. His name was Gaylord French. Name like that? Cop or florist or college professor.

There at the jail booking area I said to Gaylord French, "I used to be a decathlete. I used to compete in the decathlon back in college. That means ten events."

The policeman who sat behind his desk cataloging my empty wallet and keys said, "You get yourself three more charges added to these seven and you'll be a decathlaprisoner." He didn't laugh. He acted as if he'd been waiting his whole life to say something like that.

I said to Gaylord French, "No, man, I was just saying—you're in pretty good shape, running me down the way you did. I wasn't the best decathlete, but still. I know the hundred-yard dash, and the mile, and hurdles, and the high jump. Pretty much you and I performed all those events down there in the woods." Understand that I fully know that I sucked up to the deputy.

Gaylord French said to the other officer, "Who's got a cigarette? I need to put some spit-tobacco on these bee stings. Goddamn this place for going No Smoking everywhere."

I didn't have a cigarette at that time in my life because I still considered myself a decathlete. Later on I would understand Gaylord French's impatience concerning do-gooders deciding what was right for prisoners in regards to their health. Prisoners, hell—I would be willing to bet that every goddamn do-gooder was pro-choice in regards to a woman's body and euthanasia, but they wouldn't allow for people to kill themselves slowly and voluntarily, all the while paying taxes on cigarettes so that Medicare and education could continue, with tobacco products.

The "assault on an officer" charge, by the way, should've been leveled on the yellow jackets, not me. In backwards South Carolina, where this took place, if an officer of the law falls asleep behind the wheel and crashes his cruiser, a diner waitress can get charged for not serving the officer enough coffee. True law, passed unanimously by the legislature, from what I've heard.

But this story's not about me.

The booking cop made me sign something, he took away my shoelaces, a magistrate appeared soon thereafter, and I received an orange jumpsuit. I might've received only thirty days because the magistrate said, "Barry Pendarvis. Are you related to Perry Pendarvis, of Pendarvis Cadillac?"

I about said, "Yes!" like that. I about said, "My daddy could get all y'all Cadillacs if you let me loose and we forget this ever happened." But my old track coach's voice came into my head right about then—damn him!—saying, "Become the javelin, and soar beyond up-till-now unfathomed illusion."

I said to the magistrate, "No, sir. I'm not related to anyone here."

Gaylord French stood there and said, "I need to get some Benabryl." Benabryl! Like part Benadryl and part Brylcreem. I got lost in thought thinking about an old-fashioned hair styling gel that repelled stinging insect pain.

I said, "I'm here because I got one of those post-graduate Clean Up South Carolina fellowships." The magistrate and Gaylord French looked at me as if I'd spoken in a foreign tongue. I should point out that—maybe this is everywhere, I don't know— no law experience, or even college education, is required to become a magistrate in South Carolina. They're appointed by the governor, who doesn't have to have a college education either, but should possess working knowledge of how to drive a tractor, run a spinning frame, quote the Bible in a believable fashion, and see no need whatsoever for libraries. I said, "I graduated from college, and I'm taking a year off to pay up my student loans. There's this program. It's like the Peace Corps. Except not about peace. Or the United States."

"So you was burning up campaign signs, and that's considered trash in your opinion," the magistrate said. I would mention his name, but I never learned it, and the fake-copper nameplate on the desk read "Big Man."

Gaylord French said, "Thinks our people is trash, running for office, represent us all over, good citizens." You should've seen his face. He had those yellow jacket stings ringing his eye sockets in a way that looked like Maori warrior tattoos.

Here I did like, "Well, I haven't officially started my job yet, and I figured that if litter stood on the side of the road, then it should be picked up. I mean, the signs I gathered up were from a primary that took place a year ago."

Call me a yellow dog democrat, but I thought that the two million republicans running in the primaries for governor, lieutenant governor, secretary of education, first district congressional seat, senate, county council, et cetera, should've contacted their wrongheaded volunteer supporters to pick up those roadside campaign placards at major and minor intersections, and correctly disposed of the things, or at least stacked them up and saved them for the next election. I had moved into the rent-free Clean Up South Carolina apartment that they gave me, went scouting around, as twenty-two-year-old ex-decathletes might do, for good beer joints. I found one, I drank some drafts, and I thought about how I couldn't believe a guy at the University of Oregon almost amassed 10,000 points in the decathlon whereas I could never break 7,000.

I don't want to make any generalizations, but I would be willing to bet that behind most bashed-in mailboxes, shot-up stop signs, and toilet-papered trees stood either a future- or ex-decathlete.

I would also contend that drunken ex-decathletes don't remember the unimportant inviolable proceedings of an admonitory magistrate who enters a faux courtroom in a jail's side room bent on gavel-banging, driven to hold a better office in a more convenient and prestigious district.

Whereas I thought I got thirty days because the magistrate saw in my face an otherwise honest man, I learned later that the harshest sentence a magistrate can offer is thirty days, or a fine not exceeding $500. Maybe Big Man bought a lemon from Perry Pendarvis and took it out on me.

Sarly Fink was my cell mate. He's still there, probably, or down in Columbia at the big prison. One can get on the computer these days, type in "SCDC"—which stands for South Carolina Department of Corrections—find the site, and enter a name. I've done it, sure, but Sarly Fink doesn't appear. Has he died? Has he been transferred to Angola or San Quentin? Maybe he's been truly rehabilitated, like some kind of success story that's never been reported.

Sarly Fink had a lawyer and everything, according to him, but a jury found him guilty of passing bad checks, or DUI, or forgery, or selling beer to minors, or fishing without a license, or tampering, or not paying taxes, or driving without a license, or killing an endangered species that attacked him, or spooking neighborhood children mercilessly.

This is his story. Sarly Fink told a lot of them, and I believed one.

Again, it was the county jail. We wore orange jumpsuits. Some of us worked the kitchen, some the recycling center, and others on a chain gang without the chains. Sarly Fink and I picked up roadside garbage, just like I would've done, of course, had I honored my Clean Up South Carolina post-graduate fellowship. Here's something I learned: It seems like redneck litterers prefer Busch Light, Hardee's hamburgers, and Slim Jim Giant Jerk beef jerky strips. We stabbed our nail-sticks into more of those objects in a day's time than, say, cans of Sapporo, Big Mac boxes, or Mallo Cup wrappers.

"I'm paying for something else I done," Sarly Fink whispered to me on the first day out. "I fucked up, and God's holding a grudge."

I know there are a bunch of those nightly cable TV shows about convicts stuck together holding hands and whatnot in eight-by-ten cells, but Sarly and I weren't in this type of situation. Maybe jailhouse homosexuality becomes an issue *after* thirty days, I'm glad to say.

I picked up a used diaper and shoved it in the canvas bag and said to Sarly Fink, "Yeah, yeah, yeah. God's against all of us."

"Listen to what I have to say," he said. "I want you to ponder my story."

There were some other encaged fellows with us. Most of them bragged about the women who awaited them on the outside. Sometimes I imagined pole vaulting over the razor wire, running off, and meeting up with incarcerated men's supposed girlfriends. Sometimes at night—I didn't sleep much—I imagined shoving a shot put into the mouth of Sarly Fink.

People kept honking the horn as they drove by. I probably lost a few years of my life from what these thirty days did to my nerves. I said, "Go on, my man."

You wouldn't believe how many ticks live in roadside high grass. I'd say that three ticks show up about every ten steps. I kept pulling them off of me—and thinking how I needed to tell Clean Up South Carolina how it wasn't fair to offer a post-graduate fellowship without Lyme disease protection—and seeing them on Sarly Fink. I told him, but he kept walking, high-stepping, looking for trash.

"I sucked other people's crap," Sarly said finally. "That's what I done for a living. It's what I do now, and what I will do in the future. I got the equipment."

I said, "Look at how bleached out that dead deer's skull is," and pointed.

He stabbed it. Sarly said, "Hear this, Barry. I ain't proud of it all."

"I'm not proud of my quarter-mile time," I said. What could I say?

"I've been thinking about telling a psychiatrist all about it so we can write my story."

We continued walking through sweet grass taller than the average third-grader. I tried to concentrate there on the side of the road, but looking back I probably thought only about how I would soon no longer be a decathlete officially. I felt pretty sure that some kind of federation stripped people of what they called themselves if said people didn't compete over a certain period of time. Like an accountant can't call himself one anymore if he forgets to punch in some numbers over, say, two hours.

I found a 16-ounce beer, half full, and drank from it. That's how I was back then.

"I kept track of people," Sarly Fink said. "I drove around and looked. I watched. People always looked down on me for what I done for a living, and I reciprocated duly."

I didn't say anything about how "reciprocated" might be a big word. Reciprocated? I said, "Is that a copperhead down by your foot?"

Sarly said, "Man and woman. Husband and wife. Rainfall for a month. Septic tank needs cleaning out 'cause they ain't played by the septic tank rules for years. Do you know septic tank rules, Barry? There are rules. No grease dumped down the drain, for one. There are eighteen others. Anyway, they call me up like it's my fault. So I show up with a box of rubbers in my truck and have them opened and unstrung, you know. People who yell at septic tank cleaners ain't going to come out there and look at their own shit, you know."

Of course I pretended to know what the hell Sarly Fink meant. Was he speaking in some kind of stream-of-consciousness? Was he imagining things? I said, "I'll be damned."

"Let's say a married couple needed their tank cleaned. I'd show up, and dig a foot or two down to the coffin lid, you know, that covers the tank's opening—right there when the pipe leads from the house. If I felt they didn't respect me and mine, I'd drop ten or twelve opened rubbers down there to float atop the water, maybe stick two hanging right there from the pipe like they'd not finished their journey. Then I'd call the man and woman out and say, 'Y'all shouldn't throw all these here condoms down the commode.' You see what I'm talking about? That's what God's mad for."

I said, for no reason whatsoever, "My least favorite event's the long jump. I think it has to do with a fear of fouling there at the board."

"So then a woman would say, 'My husband don't wear no rubbers,' and a husband would say the same. He thinks some old boy's showing up when he's away, you know, screwing his wife. And she thinks that a woman's showing up when she's off somewhere. Do you see what I'm saying? Can you picture the scenario in your mind's eye?"

Telling Sarly's story later, I see one of his eyes twitching, maybe sweat draining down the sides of his face. I didn't say, "That's kind of cruel," though I thought it.

"I bet I done this little trick a couple hundred times. See, then they would divorce because they don't trust each other. That's what happens. They divorce, the house comes up for sale cheap, and I buy it. Or at least I had plans to buy those houses and resell them later, but I never had the money."

I turned around to look for the guard, who wasn't paying attention. I said, "Wait. You threw rubbers in the septic, and then asked a husband and wife to come look at the things?"

"College boy. I told them they shouldn't dispose of rubbers down the commode, among the seventeen other things. Feminine hygiene products. Paper towels. Grease. Rocks."

"I get it. They accuse each other of cheating. If a husband's cheating, he doesn't want to get another woman pregnant. Same with the wife."

"Not to mention the transference of likely sexually transmitted diseases. The clap. Gonorrhea. Herpes. Syphilis. Those other ones. I believe there are eighteen of them, too."

I said, "Huh. That is bad. Thanks. I mean, I felt bad for getting drunk, stealing those signs, burning them on the roadside, emitting toxic fumes into the atmosphere which would harm the ozone layer, and the rest of it. Not so much, though, after your story."

"It ain't all about loitering and shoplifting," Sarly said. "I'm paying for what I done to innocent victim married couples, just because I knew how they said things behind my back like how they didn't know how anyone could clean up other people's shit and the like. I know that I'm not a nice person."

I walked onward. I couldn't tell if tears mixed with Sarly Fink's facial perspiration. Finally I said, "There's rape and murder. Those are worse than what you did." I tried to think of at least eight more things worse than ruining a good marriage, but couldn't. Sarly Fink's actions, in my mind, tied with kidnapping.

The guard yelled at us to keep moving. "You won't learn this in school," Sarly said, "but it's always best to live in a house connected to the city sewer."

I did my time and made a point to disregard politicians altogether for the rest of my life. In a way, I came to believe, people who run for elected office are exactly the same as Sarly Fink. They promise to clean up a sudden mess, and in the process point out some kind of unforeseen disaster that was a predecessor's fault. Sarly Fink put out roadside signs for his septic services, as did political hopefuls. The world, or at least America, or at least the South, seemed to rely on such odd connections.

This is my story: I went AWOL from Clean Up South Carolina, got a number of blue-collar jobs, and paid back my student loans in a traditional manner. I became a citizen, more or less, and only tore down political signs if I thought they obstructed a driver's view of oncoming traffic.

All political signs, by the way, obstruct someone's view.

Eventually I went to grad school and got a master's degree in something called American Studies, with an emphasis in Class Struggles and Unspoken Caste Systems. My thesis, I swear to God, is titled "No Shit: Divorce Rates Vis-à-vis the Disappearance of Outhouses in the Rural South." You can look it up on Google. While you're at it, see how Gaylord French died in a mysterious explosion in a mobile home owned by a man who owned a florist's shop.

I got a job teaching at a technical college where the unscholarly and unathletic matriculate in hopes of transferring to a state university so they can undertake useless political science courses, go to law school, and eventually represent me on some level. Not that I'm one with any of the mostly Asian religions, but I start each day with a mantra of sorts, a chant that goes, "Sarly-Fink-Gaylord-French-Big-Man, Sarly-Fink-Gaylord-French-Big-Man."

Sometimes at night I go out to my campus with a flat screwdriver, pry out a small water meter cover from the sidewalk, and throw it like a discus. Then I run away, jumping over hedges, benches, and signs placed sporadically to remind students of upcoming orientation events.

COLUMBARIUM

Not until my father walked into the post office—or perhaps it was a few days earlier at the bastardized crematorium—did I understand how much he despised my mother's constant reminders. For at least fifteen years she substituted "No," "Okay," or "I'll do it if I have to," with "I could've gone to the Rhode Island School of Design" or "For this I gave up the chance to attend Pratt" or "When did God decide that I would be better off stuck with a man who sold rocks for a living than continuing my education at Cooper Union?" I figured out later that my parents weren't married but five months when I came out all healthy and above-average in weight, length, and lung capacity. To me she said things like, "I should've matriculated to the Kansas City Arts Institute, graduated, and begun my life working in an art studio of my own, but here I am driving you twenty miles to the closest Little League game," or "I had a chance to go to the Chicago Art Institute on a full scholarship, but here I am trying to figure out why the hell X and Y are so important in a math class," or "Believe you me, I wouldn't be adding pineapple chunks, green chiles, and tuna to a box of macaroni and cheese for supper had I gotten my wish and gone to The Ringling School of Art."

I went through all the times my mother offered up those blanket statements about her wonderful artistic talents—usually by the fireplace while she carved fake fossils into flat rocks dug out of the Unknown Branch of the Saluda River—there at the post office while my dad and I waited in line. She sold these forgeries down at the Dixie Rock and Gem Shop, or to tourist traps at the foot of Caesar's Head, way up near Clingman's Dome, or on the outskirts of Helena, Georgia. My mother's life could've been worthwhile and meaningful had she not been burdened with motherhood; had she not been forced to work as a bookkeeper/receptionist/part-time homemade-dredge operator at the family river rock business; had she not met my father when her own family got forced to move from Worcester, Massachusetts, because her daddy was in the textile business and got transferred right before my mother's senior year in high school. There were no art classes in the schools here; she could only take advanced home ec and learned how to make fabric and dye it, just as her father knew how to do at the cotton mill, more than likely.

"I could've gone to the School of the Museum of Fine Arts in Boston had I not been forced to take an English class that I'd already taken up in Massachusetts and sit next to your father, who cheated off my paper every time we took a multiple-choice test on *The Scarlet Letter*. I blame all of this on *The Scarlet Letter*, and how your dad had to come over on more than one occasion for tutoring," my mother said about once a week.

I didn't get the chance to ever point out to her how Nathaniel Hawthorne lived in Massachusetts. A year after her death I figured out the math of their wedding date and my birth, and didn't get to offer up anything about symbolism, or life mirroring art, et cetera.

My mother died of flat-out boredom, disdain, crankiness, ennui, tendonitis from etching fake fossil ferns and fish bones into rocks, and a giant handful of sleeping pills. Her daily allotment of hemlock leaves boiled into a tea probably led to her demise, too, if not physiologically, at least spiritually.

According to my father, the South Carolina Funeral Directors Association didn't require normal embalming and/or crematorial procedures should the deceased have no brothers or sisters and should said dead person's parents both be dead. Looking back, I understand now that my father made all this up. At the time, though, I just sat on the bench seat of his flatbed, my mother in back wrapped up in her favorite quilt inside a pine coffin. "We're going up to Pointy Henderson's, and he'll perform the cremation. Then we'll scatter your mother down by the river so she can always be with us."

Mr. Henderson was a potter and president of the local Democratic Party. About once a year he came down from the mountains and enlisted young democrats—and we all joined seeing as once a year, too, he held a giant shindig that included moonshine for everyone willing to either vote right or, if underage, at least put yard signs up.

"Cremation takes two to three hours at 1400 to 1800 degrees," Henderson said when we got there. "I did the research long ago." He got his two daughters to heft my mother off of the truck and carry the box to the groundhog kiln, which appeared to be dug into the side of an embankment. "My fire reaches near two thousand degrees on a good day," he said. "After Mrs. Looper cools, I'll go to ashing down the hard bones, if that's all right."

My father nodded. He'd done his crying the night before, as had I. "We'll come back in a couple days," my father said.

"You and me's kind of in the same business, I guess," Henderson said. "You take rock and sell it to people want paths to their front doors and walls to keep them out, and I take clay and sell it to people who want bowls on their tables."

I didn't get the connection. I guessed that clay was kind of like ground-down rocks, to a certain extent. I looked at Mr. Henderson's daughters, who were my age, and were so inordinately beautiful that no one spoke to them in school. If Homer came back to Earth and met the potter's daughters, he'd've had to rewrite the Siren section of *The Odyssey*. One of them said, "Sorry."

I said, "I'm a democrat," for I could think of nothing else. "I'm thinking that some laws need changing."

The other daughter said, "Sorry."

My father and I drove back home, as they say, in silence. Right before my mother slumped over in her chair dead at the age of thirty-three, she had set her last pancake-sized rock, a fake millipede etched into it, down on the stool. For her carving tool she'd been using a brand-new single-diamond necklace my father bought her. I don't know if her engagement ring, which she normally used for such forgeries, had worn out or not. My father had bought the necklace as a way to celebrate a new account he'd won—as the sole river rock supplier for an entire housing tract deal down in Greenville that would include a hundred patios and driveway-to-front-door paths.

I sat at the kitchen table reading a book about three out of the four ancient elements. My mother had just gotten up to go to the bathroom, I assumed. She said, "I could've gone to the Maryland Institute College of Art. Here I am walking to the bathroom one more time."

Those were her last words, as it ended up. "Mom's last words were 'Here I am walking to the bathroom one more time,'" I said. My father, without offering a reason, performed a U-turn in the middle of highway 108 and drove back to Mr. Henderson's. I said, "I guess she didn't know those would be her last words."

"Maybe she was a visionary. Maybe Heaven's just one giant toilet, Stet. I don't mean that in a bad way." I knew that he *did* mean it that way, though. My father didn't cotton to there even being a Heaven or Hell. In the past he had said, "If there was a Hell in the middle of the planet like some idiots believe, I think I'd've seen a flame or two shoot out from as deep as I've dug for rocks over the years."

We drove back up Mr. Henderson's rocky driveway not two hours since we first arrived. He had already shoved my mother into the chamber. My father told me I could sit in the truck if I wanted, which I did at first until I realized that I had something important to say to the potter's daughters, something that might prod them into seeing me as special. Something that might cause both of them to be my dates at the prom in a few years. I got out and stood there. Mr. Henderson explained something about the firing process, about the wood he used, something about how he can perform cremations cheaper than making his own pots because there's no glaze involved. His daughters walked up and stood with us twenty feet from the kiln door. I said, "My mother was an artist."

They said, in unison, "Sorry."

Smoke blew out of the kiln's chimney and my father said, "Well I don't see any smoke rings going skyward. Which means I don't see a halo. Come on, son."

Not until I had graduated from college with a few degrees— my father had told me to get my fill of education before coming back to run the family river rock business—did I understand the backtracking to Mr. Henderson's makeshift crematorium: My father wanted a sign from the Otherworld, just in case his final plan bordered on meanness or immorality.

I'm not sure what we spread down by the Unknown Branch of the Middle Saluda River. It's not like I shadowed my father for two days. I imagine he flung plain hearth ash down on the ground. At the post office, though, my father told Randy the post office guy, "They all weigh the same. You can weigh one, and the postage will be the same on all of them."

There were six manila envelopes. Randy said, "Don't you want return addresses on these?"

"I trust y'all," my father said. "I trust the postal service."

To me Randy said, "You applying to all these colleges?" He sorted through the envelopes. "I guess you are, what with all these admissions departments."

I said, "Sorry," like a fool, for the words of the Henderson girls rang in my ears still. I'd learned long before not to contradict my father. A man with a river rock business doesn't keep many belts around. I could go throughout life saying my father never spanked me, but I couldn't say that I'd never been stoned, in a couple of ways.

Driving back home my father said, "She got her wish. She finally got to attend all those art schools." Then he pulled off to the side of the road, past a short bridge. Beneath it ran a nameless creek. I got out, too, and together we took drywall buckets out of the back of the truck, trampled our way down the embankment, and scooped up smooth rounded mica-specked flagstone, each one the size of an ice cube, each one different in glint.

I WOULD BE REMISS

At this, the completion of *No Cover Available: The Story of Columbus Choice, African-American Sushi Chef from Tennessee*, I will not thank God, like all those athletes and musicians do on TV in hopes that it'll make them appear like a neighbor one would wish to know. I'll try to make this short. If I were the kind of monotheist I was brought up to be, I would have to begin with Adam and Eve, and get through all the long history of begats right on up until I handed the manuscript over to my publisher. For in any person's biography, everyone who's ever lived on the planet plays some minor part in said person's life. But I lean toward believing in evolution. So that'll save some ink.

I want to thank a girl—not a *woman*, at least at the time—named Juanita Wilkins who sat in the very first American History 101 class I taught at Tennessee Valley Community College and got all mad at me for "dissing" her, as she told the dean, for using inappropriate politically incorrect language and claiming that I had offered to trade sex for grades, et cetera. Juanita Wilkins, who then got caught for lying about all that, got kicked out of school, and caused the dean to tell me never to "dis" a student in front of her classmates ever again, and that this warning would go into my file, which made me walk off the job that day newly intent on my researching *No Cover Available: The Story of Columbus Choice, African-American Sushi Chef from Tennessee.*

Let me make certain that this is clear: We'd gotten to the Civil War, which happens to be a major part of American History 101 at Tennessee Valley Community College, if not everywhere. Juanita Wilkins, who is now a phlebotomist living in the area, said that racist word. She said our economy would be better if we still had slavery, et cetera. I made her leave the classroom, and wouldn't let her return until she apologized to the class and me. This was one of those Tuesday/Thursday classes all the kids like, and it was on a Thursday when the occurrence took place. So she had Friday, Saturday, Sunday, and Monday to mull over things, and she came back on Tuesday to apologize. To be honest, Juanita did a pretty good job, but I think it might've had to do with her being a second semester student who'd already taken the Public Speaking class that's required of all TVCC students. I let her back in. When we took our midterm exam, she made an F, and she made an F on her term paper, basically because I realized right away that she plagiarized. Who would hand in a term paper called flat-out *Abraham Lincoln: The Prairie Years and the War Years* that came to 800 pages? She typed the whole thing up, too, to make it look like her real work. What kind of phlebotomist-to-be can type 800 pages in a few weeks? This was before the age of computers, at least at Tennessee Valley Community College. It's not like she could've scanned Carl Sandburg's book, or whatever it is the community college students are doing these days.

Juanita failed the class, she told the dean that I'd offered to give her a B if she gave me a blow job, and I got called in to tell my side of the story. When Juanita Wilkins went in for her meeting with the dean she said to him, "I can't even be in the same building as Mr. Stet Looper," and then the dean looked up what Juanita signed to take for classes in the Fall. Right there he saw "American History 102—Looper," and he said, "If you can't stand being in the same building, then why'd you sign up for another one of his courses?" and she said, "Oops, I guess you caught me," and then she got kicked out, though I guess they let her back in at some point—maybe on a probationary status—seeing as she became a phlebotomist, and there's not another Nurse's Aid major within another hundred miles of here, I doubt.

So I quit. And I started right away working on this biography. So I want to thank Juanita Wilkins for a serendipitous moment.

Going backwards, I want to offer many thanks to my old tenth-grade English teacher back in South Carolina, Mrs. Rena L. Stone—her real name—who once told me that it didn't make a difference where I put the apostrophe in a word like "didn't." She, too, used to say after every student's book report: "I have read that book, and it is a very good one!" like that, all excited. So a couple of us started making up titles and plots and characters, and spun whole tales about mountain lions eating entire Appalachian-dwelling families and whatnot, just so we could hear Rena L. Stone say, "I remember how scared I got when *I* read that book," and so on. My entire craft of telling good tales—or learning how to *avoid* what's not necessary in a biography such as *No Cover Available: The Story of Columbus Choice, African-American Sushi Chef from Tennessee*—emanates from an eleven o'clock tenth-grade English class.

I wish to offer boundless gratitude and praise to my agent, Cherry "Chart Topper" Chitwood—working out of Signal Mountain, Tennessee—for her gentle prodding when it looked like my obsession might take longer. Who says everyone needs one of those fancy, easily distracted New York City agents? Speaking of which, oddly enough, I would like to offer sincere clemency to the 421 agents who told me I'd be better off starting with either A) a biography of someone already famous; or B) a novel; or C) a story of people living a hardscrabble life in Appalachia during the 1920s; or D) a book of linked stories; or E) a collection of poems; or F) a cookbook featuring the recipes of Appalachian hardscrabble citizens living in 1920. May you all thrive, and find another biographer with a bestseller in his or her head!

Eternal gratitude toward Ray Simmons, Blister McCovey, Boyd McJunkin, Leslie Spivey, Myra Cummins, Dev Patel, Moe-Moe Autrey, Bill Finster, Lefty Hopewell, Punt Hutto, Williemina Goode, and Virag Parthasarathy, for providing me work as a housepainter, janitor, roofer, floral-delivery driver, lawn-maintenance guy, motel desk clerk, housepainter, janitor, roofer, telemarketer, and motel desk clerk—all noble professions that allow for biographers to work on tomes such as this one. I am indebted to you all, and apologize for perhaps shirking my duties at times in order to pull out my Mead notebook to sketch out such chapters as "Simon Hirsch Taught Me Cooking in Vietnam," or "That Sea Cucumber Turned Sour!" or "Fuck You, Whitey, I Don't Serve Barbecue Here."

I need to offer gratitude to the school board for allowing me to substitute teach in the school system on a sporadic basis, right on up until I accidentally wore some of those stick-on eye-black things that I wrote something on that wasn't "John 3:16," and scared the townspeople. I'll get to thanking the appropriate people about that incident later on, if I have A) the time; and B) the ability to write it out in a way that doesn't make me sound like a pervert.

Eternal gratitude plus one day to all of those stamp-hoarding editors who wouldn't even send back my SASEs to say they weren't interested in my book, because it's true what they say when they say "the best revenge is living a served cold good life." I hope all of you editors end up in Hades with Columbus Choice's lynch mob and have to talk to them endlessly about rope and knots.

I would be remiss not to mention that I really don't despise or blame the editors. No, I fault the idiotic book reps. Why are they even called in for an opinion in regards to a novel or biography's worth? Allowing book reps to have a say in the acquisition process is on par with letting stockboys tell farmers what they should plant, and how they should tend their crops, if you ask me.

Tad Milkins needs to receive a special thumbs-up for letting me overstay my welcome at the Frozen Head State Park Campground, on the outskirts of Harriman, Tennessee, back when I had no other place to live. I am sorry, Tad, that you had to live through all my stories about my ex-wife, and I want you to know how much I appreciate your keeping an extension cord with a drop light attached all the way out to my two-man pup tent so I could scribble down ideas and paragraphs in the middle of the night, amid James Earl Ray conspiracy theorists who camped alongside me in their wonderful Northface dome tents and wished to be left alone before making their pilgrimages to nearby Brushy Mountain Correction Complex, once known as the Brushy Mountain State Penitentiary, which won't even be in operation by the time *No Cover Available: The Story of Columbus Choice, African-American Sushi Chef from Tennessee* ends up on independent bookstore shelves around the country, plus those other places both real and internetic. I also want to extend my good wishes to Tad for lying to that Department of Natural Resources officer about my having a fishing license when I got caught working the Emory River, trying to get enough to eat back between working for Dev and Moe-Moe. And I apologize for taking your sister out to the CCC dynamite shack along the South Old Mac Trail. Those were questionable times for me—and your sister, from what I could tell—and I owe you. But you're not an uncle yet!

No biography of Columbus Choice can be completed without a tip of the cap to Franklin Delano Roosevelt, who helped start the Tennessee Valley Authority, who helped America fight people like the Germans, Japanese, and Koreans—which made it impossible *not* to fight the North Vietnamese—who caused Columbus Choice to want to get out of the Harriman/Oak Ridge, Tennessee, region and join the military, seeing as there would be more African-Americans in Saigon than in Roane County. Mr. David Eli Lilienthal deserves a pat on the back, also, for being "Mr. TVA," as he's been tabbed by Wikipedia, as by other people equally enamored by the New Deal.

Next door to Harriman stands famous Oak Ridge, Tennessee, known as *the Atomic City, the Secret City, the Ridge,* and *the City Behind the Fence.* I'm sure that it affected Columbus Choice more than a little bit. If I'd've known Mr. Choice personally, before I partook writing his biography, maybe I'd've asked him why he didn't call his restaurant Secret Sushi Behind the Fence, or The Atomic Nigiri Behind the Secret Fenced City, or something along those lines. Maybe he would've made more friends and money, and not ended up hanged way up on Bird Mountain, elevation 3,142 feet.

I have undying gratitude for a redneck driving one of those old, sky-blue Ford F-100 trucks with a Confederate flag license place on his front bumper. He tailed me—I suppose—because I had an Obama sticker on my back windshield. In the end it gave me a sense of utter fear, and I realized what Columbus Choice must've felt when the last two white faces he ever saw stopped and said, "Need a ride? Get on in," and took him to Bird Mountain.

I wouldn't have finished my project had it not been for Google, and I want to offer a peck on the cheek to whoever types in all those ancient articles from local newspapers. If y'all ever need a good typist, I would encourage you to contact Ms. Juanita Wilkins, phlebotomist.

It pains me to say this, but I need to offer unremitting gratitude to my ex-wife Abby, whom I met back in college. Abby urged me to get my master's degree in Southern culture studies at the University of Mississippi-Taylor, though I feel pretty sure now that she thought it would mean I'd be bringing in something like fifty thousand dollars a year, and looking back on it, all she wanted for me to do was go off to those biannual two-week residencies down at Ole Miss-Taylor so she could continue her ongoing affair with somebody I never knew.

I would be remiss to forget Ms. Billie Holcombe, who got me in touch with her prison-guard sister, Anita Reid, who got me in touch with another guard who asked that I never use his name in *No Cover Available: The Story of Columbus Choice, African-American Sushi Chef from Tennessee.* This particular guard—let's pretend that his name's Mark Sanford—took some of my money and arranged for me to talk to Jack Plemmons, one of the two men convicted of lynching Columbus Choice. Jack wanted to make sure that I thank Sid Plemmons—his brother and co-killer—but I can't thank Sid seeing as he went off and died before I took on my project. I certainly cannot thank Eugene Bobo, who sliced Sid Plemmons's neck with a shank—a homemade knife made in prisons all across America—devised of a sharpened toenail clipping taped to a tongue depressor. Who makes knives out of a sharpened toenail clipping?! Anyway, I need to thank Billie and Anita, for I would've never been able to sit face-to-face—between Plexiglas—with Jack Plemmons and have him tell all his lies about how Columbus Choice had been sneaking into Jack's pastures at night in order to deplete his farm ponds of bream and crappie, in order to have enough fresh local fish available for when the less-adventurous diners from, say, the Tennessee Department of Transportation came inside at lunch break, scared of hokkigai and hamachi, and so on. Of course Jack kept eye contact the entire time he told this story, for he too had been a graduate of the Tennessee Valley Community College, and had undergone their rigorous Public Speaking requirement.

My father deserves a nod, for he always said to me, "Stet, you can be whatever you want to be in America." I remember always thinking, Anything? I can be anything?! Back then I wanted to be a banker, or a track coach. When I took those tests on What You Should Be, it came out "banker" and "track coach." At least that's what my guidance counselor told me. I never saw the official results. There had to be some kind of connection there. Would a person prone to stealing money become a banker *and* track coach? Why wouldn't the result simply come out "robber"? At the Brushy Mountain State Penitentiary, according to Jack Plemmons, there were running bankers inside. He said that his brother used to chase this guy down in the exercise yard all the time.

I have undying gratitude to Ms. Robin Hirsch, who told me all about how her father Simon worked as a cook in the Special Forces, and how he found ways to make up "Southeast Asian Kani," and "Toro Vietnam," and "Haddock Hanoi," and "Flopping

Kosher Laotian Spicy Anago," and "Chairman Mao's Fishy Balls." I am sorry that I never got the time to meet Chef Simon Hirsch, as he ended his life before I even thought of starting research on Columbus Choice. But I can tell you this: My mouth watered the whole time Ms. Robin Hirsch told me about her daddy's recipes. I didn't get to include it in the book, seeing as *No Cover Available: The Story of Columbus Choice, African-American Sushi Chef from Tennessee* was about Columbus Choice and not about Simon Hirsch, but Robin found her father face-down dead of an unexpected heart attack in the middle of a pot of the leanest breast of flanken, simmered and served in broth, with a matzo ball, Krelach, noodles, peas, and carrots. What a way to die! Except for the third-degree burns, I suppose. Unlike Columbus Choice, Simon Hirsch got buried within thirty-six hours and wearing his tallit, so maybe it wasn't that bad an experience for those closest to him. I would like to think that within those thirty-six hours Simon Hirsch had time to think about how he taught Columbus Choice the finer aspects of Kosher deli- and sushi-cooking, and how he changed the life of a young African-American man, and how he (Simon) grieved for the way Columbus got lynched.

I'd like to, but like I said I'm not much into the monotheistic Christian ways of thinking, and I'm pretty secure in my belief that Simon didn't think much of anything once he succumbed.

Lately I've felt like a Buddhist for some reason, so I would like to thank Siddhartha Gautama and the Dalai Lama.

For patience and intelligence, I'd like to thank Dr. Theron Crowther, my mentor, for steering me away from my original low-residency in Southern culture studies master's thesis, *The Curious Life and Difficult Times of Mexican-American Fireworks Store-Owning Jorge "Short Fuse" Villegas: Love and War, Sparklers and Hatred*. Dr. Crowther knew intuitively what a problem I might have interviewing illegal aliens. He understood the inadequacies I might have seeing as I never took Spanish seriously when I attended Vanderbilt University—Go Commodores!—on a football scholarship as a punter who got a bad case of the shanks and only remained on the team for half a season. Dr. Crowther taught me how to ask the mysterious questions needed: Who, What, How, Where, When, and Why. He taught me how to read an interviewee's facial expressions—if a person kept looking off to the left, it meant he lied. If a person kept looking off to the right, it meant he lied. If a person made eye contact in a way that made the interviewer uncomfortable, then the interviewee was lying.

It's not like I tested for being a part-time track coach for nothing: I would like to extend a high-five to my high school track coach, Junebug Pinson, who told me that I could break six-four (now called 1.9304 meters) if I quit trying to be a punter. He also said I could do something else besides being a high-jumping punter if I watched the evening news, read the morning paper, and quit making up book synopses for Mrs. Rena L. Stone.

Kudos, too, to my classmates at Ole Miss-Taylor, all of whom will have their master's theses published one day, I feel certain! I couldn't have continued with this project had I not had the moral support from everyone sitting around the campfire in Taylor, Mississippi, telling stories about what we'd uncovered over the previous six months. I want to thank Ben D. Strawhorn, especially, for teaching me how to heat rocks correctly in an open fire pit and using them to cook on. Catfish ended up being a lot easier than I thought.

And I need to apologize for stringing out my low-residency residencies for so many years, keeping other scholars from gaining admittance to the Most Highly Selective Southern Cultures Studies Program in the Nation, according to *U.S. News and World Report.*

Before things "reached the top of a Chinese rain barrel," as Jack Plemmons said were Columbus Choice's last words—which is to say my life had gone to the bottom of a charred Tennessee barrel found frequently in Lynchburg, and then I continued downward all the way through the center of the earth, and then I punctured through the bottom of a rain barrel in Guandong province and crawled the last few feet until I knocked the top of said barrel off—I want to thank my pre-Frozen Head State Park Campground landlord, Mr. Lester "The Protester" Townes, who allowed me to paint the entire Atomic Arms apartment building instead of paying rent for a couple months. Painting a cheaply built, wooden, two-story row of twenty-four residences that sometimes truckers confused for a bad motel way off highway 62 gave me the quiet moments needed to mull over all the intricacies of an African-American GI with cooking skills taught him by a Jewish soldier from Brooklyn, and how some of the coincidences and chance encounters brought into one's life are ineffable and inexorable and inescapable and ineludible and inevitable and inexhaustible and inexplicable, not to mention beyond reason. Lester Townes's duskly ritual of splitting a twelve-pack of Old Milwaukee and a pint of Jim Beam with me only furthered my imagination and resolve, though it might've A) caused me to slow down the painting, and B) injured my vital organs.

Warm feelings to recent divorcee Wymona, who lived at the Atomic Arms, for letting me borrow her fine, New World Dictionary during lunch breaks and siestas in order to use scholarly words (see paragraph above) throughout. I wish I could remember Wymona's last name. Maybe I knew it at one time. Perhaps I suffer from periodic bouts of *dementia pugilistica*—in the dictionary—from having cornerbacks ram into me while I was trying to punt a football, or for misjudging a high jump bar and missing the pit. Maybe I should go get a blood test from Juanita Wilkins and see if I'm missing some vital platelets or something.

I would be remiss not to offer a big drunken smooch and some dry humping to all of those writers conference and colony directors who didn't see me as worthy of their time. If I'd gone to Yaddo, Breadloaf, MacDowell, Provincetown, and the other twenty-seven "colonies" or "conferences" I applied to back when I lived in the Frozen Head State Park Campground, then I'd've succumbed to their perfect afternoon cocktails and toddies and spent all my time trying to unzip some poetess's Dickey work pants, or trying to run from men who saw something exotic in a Tennessee ex-punter's drawl, and I never would have gotten Columbus's story right. So endless doffs of a beret to y'all.

I want to thank the good people at Mid-State Nursery for providing me needed information in regards to planting tomatoes, cucumbers, spinach, and jalapenos in five-gallon drywall buckets so that I had enough nourishment over a few years to complete my project. I would like to thank Columbus Choice's best friend in Harriman, and owner of Nuclear Fish Wholesale—Harold Holcombe—for giving me that recipe on how to make cucumbers into kosher dills. As for Harold, let me make it clear that I would've never completed the biography had he not told me all of the things that occurred to Columbus Choice that didn't come out in the court trial—occasions that I couldn't fully include in the text of *No Cover Available: The Story of Columbus Choice, African-American Sushi Chef from Tennessee*. For instance,

Mr. Holcombe made it clear that he had no problem whatsoever with blacks and whites carrying on a heterosexual relationship, and Mr. Holcombe's sister Luanne concurred that her brother felt that way. And that she didn't have an affair with Columbus Choice, unless harmless flirtation meant adultery.

I owe a debt of gratitude to Dr. Hajar Fard, at Roane Medical Center's emergency room, for treating my stomach ulcer and kidney stones, and providing me with diet tips that exclude cucumbers, tomatoes, spinach, and peppers. Writing a 550-page biography on an African-American Tennessee sushi owner is hard enough without constant torso pain. Rest assured, Dr. Fard, that I will pay my medical bills once the royalties stream in. And I stress *stream*!

Also, I need to thank Brenton Burry, attorney-at-law, for utmost representation and teaching me not to hold my hands together at a trial in such a manner that might make jury members subconsciously view me as guilty for blowing a .18 on the drive back from Yolanda Choice's juke joint back when I needed to ask some questions about her father over a three-day period. Should it ever happen again, Counselor Burry, I promise not to yell out "Drinks on me!" again, should the foreman announce "Not guilty." Maybe I ran into some luck by choosing the breathalyzer instead of having a blood sample drawn by Juanita Wilkins, phlebotomist.

Many thanks to Mrs. Gloretta Knoblock at the Harriman Public Library—built in 1909—for her helpful advice in regards to xenophobia, prison systems, edible fish, military mess halls, rope knots, and alcoholism. Also, thank you, Ms. Knoblock, for letting me drive the bookmobile, on a trial basis, for two weeks. To this day I'll maintain that A) I didn't tell the kids to read *Animal Farm*, then offer up, later, reasons why the novel stood for how a socialistic government might be better than a capitalistic system; and B) I didn't try to "live" inside the bookmobile at night.

My publisher says I have thirty days to finish up these Acknowledgments before they have to shove them into the "back matter," so I hope I have time to thank everyone. The last thing I want to do is be one of those writers who A) sends things in to his publisher past a deadline, and B) forgets to remember the people, places, and things that brought him into being the kind of biographer that he became.

I want to thank whoever came up with the term "deadline," which I can't find in Wikipedia, Google, or the OED—not necessarily in that order.

Friends and family members who lent support and encouragement are too numerous to name here, but I am particularly indebted to Mr. and Mrs. Walker Hitt, plus their fine daughter Cassandra at State Line Office Supplies for pointing out how, like at a funeral home when it's time to pick out a casket, they arranged their rolling ball pens down the Pen Aisle in such a fashion that, as long as one had some time, one could get past the really expensive ones and find, there at the end of the aisle, passable writing instruments that had been remaindered or discontinued. The same goes for their knowledge of legal pads, typewriter ribbons (call me old-fashioned and stubborn, but I had no idea that this "computer phase" would actually last) that no one stocked anymore, and sticky notes so I could keep track of what went on while writing.

Furthermore, I am deeply indebted to Cassandra for listening patiently to sections of the biography, and for her comments— particularly during those trying days when I couldn't get the chapters "Skinless and Boneless," and "That's Not the Smell of Aji!" down on paper right. Thanks beyond thanks, too, for Cassandra's keen advice concerning whether or not I should've moved out of the Atomic Arms apartment complex in Harriman and live a less expensive lifestyle at the Frozen Head State Park Campground, out closer to Oak Ridge and the Brushy Mountain State Penitentiary. May State Line Office Supplies prosper, and grow into a chain across all Tennessee!

I would like to express my gratitude to the Patel and Parthasarathy families for offering me a discount when I wished to "check in" to their respective motels in order to "acquire some quiet time" so that I could "get some work done." Thanks, too, to both C.H. and P.S.—I promised I wouldn't tell your friends or family—for aiding me when I got all pent up to the point where I didn't think I could continue with what ended up being 550 pages of *No Cover Available: The Story of Columbus Choice, African-American Sushi Chef from Tennessee.* I know that y'all know that my name wasn't really "W.J. Cash," and I thank you for letting me sign in for two-hour increments.

Eugene Stansell, from the Highway 62 Super Stop, deserves my undying gratitude for warning me about taking Tylenol should I be drinking too much. And I would like to thank his brother Floyd, who operates the Highway 62 One-Stop Auto Repair next door, for cherished advice concerning tire tread and oil changes, plus that seamless Bondo job on my car from when I ran off the road, dodging a deer, and scraped the passenger side from fender to bumper on Old Lady Crenshaw's rock-encumbered mailbox that must've been designed by the same guy who did the Washington Monument. And I would like to thank their sister, Patricia, for allowing me to pick her brain when it came to what ended up being a linchpin of a chapter in *No Cover Available: The Story of Columbus Choice, African-American Sushi Chef from Tennessee* titled "Columbus's Oyster Conundrum."

Though not technically "friends" or "family members," I want to thank the editors of the *New Yorker, Atlantic Monthly, Harper's, Paris Review, Georgia Review, Southern Review, National Geographic, Nation, Economist, South Carolina Review, Appalachian Heritage, New Delta Review, Arkansas Review, Shenandoah, Epoch, Mid-American Review, Playboy, Oxford American, Esquire,* and some others. Although all of you rejected individual chapters of this book, I could read between your standard rejection letter lines that you wished for me to continue my important tome. And I would like to give a special thanks to Steve Wickett and Danny Gillis for understanding that the story and plight of Columbus Choice was worthy of sharing on their most excellent blog dungbeetleworkinghard.com. Salut!

A hearty heartfelt heartwarming hug to Ida Flokiewicz and Maria Cherepanov—both names that prove I have a regular New York publisher, seeing as those kinds of surnames don't exist in either A) Tennessee; or B) the world of vanity-self- publishing—in the "jacket designing" department. I'll be the first to admit my error in thinking that my book, *No Cover Available: The Story of Columbus Choice, African-American Sushi Chef from Tennessee,* should have had a photograph of a black man wearing a bandana on the cover, or a black man pointing at a Dynamite Roll on the cover, or an empty noose, or a photograph of the Tennessee hillsides north of

Chattanooga and west of the Smokies, or a picture of someone standing with a fishing rod in his or her hand on the banks of the Emory or Clinch River, or members of the fucking idiotic KKK in their hoods with a burning cross in the background, or Sammy Davis, Jr. about to bite into a photoshopped piece of sashimi, or a soldier running for cover while bullets ricocheted around him, or a tuna hanging from a rope, or an octopus with a knife jabbed into it, or an African-American male looking off into the distance to a land where no one will judge him by the color of his skin, or a bowl of kani salad languishing on a picnic table covered in ants, or a two-lane Tennessee road leading to nowhere until the end of the asphalt turns into a pinpoint, or a mound of fresh dirt on a gravesite, or me.

I want to thank Ida and Maria for talking me into understanding how *No Cover Available: The Story of Columbus Choice, African-American Sushi Chef from Tennessee* would never sell without, and how it deserved, a cover that depicted a full-blown photograph of a stray dog with the wind at its back, and an American-made sedan driving off toward the horizon. That's the thing about people in the art departments of publishing houses working hand in hand with their PR departments: *They know what's the right thing.* Listen, if the government were headed up by people with backgrounds in publishing's "jacketing design" realm, I'd be willing to bet that other countries wouldn't hate us as much. There's no telling what the American flag would end up looking like, but that's another story.

My editor, who has asked to remain anonymous, deserves a lifted glass of champagne. I cannot express my regret that she's decided to accept and publish *No Cover Available: The Story of Columbus Choice, African-American Sushi Chef from Tennessee* as her final work with this particular publisher. I am fully awestruck by your saying to me, "This book will show them a thing or two!" Please believe me when I say that, should a movie ever be made of my life, then I will make a point to have a Leading Lady of Hollywood play the part of the editor. I'll request to have the Leading Man of Hollywood play the part of Stet Looper, biographer, and have about the Twentieth Most Requested Leading Woman of Hollywood play my ex-wife who endured my thinking about, then writing, *No Cover Available: The Story of Columbus Choice, African-American Sushi Chef from Tennessee*. Kudos galore!

I would like to thank the Tuskegee Airmen.

I owe thanks to Booker T. Washington.

When I showed up to interview Jack Plemmons at the Brushy Mountain State Penitentiary—who still maintains his innocence in regards to lynching Columbus Choice—someone told me that I needed to wear good rubber-soled tennis shoes because the guards might think I wished to steal in a "shiv" or a "shank," much like the sharpened toenail clipping taped to a toothbrush handle that ended up being used to slice the neck of Sid Plemmons, Jack's brother and cohort in the lynching of Columbus Choice. So I went immediately down to Mid-State Shoes and got me a nice pair of running shoes that didn't have those light-up flashers on the heels. Who knows if there's some kind of Prison Wish List when it comes to light-up shoes? I'm no expert—I only have a low-residency master's degree in Southern culture studies—but I would think that no prisoner with any brains would want a pair of glow-in-the-dark shoes to wear while escaping. Anyway, I got some regular Nike training shoes with waffle bottoms and strode right in the gates.

So I want to thank a man named Phil Snoddy for selling me those shoes, and for all of his advice about how I might perfect some kind of toe-heel-toe thing should I ever involve myself in a middle distance race the likes of the 800 or 1500 meters. The chances of my getting into shape and entering an all-comers race are pretty slim, Phil, but you never know when I might undertake a biography of, say, Haile Gebresalassie, so thanks for everything you did for me in regards to fitting my running shoes correctly.

I would like to thank Tommie Smith and John Carlos on the Olympic stand in Mexico City.

I am deeply indebted to Visa, MasterCard, Discovery, American Express, and four other Visa cards. When the royalties come in, I promise to pay off more than a minimum balance. Well, as far as you're concerned, American Express, I'll just pay you off in full, I suppose. What's with the policy that everything must be paid in full? That's not even American, if you ask me. It's *express*, but it's not American.

I would like to thank John Maynard Keynes.

Boundless gratitude and praise should be offered to my old ex-stray dog Dooley, who—in his way—pointed me in the direction of Columbus Choice's life and death. This is a funny story that perhaps I should've included in the text of *No Cover Available: The Story of Columbus Choice, African-American Sushi Chef from Tennessee*: Before phlebotomist-to-be Juanita Wilkins got thrown out of my class for saying a racist term back when I taught America

History 101 at Tennessee Valley Technical College, which later caused me to walk off that job because she went to the dean and said I'd molested her or whatever and then recanted her story when she got caught, Dooley and I were taking a walk across the campus. I had him on a leash because of the squirrel population. I had him on a leash because, at the time, I didn't own any Nike waffle trainers. Dooley came across a stray piece of sandpaper and started sniffing it. I said, of course, "Don't eat that. It's not a dog chew." Dooley wagged his tail. This white woman came by from the opposite direction—I forget her name, but she worked as an instructor in the Machine Tool Technology department—and she said, "That dog got some Japanese in him. That dog think that sandpaper a piece of nori, like what served over at Columbus Choice's Sushi over in Harriman." And I said, of course, "What? Where are you from?" And she said she was from Oak Ridge originally, and then she told me about how she had a second cousin who had a friend who had an aunt who had at one time been engaged to *both* of the Plemmons brothers, et cetera, before they lynched Columbus Choice for supposedly stealing freshwater fish. As we talked, Dooley ate the sandpaper. Later, when I was trying to clean up all his vomit on the floor of my apartment, I couldn't get the Machine Tool Technology woman out of my mind. I called up my estranged wife, Abby, to tell her all about it, and she said, "You need to get rid of that dog." I didn't. He was my lucky charm, and while I was doing research for *No Cover Available: The Story of Columbus Choice, African-American Sushi Chef from Tennessee,* Dooley rode shotgun. So, Dooley—I hope it's another fifty or sixty years, but I look forward to seeing you in the afterlife.

For invaluable insight into the upbringing of Columbus Choice, I would like to thank his brother, Leroy, Jr. First off, I want to thank him for teaching me that his and his father's name weren't pronounced like *Lee*-Roy, but more like Luh-*ROY*. Without Leroy Choice's willingness to tell me all about his brother's travails in the Army, and his life as a sharecropper's son in northern Mississippi, I doubt that I would've completely captured a sense of Columbus's obsession to succeed as the only sushi restaurant-owning black man in Tennessee. Also, I want to thank Leroy for his patience in regards to listening to my story, and his openness when it came to showing me the painful photographs he owned of Columbus hanging from a tree.

I want to thank Malcolm X.

I am indebted to the memory of Medgar Evers, whom I can see in that casket, which makes me think of how funeral home directors play on people's emotions, which makes me think of Mr. and Mrs. Walker Hitt's daughter Cassandra and how she toyed with me while I was finishing up my story.

A thoroughly researched biography such as *No Cover Available: The Story of Columbus Choice, African-American Sushi Chef from Tennessee* cannot be written alone. Sure, I'm the one who sat in the apartment, tent, bar, truck, trailer, or elsewhere scribbling down ideas, forming entire sections, and wondering if Columbus Choice would be proud of me should he still be alive, but just about everyone I've ever come across has played a part in the work, naturally. Take the woman who served me a western omelet those times at the Huddle House in Kingston, just down the road from Harriman: She said to me, "Do you like ketchup with your eggs?" and it made me wonder if Columbus Choice liked ketchup with his eggs, or if his blood looked like ketchup after he'd been hanged and stabbed to death. Take the man I met at the Day Old bread store in Oak Ridge who came up to me and asked, "Does that look like mold to you?" Well, it made me wonder what Columbus Choice did when his fish turned south, especially in the beginning when he didn't have a lot of customers who trusted an African-American man running a raw fish place in the middle of Tennessee. Take the man who cut my hair so I would have a decent author photo, a barber named Mr. Drake, who clipped a little too closely on my temples, which made me think of Temple Drake in Faulkner's novel, which made me think of corncobs, which made me think of grits, and how they probably weren't served in Columbus Choice's restaurant, which made me wonder if he'd've been accepted in the community better should he have offered them on his menu. I could go on and on. I *will* go on and on.

I am grateful to Cap'n Will Caldwell over at Tennessee River Marina and Boat Supply for showing me exactly what kind of water ski tow rope Jack and Sid Plemmons used to wrap around Columbus Choice's neck—durable 12-strand, quarter-inch polypropylene—and for his good-natured advice for me to stay out of people's affairs in and around the Tennessee Valley. When the royalties start streaming in, Cap'n Will, I promise to come by your place and buy me one of those used Sea Rays!

Because the Plemmons brothers went to great extents to make sure they killed a man who, as the evidence proved, *didn't* deplete local farm ponds at night, I am thankful to Rex Palmer at Palmer's Pawn and Gun for showing me his selection of nine millimeter pistols like what the Plemmons brothers used, and which may or may not have been bought or stolen from Palmer's Pawn, plus the beautiful serrated knives like the one used to stab Columbus Choice long after he'd probably died from asphyxiation and bullet wounds. I must say, though, Rex, that I *cannot* thank you for asking me to take a look at your jewelry, seeing as I came across what I feel pretty sure was the exact wedding band and engagement ring I'd given to Abby back during happier times. I'm not sure if it's worse to see a specially designed wedding band standing upright in a pawn shop display case or on the ring finger of a complete stranger woman. But I thank you from the bottom of my heart anyway, even though I had to undergo horrendous flashbacks of a woman packing up her belongings, saying things like, "You're a loser," or "The marriage vows didn't mention anything about odd obsessions," or "I knew I should've listened to my mother, father, siblings, friends, neighbors, and people I'd never even met," before going off to follow her personal dreams, which, I am convinced, weren't as lofty as publishing a book. As a matter of fact, I know that Abby wanted only to become a real estate agent in an area that thrived, seeing as her lisp kept her from being a TV anchor-woman—which probably makes me a bad person for being happy that she moved to Florida right before housing prices dropped because of everyone signing on to ethically questionable loans that they couldn't afford.

Lang Gurley over in the seafood department of Food City deserves special recognition for teaching me the importance of foods that're high in omega-3 fats, which he considers to be "brain food." I admit that before I partook of salmon on a daily basis I sometimes felt as if I couldn't do a crossword puzzle in the local weekly papers when the clue was something like "Hemingway's *For Whom* blank *Bell Tolls*," or "Shakespeare's *As You Like* blank." After a good month of salmon croquets, salmon patties, stir-fried salmon added to Kraft macaroni and cheese, et al, I could do a Sunday *New York Times* crossword over a week's time.

I want to thank Lang Gurley, also, for his insights as to Columbus Choice's personal views on clams and crabs.

I want to offer a backhanded acknowledgement to Coach Runyan from back when I was in the seventh grade participating in the annual Punt, Pass, and Kick competition. I finally figured it out, and it's made me the scholarly biographer that I am today: Runyan, you let some air out of my balls so I would always lose the competition to Gray Chadwick Cade, because his daddy had all that money and donated the aluminum bleachers to the visitors' side of the football field. I always wondered how come my punts and kicks only went twenty yards on Punt, Pass, and Kick Day, when normally I could whip Chadwick's butt. So I thank you, Coach Runyan. A) Your little trick made me practice harder, to the point where I made the team at Vanderbilt and lasted almost half a season, and B) It gave me some kind of subconscious drive to always figure out the reason why some things didn't work out as they normally do—much like the Scottish philosopher David Hume did when he figured out the "blocked habit of expectation"—and, in turn, that's what got me through Columbus Choice's biography. So a multitude of slaps on the butt to Coach Runyan.

I am grateful to Emmett Till.

I am indebted to my father's uncle Stan, who in 1966 got caught for manufacturing phony poker chips to look like the ones used at the Golden Nugget in Las Vegas, Nevada. On a family vacation out to the Grand Canyon one time, my father took my mom and me by the Nevada State Prison in Carson City to visit Uncle Stan, and I feel certain that my experience there inured me in such a way as to not be fearful of the Brushy Mountain State Penitentiary clientele when I needed to visit Jack Plemmons, Columbus Choice's alleged murderer. I should mention that Stan "the Man" owned a die-cutting operation, and that after he got caught for trying to replicate poker chips, he was paroled and immediately went into business mass-producing shims that could be used for breaking into cars. I'm not so sure that he got in trouble for manufacturing the shims, but he did get in trouble for *using* the things and operating some kind of chop shop on the Nevada-Arizona border. Stan taught me about irony, which is a useful "tool" in the writing trade—at the Nevada State Prison, he helped make license plates. All of the state of Nevada's license plates are made in Carson City, and if you don't believe it you can look it up on Wikipedia. (I'm sure that that's what my copyeditor is having some kind of fact-checker do right now.)

I wish to thank Neil Young for his song, with Crazyhorse, "Stupid Girl." I can't say how many times I listened to that song after Abby left me, and how many times I played it for Dooley when he was ignored by some bitch on the streets of Oak Ridge.

Slim Pender deserves accolades for letting me visit the spot on his land where Columbus Choice got lynched. I could really feel the vibes there, even though Slim cut down the oak tree right after the Plemmons brothers' trial. I appreciate Slim letting me run my hands all over the beautiful chest-of-drawers, nightstand, armoire, picnic table, high-boy, and three crosses that he puts out in the yard on Easter to represent where Jesus and those two thieves got crucified, all made from the oak tree where good, entrepreneurial Columbus Choice was found hanging. Now, Slim, I don't want to say anything about how I think you're a xenophobic, bigoted, card-carrying member of the KKK but maybe I ought to do so. Come on, man. I saw you smiling when I ran my palms against that wood. I saw you laugh when I got teary-eyed and shook my head in disbelief.

I want to thank Monetta Jones down at the One Spot Café for teaching me that French fries can be eaten with tartar sauce instead of ketchup, and for letting my only friend, Dooley, come inside seeing as the café already had a C rating and couldn't get much lower even if an inspector came in and saw an ex-stray dog there beneath a tabletop, licking his balls.

I would like to thank Richard Nixon for not keeping his promise in regards to getting the troops out of Vietnam by 1971, for in doing so, most of the young men in my hometown were off in Southeast Asia, which meant that the Abracadabra Drive-In Movie wasn't filled to capacity ever on weekends, which meant the owner had to cut prices down to something like a dollar a car, which meant that my parents went there often seeing as my father's eyesight and flat feet kept him 4-F, and so I was conceived in the back seat of a Dodge while my parents attended a *Two-Lane Blacktop* and *Willard* double feature. Of course I find this symbolic, for writing my thesis—which became my book— probably came to me, I believe, in a strangely genetic way. First off, "blacktop," contains the term "black." The movie *Willard* had to do with rats, which might be considered "fresh meat." In order to write about Columbus Choice, I had to drive all over the Harriman/Oak Ridge/Roane County region of Tennessee, which is made up of nothing other than two-lane asphalt. I don't want to say anything bad about Columbus Choice's restaurant, but I would imagine that he had to stay in control of vermin, viz., rats. At the Abracadabra Drive-In Movie theatre, from what research I've done, the concession stand offered popcorn, hot dogs with chili, Milk Duds, and Butterfinger candy bars. I bet there were rats inside that concession stand, too! My father once told me that the whole reason I got conceived was because he said to my mom, "You want a butter finger?" and he didn't mean the candy bar.

So I am boundlessly grateful to whoever was in charge of constructing the back seat of Dodge Darts, from welder to seamstress. I couldn't have done it without y'all. Plus Claude Freeman for having the business acumen to open the Abacadabra. Plus Gilbert Ralston for writing the novel and screenplay for *Willard*, and Will Corry and Rudy Wurlitzer for writing *Two-Lane Blacktop*. Plus all the actors involved who wouldn't ever be able to do anything worthwhile without the writers, outside of mime. I especially want to thank any of the sound effects geniuses—my parents might not have ever screwed had it not been for loud noises all over the Abracadabra speakers that masked their lovemaking sounds. I would like to thank the directors of those two movies, also—Monte Hellman and Daniel Mann—and please know that I would be honored should either of you ever want to direct a movie version of my biography.

Where I grew up in a small South Carolina town far, far away from the industrialized, modern conveniences of Tennessee, a man named Mr. Pinky Jervey ran a little juke joint roadhouse that may or may not have been built on slave burial grounds. Now, I don't know if Pinky—he got his nickname from a persistent and near-lethal case of conjunctivitis—couldn't read altogether, or quit trying due to the stress it put on his eyeballs, but not once did he ever check my ID when I rode my bicycle over there. I got beer, and I drank it in the woods alone until I heard that it was a sign of alcoholism if one drinks by himself. I was fourteen and fifteen at the time. When I heard about the "drinking alone" stuff, I started taking my dog with me, who lapped at the tops of beer cans as if they'd been smeared with canned Alpo. In a previous life I'm pretty sure that dog—politically incorrectly named Gypsy— might've been either a drunk or a porn star. Anyway, I want to thank Pinky Jervey for his indirect part in my writing life. In a bunch of the reading that I did as a lackluster and failed punter on the football team at Vanderbilt, both in history and in English classes, I came to understand that a bunch of Southern writers might've had a little problem with the booze. So I feel as though Pinky abetted me in ways that he would have never known way back when he played Ray Charles and Ronnie Milsaps inside his bar relentlessly.

A number of peripheral, seemingly random events and acquaintances helped me immeasurably while I wrote *No Cover Available: The Story of Columbus Choice, African-American Sushi Chef from Tennessee,* and I wish to acknowledge all of them heartily. For example, on many occasions I would go over to the Atomic Gas 'n' Go for coffee in the morning, and stand around talking to Mr. Beach Beacher, who drove a 1962 Studebaker Gran Turismo and parked it across three spots out front. He'd had an idea back in something like 1999 that he could use up all of his savings for such a car—what a car!—restore most of it himself, and then win money in various vintage car shows and fairs and competitions of one sort or another. Beach Beacher wore a red, short-sleeved, Studebaker shirt with two front pockets every day, advertising that he owned the car parked out front should anyone come inside the convenience store for a scratch-off card, and be all gung-ho to say something like, "Hey, does that Studebaker out front have a V-8 engine?" and whatnot. Now, Beach Beacher always seemed perturbed that people forever wanted to reminisce, argue, or use the opportunity to say something mean about foreign-made automobiles. I watched from my stool, drinking regular Folger's coffee, as Beach Beacher—and that was his given name, according to his obituary, not some kind of childhood nickname—snapped at his interrogators. I thank Mr. Beach Beacher, for it will remind me that if you make a big deal about parking sideways in a vintage vehicle and wear a shirt that might as well be made of neon, then you're asking for people to interrupt your thoughts. Just like how if I don't want to ever talk about the tragic life of Columbus Choice, then I shouldn't go and publish an entire biography of the great man. Anyway, to Beach Beacher, I offer my thanks, and I hope that you know that after you affixed the garden hose to the muffler of the 1962 Studebaker Gran Turismo and died, your son sold the car to a retired nuclear physicist from over at Oak Ridge who keeps it parked outside the One Spot Café in Harriman from about nine in the morning until after the lunch crowd. I know only that his name's Dr. Heinrich-something. I guess I'll learn his family name when I notice it in the obituaries one day, after he too understands the pressures of discussing 289 cubic inch engines and Flight-o-Matic automatic transmissions every day to strangers. I'm hopeful that when surrounded by history and civil rights buffs wanting me to sign copies of their books, I never tire from talking about fatty tuna.

For making me feel better about myself, I wish to thank the people I saw nearly daily in and around the Harriman-Oak Ridge area: the guy who always walked around on stilts wherever he went, and who tried to sue every bank under the Americans with Disabilities Act because their ATMs were too low for him to use;

the guy who rode a unicycle wherever he went; the woman who rode, alone, on a bicycle built for two; the woman who stood on the street corner outside Rex Palmer's Pawn Shop, staring up at the sun, without sunglasses, tears running down her face; the last remaining "shell-shocked" soldiers from World War II who left their long-term residential facility and walked around town wearing motorcycle helmets; the guy who carried a surfboard wherever he went—the one wearing the puka shell choker, not to be confused with the guy who carried a surfboard around wherever he went yelling out the theme to *Hawai'i Five-O*, seeing as he kind of grated on my nerves, which indirectly kept me from concentrating while working on the Columbus Choice biography; the woman who wore galoshes every day, no matter what the weather, forever prepared since the Great Flood of 1971.

I must offer a zealous thumbs-up to Eric Burden's version of the Nashville Teens' classic song "Tobacco Road."

Among Columbus Choice's closest friends in childhood who outlived Columbus Choice, I want to single out for special thanks the third leg on his high school track team's 4X110 relay team Julius "Cube Steak" Goode for information on the anchor leg's soft touch when it came to receiving, then grasping, the baton; his senior prom date Ms. (now Mrs.) Jackie Puckett (now Holloway) for information on her date's soft touch when it came to pinning a corsage on her dress; Ludie Latimer for information concerning Columbus Choice's short-lived attempt to play the cornet in junior high school, then how he changed over to bassoon so as not to have to deal with marching band and the inherent, ubiquitous, inexorable (my words) practice sessions every afternoon; Marquette "Drumstick" Carter, the first leg on the 4X110 relay team,

for information on Columbus Choice's early competiveness, and
the changes that Marquette noticed once Columbus came back
from the military; Vanita Tolbert for information about how, in
the sixth grade when she wore white pants and had her very first
menstrual period during math class and went up to the teacher
(Mrs. Blocker? Mrs. Baten?) so the rest of the class had a good
view of what happened on the back of Vanita's pants—and when
a couple of the boys in the class (Cube Steak? Drumstick? Ludie?)
yelled out, "Nita's butt bleeding, Nita's butt bleeding!"—Columbus Choice got out of his desk, took off his coat, and wrapped
it around her backside in a manner both brave and chivalrous;
Sherry Leverette, Columbus Choice's sixth-grade girlfriend, for
information on how he might've been the first "player" in the
African-American community.

For invaluable advice concerning pure-tee fear, I need to tip my
cap to Juanita Wilkins's father, Bernard. In writing such a sad,
tragic, fate-filled biography, it ended up important for my knowing pure-tee fear, in order to slightly comprehend Columbus
Choice's adrenaline levels and heart rate when a gun was pointed
his way.

Among Columbus Choice's closest friends in adulthood, I want
to single out for special thanks Wesley Fulmer, of Fulmer's Work
Clothes Supply, for information about Columbus Choice's need
for a three-pocket apron; to Bentley Canfield, of Canfield's Restaurant Supply, for information concerning how Columbus preferred those flat, no-roll pencils that carpenters normally use on
jobsites; to Dean Willis, of Exotic Pets of Oak Ridge, for his unof-
ficial prognosis that Columbus Choice suffered from both arach-
nophobia and ophidiophobia, but that he came into the store

totally obsessed with the lives and habits of most amphibians, and had a special connection with a pair of tiger salamanders (they can live to be twenty-five years old!), who finally died—one right after the other, as if they were love birds, or doves, or beavers, or ospreys, or voles, or any of those other matrimonially significant animals—which caused Columbus to become significantly depressed, which happened (was it a coincidence?) right before he went off with the Plemmons brothers on that ill-fated trip.

I have read enough biographies of famous biographers—which makes them *autobiographers*, also—to know that most writers suffer physically, mentally, financially, and matrimonially, just like I did while undergoing my long work project. I have to admit that—because not everyone in mid-central-southern Tennessee has cable access and watches *Antiques Roadshow, Treasures in the Attic, If Walls Could Talk, Junkin'!, That's Not a Bedpan, At the Auction, The Appraisal Fair, Don't Throw that Away!, Forever Tarnished and Crazed*, and/or *Flip This Knick-Knack*—I ended up being able to make ends meet after I lost that job teaching History 101 at Tennessee Valley Community College because well-meaning people threw away their so-called junk out on the edge of Highways 29, 27, 61, 62, 162, 58, 328, 299, the Oak Ridge Turnpike, and Margrave Drive over in Harriman. So I want to thank all those people who placed their Stickley furniture and Queen Anne chairs out on the roadside, which I shoved into my car, didn't restore seeing as I knew enough as to not compromise the patina (or pati*ni*), and then sold to a man in Chattanooga, who knew a man in Nashville, who knew a man in Memphis, who knew a woman in Chicago, who knew a woman in New York City, who probably sold everything to a man in Atlanta—somebody like Ted Turner.

I would be remiss in not thanking Ted Turner for starting the entire cable TV industry, which enabled everyday people to start up stations like Home and Garden Television, Style, Oxygen, Lifetime, the Learning Channel, Arts and Entertainment, the Discovery Channel, and so on, which air programs daily like *For What It's Worth*, et al.

I would also like to thank the people who developed and aired the Food Network, seeing as I learned many, many new tricks and recipes in regards to cooking on an electric eye, and then a gas stove, and then on an old-school Coleman MatchLight two-burner propane stove. Maybe one day I'll be one of your celebrity chefs, after *No Cover Available: The Story of Columbus Choice, African-American Sushi Chef from Tennessee* becomes well known, et cetera. Maybe y'all will come down here and I'll show you some of the things that kept me alive while I worked on Columbus's biography.

Here's a taste, so to speak: Kraft macaroni and cheese with a can of Campbell's oyster stew thrown in. Stir thoroughly. I call it "White Trash Calabash." Here's another: Kraft macaroni and cheese, a can of Chicken of the Sea tuna packed in spring water, Dole pineapple chunks, and green chiles. Mix well. I call it "Elbow Chicken of the Hawaiian Sea, Amigo." There are other recipes that involve Vienna sausages, potted meat, and a variety of food that Columbus Choice, I know, wouldn't approve of, seeing as he was such a gourmand before he got lynched by the Plemmons brothers. Anyway, I thank the people of the Food Network all the way to a boiling point.

Juanita Wilkins, ex–History 101 student and current phlebotomist, told me one time that she'd invented a hangover cure that involved day-old Kraft macaroni and cheese, day-old bread, Spam that accidentally got left out overnight, all mixed in with day-old coffee that she called Mysterious Caffeinated Wonder Pasta, but you'd have to get in touch with her if you ever wanted to try it. She'd be good on any of your programs, seeing as truckers and housewives with a curious lesbian side might like to look at her.

———

It would be a frightful error if I forgot to include Dr. Sammy Alexander for his free foot diagnosis over at the Oak Ridge Medical Clinic, and for telling me that I didn't A) contract diabetes; or B) have some kind of disease caused by toxic chemicals dumped into a variety of creeks and rivers where I'd washed by socks and shoes at one time or another. Who would've thought that tea tree oil could eradicate toenail fungus? What a miracle drug! Thanks for the suggestion and insights, Dr. Alexander. And I didn't have to go into one of those chain drug stores and feel like a leper, standing in line with an expensive tube of Fung-Off for everyone to see and make judgments as to my hygienic practices or lack thereof. And thank you, too, for helping out with my good friend J.W. when she couldn't afford those women's clinics in Memphis or Nashville or Chattanooga.

I am indebted to Python Dave McCarter for his fine tattoo artistry on my biceps over the years at Ink Well. At least the *heart's* still there with the arrow through it!

Goodwill Industries and the Salvation Army Thrift Store deserve a heap of recognition for offering down-on-their-luck hard-working biographers a place to purchase clean, like-new men's dress shirts for a dollar each. I found it terribly important to feel successful, though I had not been successful whatsoever at this point, in my writing endeavors. Furthermore, I wish to thank all of the thrift store associates for being lenient when it came to "senior citizen discounts." I'm not too proud to say that it got to the point where it was cheaper for me to buy new used shirts and throw them away than it was to waste all those quarters at Nuclear Wash-o-Matic.

Maybe even more important for a biographer is the fine selection of books to be found at Salvation Army and Goodwill Industry thrift stores. It can be difficult to own a bookcase when living in a campground, so I advise any future biographers out there to buy one book at a time, then donate it back for tax purposes (always have hope that one day you'll make enough money to pay taxes!), or choose one of the fine cracked near-leather or stained cloth Strato-Loungers in the showroom in which to read a couple chapters at a time. If you keep a Bible handy at the Salvation Army, no employee will ask you to leave, I have found.

The Oak Ridge Oatmeal Breakfast Club, whose members served bowls of Quaker Oats each weekday morning at the Oak Ridge Mercy Center, provided Dooley and me with needed sustenance when I was in town to interview ex-employees and friends and relatives of Columbus Choice—or to read fascinating biographies of Jesse Owens, Colin Powell, and the Dalai Lama—and I offer y'all a hearty slap on the back.

I am in indebted to the Candle Corporation of America, a subsidiary of Blyth, Incorporated, for their fine, reliable product, Sterno.

I wish to thank the staff of Dermo-Laser for their expertise in Q-Switched Ruby and Neodynium YAG lasers, with three wavelengths, to break up "Abby" into smaller particles that vanished from my bicep, and then "Juanita," which I had Python Dave tattoo prematurely. I know that y'all might exaggerate somewhat when you say that it'll only feel like a rubber band snapping on the skin, but to be honest it felt a little more like a bad rope burn. Although I'm no psychiatrist, I feel certain that that notion of the rope burn urged me onward subconsciously to tell the story of Columbus Choice's lynching.

I would like to acknowledge the support of the National Endowment for the Humanities. I *cannot*, but I would like to do so. Evidently my plan of action regarding *No Cover Available: The Story of Columbus Choice, African-American Sushi Chef from Tennessee* did not sway the voting committee, or whatever they have up there at the NEH. I completely understand. I do not bear a grudge, nor do I wish to exact vengeance on any of the highly qualified members up there in Washington, D.C. I read recently that somebody received one of the NEH grants in order to work on the *Selected Papers of Reggae Icon Bob Marley*. Selected *rolling* papers, maybe. But I understand. Up until my biography of Columbus Choice hits the shelves of every college and university library in America (and Jamaica, I suppose), no one will understand how Columbus's lynching affected our fast-paced modern-day society of men and women, the bigoted and the rational.

I would like to offer thanks to the support I received from the National Endowment for the Arts, but, again, I didn't receive one of their grants, so I cannot thank those people, either. I believe the NEA folks are up in our nation's capital, also. Maybe I didn't make it clear enough in my application that Columbus Choice was also a folk artist. He hung his primitive, naïve paintings—done with latex house paint on asbestos roofing shingles, cedar plank shingles, tin roof scrap, terra cotta shingles, and pieces of slate roofs. Unlike other folk artists of his generation, he didn't paint on plywood, one-by-twelve pine lumber, sheetrock, or refrigerator doors. Why? Because he got the *shingles* back when he was in the army, learning how to cook fine kosher meals from his friend from Brooklyn, who may or may not have been a tyrant in the kitchen. I read somewhere how a supposed scholar received both an NEH and NEA grant to write a biography about the artist Joseph Beuys, who supposedly crashed a German plane in World War II, got rescued by Tartar tribesmen who wrapped him in felt and fat, and then went on to make all these sculptures using felt and fat. I found the book and read it. Well, I read parts of it, enough to know that Beuys made up that story about getting rescued by tribesmen. So one guy gets two big-ass grants to work on a biography of a lying artist, and here I am in Tennessee, dirt poor, living in a fucking campground part of the time, and I can't get a reach-around from the NEA. Maybe I should've called my biography *No Cover Available: The Story of Lying Folk Artist Columbus Choice, African-American Sushi Chef from Tennessee.*

But, again, I suppose those people in Washington, D.C., know a lot more about who deserves grant money as opposed to me. Or I. See, I don't even know grammar, so maybe that should prove to me how come someone who makes a documentary of himself counting the thorns on a rose bush deserves monies as compared to an independent scholar wishing the world to understand the complex life of a black man in central Tennessee whose mission was to teach the masses about the dietary advantages of jellyfish.

I want to thank whoever runs that reality-based television program that involves a tyrant chef. Without watching that show, I might not have understood how Columbus Choice wanted to prove everyone wrong in regards to his mastery of the kitchen.

I want to thank Mr. Walker Hitt for not pressing charges, and that other guy for believing me when I said I walked into his place with a vintage Sheaffer fountain pen.

———

The Southern Poverty Law Center, founded by good Morris Dees and Joe Levin in 1971, has done some extraordinary and brave work in regards to civil rights and hatemongers. I would like to thank them for their moral support. After I wrote them all about my project concerning Columbus Choice, they informed me that they didn't tender financial support, outside of their "Teaching Tolerance" grants. They couldn't give me money, though, seeing as I no longer taught History 101 at Tennessee Valley Community College after I walked off the job due to Juanita Wilkins's misdirected allegations. One day, Southern Poverty Law Center, one day!

I hate to admit it, but I contacted the neo-Confederate group League of the South in hopes that they would pay me *not* to publish *No Cover Available: The Story of Columbus Choice, African-American Sushi Chef from Tennessee*. What the hell. Here's the letter I got back from one of those people, who say that they're not racists, et cetera, but still want to secede from the union because of black people: "Dear Mr. Stet Looper. We dont' [sic] care about no books [sic] ritten [sic] about no niger [sic] juw [sic] boodist [sic]. If you ast [sic] us, a juw [sic] boodist [sic] is nothing more than a Judas."

It went on some more. Most of it was illegible—evidently supporters of the Confederacy don't believe in typewriters, much less computers—but I'm pretty sure I made out "die, die, niger-lover [sic]" and "you cain't [sic] spell 'triggers' without 'grits'."

Have you ever noticed how "sic" and "sick" are close together in spelling? There's a reason for that. I can't claim thinking that up myself, though—I'm pretty sure I read it in "Dear Abby" one time. Anyway, they didn't give me money to *not* publish the book, which makes me happy that I published it so more people will understand the hateful commitment of League of the South members.

———

I want to thank the Clash for their song "Police on My Back."

I am indebted to the drug cartels of both Mexico and Colombia. When no one else would send me money to complete the biography, I had no other choice but to go find the sunken motorboat of Juanita Wilkin's cousin, Willie Wilkins, who once transported marijuana and cocaine up and down the rivers of the Tennessee Cumberland Plateau. Willie took three years of Spanish in high school, and got tabbed to be a runner, somehow. I'm serious. I figured this out sans the help of his cousin: the Hispanic population had infiltrated the entire southeast because no one else had the work ethic to pick peaches, apples, burley tobacco, and so on. One of Willie's classmates had a friend, who had a relative, who had a friend, and so on. Next thing you know, a guy named Guillermo is saying in Spanish to Willie, "Would you be interested in picking up some drugs and then trafficking them upriver to some people, who will traffic the drugs upriver to some people," and so on, until the drugs reached Cincinnati, or Detroit, or Woodland Caribou Provincial Park up in Ontario.

Willie got to taking the drugs, as they say. He became an addict, something I can understand, what with my booze problems. He got to where he took little slivers of the cocaine and ingested them into his nostrils, as cocaine people are wont to do. He pinched off pieces of bud and smoked it in a pipe, much like the pseudo-Rastafarians who read such books as *The Selected Papers of Reggae Icon Bob Marley* feel obligated. That's what Spanish-speaking Willie did. Some educators believe that all of us need to know a foreign language, but I'm here to point out that people who concentrate in Spanish might turn to marijuana and cocaine usage, and those who're inclined to learn whatever they speak in Afghanistan lean toward heroin. I don't want to make any vast generalizations, but anyone enamored with Southern culture might be prone to scouring pastureland in order to harvest and partake of the psilocybin mushroom.

And Willie, of course, got paranoid. He dropped off drugs one day and took in some money. He dropped off some drugs, and he took in some money. He dropped off some drugs, and he took in some money. I can see him doing all this. His long mullet hair flew in the wind, and he had no one behind him water skiing. I don't know if DEA (Drug Enforcement Administration) officers actually followed him in a go-fast boat, or if he got all paranoid, but the next thing you know he shot a hole in his own hull, jumped out, and swam to shore. He told me all about it from the Brushy Mountain State Penitentiary, where he stayed because when he got out of the river he immediately stole a car, and kidnapped a woman, and got caught.

Listen. You take a hungry, poor biographer who can't get any financial support for his project—let's say one intent on writing *No Cover Available: The Story of Columbus Choice, African-American Sushi Chef from Tennessee*—and tell him where a sunken boat half-filled with drugs and money might be, what you have is a biographer in a scuba suit. So I thank Willie. I thank the DEA for scaring people enough to think that they're being followed even when they're not.

I want to thank that psychologist for teaching me that I can't be too proud.

I'm not sure how or why the local VFW club thought that I was a veteran of any of the foreign wars, but the bartender there, Vic Partlow, needs a pat on the back for putting up with me during those long, drought-like days when I couldn't figure out how to handle Columbus Choice's life story without becoming "involved" or "attached" or "subjective." Furthermore, I want to thank Vic Partlow for letting me in for free on the nights when comedian Mighty Max showed up on what I learned later was some kind of Crystal Meth Circuit, as opposed to the old Chitlin Circuit. Mighty Max might've been the worst comedian of all time, and I have the handheld Sony ClearVoice Plus Microcassettecorder M-470 with Auto Shut Off, which I used about every day in order to speak out what thoughts I had regarding the biography, to prove it.

Anyway, I need to thank Mighty Max, also, for letting me know that if he can make it, then anyone can make it. Listen:

Some jumper cables walk into a bar. The bartender says, "Man, you look horrible." The jumper cables say, "Don't get me started."

A sixteen-penny nail walks into a bar and the bartender says, "Can't serve you. You're already hammered."

A right-wing radio personality walks into a bar. The bartender says, "Can I get you anything?" and the guy says, "No thanks, I'm already really fucked up."

A hairbrush walks into a bar. The bartender says, "Hold on, buddy. Don't bristle up on me."

A tongue depressor walks into a bar and the bartender says, "Get out of here. You make me gag."

A blow-up rubber sex doll walks into a bar. The bartender says, "What'll you have?" and the sex doll pauses before saying, "It was just on the tip of my tongue. Well, fuck me."

A pair of pliers walks into a bar, but the bartender says, "We don't serve tools."

A screwdriver walks into a bar and orders a vodka and orange juice. The bartender says, "What are you, a cannibal or something?"

Some confetti walks into a bar and the bartender says, "I can't serve you seeing as you're already torn up."

A rectal thermometer walks into a gay bar and gets a hero's welcome.

Nine million, nine hundred ninety-nine thousand, nine hundred ninety-nine lottery tickets walk into a bar. The bartender says, "Sorry, we don't serve such losers."

A rasp walks into a bar and asks the bartender, "Can I drink here if I promise not to grate on your nerves?"

An air horn walks into a bar and the bartender says, "If you're intent on blowing, follow the rectal thermometer next door to the gay bar."

A bipolar woman walks into a bar, but the bartender says, "Last time you were here you split without paying."

An atom walks into the bar and the bartender says, "Last time you were here you split without paying, and all hell broke loose soon thereafter."

A candelabra walks into the bar and the bartender says, "Can't serve anyone already lit."

A linebacker walks into a bar. "Hey, don't rush me," says the bartender.

A bowling ball walks into a bar. He says, "I'd like a pint of Mad Dog 20/20." The bartender says, "You can drink better wine than that. You're not in the gutter anymore."

A bowling pin walks into a bar. He says to the bartender, "I'm thirsty, and I don't have any money." The bartender says, "Spare me."

A spigot walks into a bar and asks, "What do you have on tap?"

A spigot walks into a bar. The bartender says, "Sorry, but we don't serve drips."

A ceiling fan walks into a bar. The bartender says, "Draft?"

A blood drive nurse walks into a bar. The bartender says, "You want another pint this soon?"

A rabies victim walks into a bar. The bartender says, "I guess you're ready for another shot in your stomach."

A revolving door walks into a bar. The bartender shakes his head and says, "Turn around."

A bottle of Wite-Out comes into a bar. "I can't serve your type," says the bartender. "Disappear, buddy."

A chunk of fresco walks into a bar. The bartender says, "Can't serve you. You're plastered."

An ATM machine walks into a bar and orders drinks for everyone. The bartender says, "What are you, like, made of money?"

A length of bubble wrap walks into a bar. The bartender says, "I'm going to keep a close watch on you. Don't pop off."

A champagne cork walks into a bar. The bartender says, "I'm going to keep a close watch on you. Don't pop off."

Carbon paper walks into a bar. The bartender says, "I guess you'll be wanting an Old Fashioned."

A typewriter walks into a bar. The bartender says, "I guess you'll be wanting an Old Fashioned."

Dr. Kevorkian walks into a bar with a little Chinese boy. The bartender says, "We don't serve youth in Asia."

A car cigarette lighter walks into a bar. The bartender starts listing off the night's specials. The car cigarette lighter says, "Don't push me."

A golf cart walks into a bar. The bartender says, "This place is exclusive. Members only. We only serve people who drive Caddies."

A three-wood walks into a bar on Pizza Night and orders a beer. The bartender says, "You want a slice to go with that?" The golf club says, "Fuck you."

Y'all might've experienced the Mighty Max Spectacle yourselves, and if so, I hope you remember that the reason he is on this planet is so that the rest of us will understand how we can be anything that we wish to be. We could become vice president. I know for a fact that after witnessing Mighty Max a third or fourth time, I convinced myself that I too could be a stand-up comedian, and found myself straying from the task at hand.

———

When looking back on my own life, I think that I have a four-person gang to offer my unremitted appreciation when it comes to molding me into the biographer I am today. Sure, I know that when every biographer is asked, "Who do you see as your mentor?" or "Whose work got you into writing?" and so on, they usually come up with the standard answers: Thucydides, Dame Edith Sitwell, Samuel Pepys, and Doris Kearns Goodwin. (One time I asked Abby what she thought of Pepys, and she said to me, "They're all right, but I like traditional Hershey's Robin Eggs better.") Anyway, whenever someone should ever ask me what got me into writing about real things that happened, like I pointed out to the best of my ability in *No Cover Available: The Story of Columbus Choice, African-American Sushi Chef from Tennessee,* I only have to offer this as an answer: The Inventors of the View-Master—Fred and Ed Mayer, plus Harold Graves and William Gruber. I'm sure that they're all dead by now, but I want to thank them for offering me the opportunity growing up to see vivid, lifelike, 3-D images of places like the Great Pyramids, the Eiffel Tower, Big Ben, Stonehenge, Carlsbad Caverns, the Grand Canyon, and comedienne Lucille Ball. It's all cause and effect, I suppose. My parents didn't want to buy a television, so they got me a View-Master. I looked at these places far, far away from my home in South Carolina and knew that I wanted to go places. So I took up punting a football. And then I excelled at Forty-Five High School and got a scholarship to Vanderbilt University. And then I shanked too many fourth down punts for something like a twelve-yard average and got released from the team, and then I studied history, and then I got the opportunity to do one of those study abroad programs in Egypt, France, England, New Mexico, Arizona, and Hollywood.

And then my parents said to me, "Why should we pay good money for you to study in Egypt, France, England, New Mexico, Arizona, or Hollywood after we went out and bought you that View-Master 3-D stereogram systems so you could see all of those places already?" So I stayed at Vanderbilt and took more history classes, and through what can only be called a fortuitous, serendipitous event, sat in my third-favorite history professor's office one day when he said to me, "Damn, son, why don't you go hang out with Columbus Choice for a while," like that—meaning, "Why don't you go kill yourself?" I guess. Well I didn't know who the hell Columbus Choice was at the time. And of course I wanted to impress my third-favorite history professor. So I went and looked things up on the microfiche and on the microfilm and in the newspapers stacked up in a back room of the Jean and Alexander Heard Library—I need to thank those folks, too—because this was a time before the Internet.

Goddamn! I thought. Goddamn, this guy Columbus Choice was a black man who owned a sushi place and he got hanged, stabbed, and shot all on the same day by Sid and Jack Plemmons. I thought, Why has this not been on the national news? I thought, Will my first- and second-favorite history professors be upset with me because I don't wish to continue ongoing research on the lives of Wendell Lewis Wilkie and William Jennings Bryan?

I didn't think at the time, Right about now a baby named Juanita Wilkins is being born, and later on she will be in my History 101 course at Tennessee Valley Community College, and she will accuse me of offering her a grade for sex after she said the N word in a class made up fifty-fifty of black and white "students," and then she will become a phlebotomist in the Harriman/Oak Ridge area, and then maybe she and I will have a little bit of a relationship that will help me forget Abby.

I would like to thank the Northwestern University Wildcats football team for losing thirty-four games in a row.

I would like to thank the Prairie View A&M Panthers football team for losing eighty games in a row.

I would like to thank the California Institute of Technology's basketball team for losing two hundred seven games in a row.

I would've gone off and killed myself if I'd've realized that I'd forgotten all of the players in the Negro Baseball Leagues. I am 100% indebted to the likes of Josh Gibson, Larry Doby, Satchel Paige, Jackie Robinson, Buck Leonard, Fleetwood Walker, Cool Papa Bell, Rube Foster, Mule Suttles, et al. I want to thank the motels that allowed these heroes to spend the night while on the road, and to place a curse on the Jim Crow–hampered motels and restaurants that wouldn't allow these men through front *or* back doors.

It will be hard to believe, perhaps—it'll sound like this kind of coincidence is downright impossible—but Yolanda Choice told me that her father's father *almost* played for the Atlanta Black Crackers in 1922 or thereabouts, but he and his wife (Columbus Choice's grandmother) had a baby (Columbus Choice's father), and Mrs. Choice made some ultimatums. (I must remember to thank Arthur Schopenhauer later, especially for his remark about matrimony.) Anyway, Grandpa Choice, then in his early twenties, had to get steady work, which he did. According to his great-granddaughter Yolanda, he either worked in a cotton mill, for the railroad, or as a barber. No matter what his day job, on weekends and nights he moonlighted selling hot dogs at Atlanta Black Crackers home games. His son—Columbus Choice's father—helped out selling hot dogs from the age of six on up until the last days of the Negro League, according to Yolanda.

I don't think it takes a Doctorate in Symbolism and Irony from a non-state-supported institution of higher education to marvel at the connective tissue that goes from grandfather to father to son. In a Rube Goldberg-kind of way, the Negro Baseball League helped kill innocent, unathletic, peace-loving, Buddhist-leaning African-American Columbus Choice.

The Chicago Cubs, naturally.

I am fully aware that some of the people I met regularly during my time in the Oak Ridge-Harriman area thought that perhaps I needed the services of the closest mental health facility. I heard the whispers. People laughed at me, and pointed. Sometimes I'd get something like, "You know, Edgar Allen Poe was kind of crazy" in the middle of an exchange.

So I am fully indebted to Henry Darger, Jr., the great outsider artist and writer who penned the 15,145 single-spaced tome *The Story of the Vivian Girls, in What is known as the Realms of the Unreal, of the Glandeco-Angelinnian War Storm, Caused by the Child Slave Rebellion*, plus the hundreds of illustrations that went with it. I am hopeful that everyone who reads *No Cover Available: The Story of Columbus Choice, African-American Sushi Chef from Tennessee* will close the covers and say, "Stet Looper wasn't deranged—there were no illustrations of little girls with penises, and he's 14,000 pages shorter than Henry Darger."

So I wish to raise my glass to Mr. Darger. His unflinching obsession helped me with mine. His example let me know that it was all right, if not normal, to shuffle onward, relentless, at times blind, never understanding why an artist does what he or she needs to do, like a lucky shrew or vole that the gods decided should be born beneath, and live below, a nightcrawler farm.

———

It would be downright rude of me not to express gratitude, also, to the American sculptor Joseph Cornell, who might've been somewhat shy, but continued to make those collages-in-a-box.

I want to thank Ms. Ann-Mary (did your parents have dyslexia?) Mason at the drive-thru window at Atomic City Bank and Trust. I never wanted to admit it—and I'm sure you knew at the time, Ann-Mary—but I didn't really need all those penny wrappers, at least not most of the time. As you may or may not know, I never really trusted the banking industry. One of the reasons why I shanked so many punts in college may have been because of a gigantic Bank of America sign I could see hovering above the Vanderbilt stadium, as well as just about any Away Game stadium where Vanderbilt played. So I never trusted banks, but you, Ann-Mary, cured my distrust of bank tellers. If my dog Dooley could talk he'd want to say, "Thank you so much for doling out three or four Milk Bone biscuits every time we visited your window."

To be honest, if my dog Dooley could talk, he might also say, "My master ate some of those dog biscuits meant for me."

On a side note—just as one oftentimes needs a good bone to put in boiling water to make broth, a medium-sized Milk Bone works, too, though the end result tastes more like one of the lesser-known grains of the Midwest—say, barley—than marrow.

I am grateful to the Board of Directors, Board of Trustees, Benefactors, Friends, Advisors, and Volunteers at the Roane County Historical Museum and Senior Citizens Center, and especially to Mr. Hack Watson, Executive Director; Mrs. Luann Fleming, Director; Mrs. Patty Patterson, Assistant Director; Mr. Hut LaRue, Groundskeeper; Mr. Ronnie Waddell, Director of Maintenance; Mr. Maynard Jolly, Curator; Mrs. Maynard Jolly, Assistant Curator;

Ms. Brenda X. (what's that "X" stand for?—X-citement!) Cu-
reton, Secretary; and Mr. Hugh Gay, Docent. I understand how
difficult it probably was for y'all to actually obtain the rope, knife,
and pistol used to kill Columbus Choice and get them all on
display beneath that Plexiglas hood in the foyer of the Roane
County Historical Museum and Senior Citizens Center. I'm not
even sure it's legal. Shouldn't those objects be secured in an Evidence Room at the Roane County Law Enforcement Center?
Not that I'm complaining. Thank you all for letting me hold these
weapons. You will never know how much motivation I received
from feeling the hemp that once touched good, moral, visionary
Mr. Choice's neck. Also, I want to commend you all for understanding that every historical museum should also double as a
senior citizens center. What a great notion! You got those groups
coming in on Thursdays for Decoupage Class, and on Fridays to
play Balloon Volleyball, and on Wednesdays for Storytelling Hour,
et cetera. Later, when the old folks die off, who are they going to bequeath their old high school yearbooks to, or their butter churns, or their single trees and other farm implements, or
their arrowhead collections, or their Minie ball stash? Answer: the
Roane County Historical Museum. Great job, all.

On a side note, I took my History 101 class from Tennessee
Valley Community College down to the museum one time on a
field trip. At the time we studied the American Civil War, and I
have to tell you, y'all's collection of bullet-hole-ridden Confederate uniforms is something else. My students stood there in awe.
Except for Juanita Wilkins, who wandered over to the display of
nineteenth-century surgical utensils, which I feel certain helped
her decide to be the phlebotomist that she is today. And what
about those leeches you have floating in formaldehyde! They say
that the Clinch River once teemed with leeches, back before the
nuclear facility went up over in Oak Ridge. I guess that's one
good thing about contaminated water—it kills off leeches!

———

I would like to thank a nurse named Greta at the Roane County Plasma Center for allowing me to sell off my platelets for $18 a pop twice a week, back when I wasn't selling off found antiques, or finding money beneath the drive-through windows of fast-food restaurants. I'm no Freudian or Jungian expert, but I will admit that I probably wanted only to know more about needles and blood so that I could keep up a conversation with Juanita Wilkins later on, should I run into her and her cohorts at a happy hour festivity somewhere out by Interstate 40. And tell her to quit using the N word in class like the time she said, "[N word]s want to have more children so they can get more food stamp money from the government. We'd be better off if we still had slavery."

And then I can say, "Columbus Choice didn't have any children whatsoever."

And then Juanita, there at the Applebee's, or Chili's, or TGI Fridays, or Chief's Wings and Firewater, or O'Charley's, or Ruby Tuesday's, or any of those other places where phlebotomists might go for happy hour to wind down from a tense and hectic day of drawing blood, might say to me, "You know what, Stet Looper, M.A., you're right—I apologize for my indiscretion way back then when I was only nineteen years old and still living with my parents and subconsciously allowing my parents' and grandparents' and great-grandparents' beliefs about skin color and economics cloud my vision." And then she might decide that, yes, it is time for her to settle down with a biographer of my stature, a man well-known for *No Cover Available: The Story of Columbus Choice, African-American Sushi Chef from Tennessee.*

After we drove down to South Carolina, where we could get married without having to wait for a waiting period, perhaps we could honeymoon in Myrtle Beach, eat seafood, walk on the beach, and I could make a point not to drive by any of the "gentlemen's clubs" down there, where Juanita Wilkins could easily win any of the Amateur Night strip contests and then realize she could make a whole lot more money giving lap dances with her gigantic perfect natural breasts than she could sucking blood from tainted Tennesseans. If we did end up in a "gentlemen's club," and if Juanita Wilkins foresaw her future, she'd probably be able to talk me into it, of course, seeing as she'd taken that required Public Speaking course at Tennessee Valley Community College. Then what would a biographer like me do? How many people have been lynched in Myrtle Beach that I could research?

I am enamored by the work of the people at Rand McNally and wish to thank them for their meticulous folding road maps that one day, I'm afraid, might end up as collector's items seeing as there's A) MapQuest, and B) that Global Positioning System. Uh-oh. Goodbye, cast-off fancy antique chairs for resale, and hello, Southeastern United States Regional Map with over 20 states, 23 city insets, state parks, and historical points of interest. Anyway, while doing research, I found myself oftentimes needing to take interstates to highways, highways to secondary roads, secondary roads to state-maintained roads, and so on until I came across, for example, the site where the tree once stood before it got sawed up into furniture. Try to type in "Tree that once had a limb to hold Columbus Choice's hanging body, that's now an end table" into one of those GPS machines and see what the computerized woman's voice says back to you.

I want to thank Vasco de Gama, Ponce de Leon, Magellan, Sir Walter Raleigh, Sir Francis Drake, Hernando de Soto, and Lewis and Clark.

How can I ever repay Jimmy Houston, professional fisherman, for all his tips on catching the elusive largemouth bass? Thanks, Jimmy! I hope we meet one cloudy day when you aren't required to wear your Jimmy Houston Signature Sunglasses so I can tell you how I lured in more than a few dinners that sustained me enough to write *No Cover Available: The Story of Columbus Choice, African-American Sushi Chef from Tennessee*. Cast on, motherfucker, cast on!

And to Roland Martin. And to Bill Dance.

Although I think that they're wrong, I would like to thank every philosopher and theologian who has tried to refute David Hume's refutation in regards to teleology. I understand that this is some high-minded talk from a lowly biographer, but I need to point out how—except for trying to go backwards all the way until proving the existence of a supreme being—there's some evident and obvious truths in this teleology scam. If there had never been a World War I, then Adolph Hitler would've never been a lance corporal runner in the 16ᵗʰ Bavarian Reserve Regiment. If he hadn't received any military training, he probably wouldn't have set his goals on being some kind of "führer" and "reichskanzler." And when he became the head of Germany, America and its allies automatically had cause to believe that he had some kind of nuclear capabilities, which caused our government to begin the "Manhattan Project," which took place in Oak Ridge, Tennessee. There, physicists and their minions worked to separate and produce uranium and plutonium, which would be used to develop nuclear warheads. And so on. The Army Corps of engineers built the entire facility, and in doing so had to kick out a number of locals from their homesteads, which understandably pissed off some people vis-à-vis "outsiders" and "interlopers," which made them wary of anyone new coming into the area shoving new ideas and/or foods down their throats, which is exactly what Columbus Choice had in mind when it came to A) shamanism; and B) Japanese mayo. The heartless notion of "eminent domain" caused nothing less than an entire region's people to think that murder might be justifiable. So I offer my undying support to teleologists, and to the Army Corp of Engineers, for without their respective works, I would have never been able to complete *No Cover Available: The Story of Columbus Choice, African-American Sushi Chef from Tennessee.*

Because I am not always attuned to the fact that there are always somewhere between two and eighteen ways to undergo a task successfully—i.e., sometimes I will find myself trying to dig a square hole with a round shovel—I want to thank an unknown-named ex-hippie Nature Woman who camped two doors down from me at the Frozen Head State Park Campground back in June, right as I finished the biography. Oh, I tried to woo her, but that's another story. It's hard to woo an outdoorswoman skilled at building fires with one stick *and a callus.* Anyway, she looked like the kind of woman who'd been damaged in a previous relationship by either A) a man; or B) a woman. I could tell by her face and movements, plus her impatience.

During these couple days when she and I were campground neighbors, I couldn't quite figure out how to write the epilogue. I'd brought back a number of books to my tent (sorry, Ms. Knoblock, about that one book that Dooley peed on—I think it was the smell of mildew that attracted him) and tried to use the long-dead biographers' works as a template. It wasn't working.

And then I heard the woman apologizing over and over, plus a noise that sounded similar to tiny fingernails on a blackboard, or mice eating through a wall, or someone trying to work out the TMJ in his jaw, or an OCD person applying sandpaper to a poorly painted finial, or termites at work on compromised baseboards, or like the sound a Bendix switch makes when a car's already started and the driver turns his ignition again, et cetera. I stuck my head out of my tent and held Dooley back. I said nothing.

There are a variety of ways to exterminate slugs, but the most efficient involves a salt shaker. The hippie woman—obviously a person, much like Columbus Choice, who recognized the value and meaningfulness in all the life forms thriving on this planet—circled her personal space, squeezing the handles of a Chef'n SGB320 Grind Salt Ball. Like some kind of mantra she said, "If it makes it better, this is organic sea salt. If it makes it better, this is organic sea salt."

I went back inside my tent and finished the epilogue—as you know—by writing it *as if* from beyond the grave, *as if* Columbus Choice told the story. I awoke early the next day to find the woman gone, and her salt ball grinder—thus the reason how I know the manufacturer—left on the ground. I will keep this salt ball grinder on my desk forever, of course, as a reminder.

I would be remiss not to mention how little moments of unexpected learning provide a biographer more choices—no pun here—than he will ever know.

I would be a fool not to thank the likes of Anne Rice, Stephanie Meyer, J. K. Rowling, and those other ones—some of whom are not women—for toiling away at their bestsellers that involve vampires, werewolves, warlocks, and the like. Call me an optimist, but I am of the firm belief that young readers will finally grow out of these fantastical tomes, and want to delve into something a little more realistic, something like *No Cover Available: The Story of Columbus Choice, African-American Sushi Chef from Tennessee.*

I would be remiss to forget the influence of Rudy Ray Moore, the poet, comedian, and actor who starred in all the *Dolemite* movies. Who'd've thought that a biographer would ever thank a poet in the acknowledgments? Except for Carl Sandburg. I know that Columbus Choice would've thanked Rudy Ray Moore, also, even though—and I'm only conjecturing here—Mr. Moore never converted to Judaism, or allowed his kung fu–worthy body to rest enough in order to fully appreciate transcendental meditation.

With respect and admiration to Bruce Lee.

I am grateful to Ms. Renee Sands—and I apologize, again, for calling you "Renee *Sans*" for so long, thinking that you wanted everyone to know you as the "Renaissance woman"—and her string of tables covered in a series of tarps and plastic sheeting more complex than anything a Bedouin can construct out in the African deserts, all filled with museum-quality paraphernalia, ephemera, and collectibles at the Mid-State Jockey Lot up in Wartburg, not far from the old Brushy Mountain State Penitentiary. I'm not sure who you know on the inside, Renee, but your BMSP flatware, I should tell you, could go for a little more than a quarter a utensil if you'd break down and try the eBay route. And I'm not sure how you got a hold of the leather tie-downs and head piece for a convicted murderer in the electric chair—I did some research, seeing as that's what I do, you know, and no one's been executed through voltage in Tennessee since something like 1960—but it sure is worth the price of admission (free) to the Mid-State Jockey Lot to view and hold such things. I'm particularly awed by your collection of over 1,000 glass telephone pole insulators, and James Earl Ray's comb. I would never, ever thank James Earl Ray, seeing as he assassinated Dr. Martin Luther King, but in a way perhaps James Earl Ray gave some ideas to Jack and Sid Plemmons, who lynched Columbus Choice, which gave me all this data to report in *No Cover Available: The Story of Columbus Choice, African-American Sushi Chef from Tennessee*. What a sad, odd world we live in, Renee. Anyway, before I get all maudlin, I want to thank you for selling me that little cook set and mess kit, which I used mightily when I lived at the Frozen Head State Park Campground. And for the MREs. And let me tell you the truth: Now that I have some money coming in presently from the royalties of my biography, maybe I'll take you up on buying that goat you had on sale a while back.

Furthermore, thank you so much for letting Juanita Wilkins use some of your space to sell her hair-care products left over from the cosmetologist/beautician phase of her life. If she'd not made that extra money selling Pantene, Clairol, et cetera, she would've never been able to continue her education in the realm of phlebotomy. And if Roane and Anderson counties didn't have a phlebotomist on the payroll, where would we be now?

I would like to thank National Public Radio for their *Morning Edition* segment what seems like a decade ago about the sudden boom of flea markets and jockey lots, and how everyone selling at these places now possesses encyclopedic knowledge of, say, yellow ware and toasters, which caused me to visit Mid-State Jockey Lot in Wartburg, which allowed me to meet Renee Sands (too late) after I'd gotten rooked on a *Sanford and Son* replica lunchbox for fifty-five dollars. And then I would like to thank National Public Radio for showing up only a couple years ago, and interviewing me as I stood there like an idiot trying to sell that *Sanford and Son* replica lunchbox for a dollar—which I couldn't do, seeing as everyone there knew that it wasn't an original—and the woman asking me, "Are you here because of the economy?" and my saying, "I'm here because I'm finishing up *No Cover Available: The Story of Columbus Choice, African-American Sushi Chef from Tennessee* and I can't get any support from Yaddo, Provincetown, the NEA, the NEH," et cetera, and how, when the program finally aired after necessary editing, it came out, "Are you here because of the economy?" and my answer came out, "No cover. Choice. Sushi," which—I feel pretty sure—will remain in all listeners' psyches and/or memories once the biography hits the shelves. I guess we'll find out!

While I'm dealing with mass media, I would like to thank Fox News for being so blatantly right-wing that they'll probably find a way to support the Plemmons brothers should ever a Fox "reporter" or "anchorperson" find a need to do a "book review." I don't care. Someone once said, "I don't care if people are talking good or bad about me, as long as they're talking about me." Actually, I think my fourth-favorite history professor said that, right before he got denied tenure and was fired for fucking one of the cheerleaders, a young woman from Sevierville who always went around saying she knew Dolly Parton personally, and whom I could hear yell out "No, no, no, are you crazy?!" to the coach when he decided to punt instead of going for fourth and twenty to go from our own, say, five yard line. Screw her. I don't want to thank her for anything.

The local-news cameramen who had to go out and film the place where Columbus Choice got lynched deserve a nod, seeing as they'll be, I believe, scarred for life, like I have been. Particularly I would like to thank Buddy Kirby, who shared with me some footage that didn't get aired on TV or in the Roane County courtroom proceedings. He had walked into Columbus Choice's restaurant with his camera down low, like in one of those undercover operations. I think that he and his reporter were supposed to be just looking around scouting for a place to stand in order to do one of those human interest on-air moments. Anyway, Buddy had his camera on, maybe down around the height of his knee, and for some lucky, serendipitous moment the thing caught the underneath side of Table B8—left side of the room, eight four-tops back. Actually the camera caught Tables B 1 through 7, also, which mostly showed chewing gum stuck beneath the tables. But at #8 it was evident that someone had scrawled "6-6-76," which is the *exact date that Columbus got lynched*, and which, too, includes the sign of the devil according to the King James Version of the Bible.

Here are some questions: Why did it take the Plemmons brothers so long to get upset about the sushi restaurant? Were they that slow? How had Columbus lived for so long in the Harriman/ Oak Ridge? If the Plemmons brothers, or at least one of them, showed up to sketch that date in the bottom of the table, what had they/he ordered? Did the date have something to do with Jimmy Carter coming through the area on a campaign stop?

I never thought to look on the underside of any of Renee Sands's flea market tables or have a real-life cameraman undertake some undercover operation to conquer the scrawled or sketched or carved lettering that may or may not expose her as some kind of anti-capitalistic vendor. I had other things to think about, viz, *No Cover Available: The Story of Columbus Choice, African-American Sushi Chef from Tennessee*. Which is why I'm writing these Acknowledgments. In my editor's final publication.

Thank you, again, to Mr. Davey Hough, copywriter, for pointing out in my manuscript that it should be "The media *are* involved," instead of "is." I still say it sounds stupid, and some rules need changing.

I would like to thank the hapless linksters who paid six dollars each to walk nine holes at the Emory Golf and Country Club.

At times, early in the morning, I found it necessary and beneficial to walk the outskirts of this particular course—it's only 2,880 yards, which comes to 8,640 feet, which comes to 1.636363 miles. No one ever asked me any questions about my trespassing, really, over all those years I walked the course, watching the wealthiest residents of the Harriman area tee up, slice, and curse. Well, actually, the wealthiest men and women probably drove over to the Centennial Course in Oak Ridge and played on a regulation eighteen-hole course. I watched men and women who either A) wished to be appear wealthy; or B) had been convicted of DUIs and couldn't ride a moped all the way to the better course while balancing a bag of clubs on their laps.

No one asked questions, but plenty of them mistook me for an employee. They said things like, "Do you people know that if you water grass it'll actually grow?" or "Hey, did you see a Titleist hit over there in the woods?" or "Hey, will you tell this fool I'm playing with that it's not cheating to move a ball within one standing long jump?" and so on. They said, "Are you the concession guy? Where's your cart?" They said, "You look like a ball washer. Are you a ball washer?" and laughed the way men in plaid pants are prone to laugh if and only if they're in a group, feeling all strong and lucky and impenetrable.

I wish to thank these people for a couple reasons. First off, they indirectly caused me to write Columbus Choice's biography harder. It made me realize that Columbus would never want to be like these cheap half-course golfers, and therefore neither would I. On the other hand—and this will be difficult for me to admit—I kind of wished to *join* them in a camaraderie-filled amble across fairways forever radioactive, and the sole means of my pulling my three-wood out on the first tee box would be through finishing up, then selling *No Cover Available: The Story of Columbus Choice, African-American Sushi Chef from Tennessee.*

The part of the brain that contains all wishes must be a complex place. I wouldn't want to be in charge of it.

I would be remiss to omit the influence of Schopenhauer, Hume, Diogenes, and Bobo.

Arthur Schopenhauer once said, "Almost all of our sorrows spring out of our relations with other people," and "Religion is the masterpiece of the art of animal training, for it trains people as to how they shall think." Schopenhauer said a lot of good things, some of which, though, are misogynistic. I won't say that I've nodded my head to this one, but it has come to mind on three occasions: "In our monogamous part of the world, to marry means to halve one's rights and double one's duties."

David Hume's statement, "Generally speaking, the errors in religion are dangerous; those in philosophy only ridiculous," ran through my head every time I heard someone try to justify why the Plemmons brothers murdered Columbus Choice. It runs through my head every time I hear a church bell ring, too. At times, in the Oak Ridge-Harriman area, it's hard to delineate whether church bells ring simultaneously or the disaster sirens have been set off.

"The mob is the mother of tyrants," said Diogenes.

Jimmy Rex "Sexy Rexy" Bobo, who brings his own chair to the VFW Club because he swears he sat on a booby-trapped barstool in Saigon that blew *its own* legs off and only left him with enough shrapnel in his ass to receive the Purple Heart, once said to me, "God created Racism when He realized He couldn't handle a population explosion. None of us would agree, I doubt, but God's biggest mistake was fucking. You can't expect one lifeguard to handle every beachgoer in the world." Then he said, of course, "They been calling me Sexy Rexy before I even owned a map to *find* Vietnam," which is what he said, on average, twice per Budweiser.

I am grateful to a woman named Penny Cuthbert at Plutonium Lanes 'n' Games for allowing me to drink beer (cheapest and coldest in the tri-county area!) and never bowl a game or play Ms. Pac-man, pinball, that bowling game that involves a puck and sawdust, or Skee-ball. Thanks for letting me trade in my boots for those size 11 rental shoes, too, just so I could feel like I wasn't a total outsider, and for letting me go through the Lost and Found box. I will always cherish my Plutonium Lanes 'n' Games shirt with those tiny pockets. Whoever drew up the logo—the ball crashing through ten pins for a strike, the mushroom cloud lifting up above the pinsetter—needs to receive the Graphics Arts Award/Local Business/Attire category from the Tennessee Valley Association of Advertising Firms during their annual ceremony over at the Holiday Inn Knoxville-Downtown Convention Center. I wore that bowling league shirt with pride, and it seemed to have worked, especially when I was in the middle of the "Columbus Had No Other Hobbies" chapter toward the end of the biography. Thank you, Penny, for also allowing me to plug in my laptop right there at a table behind Lane 12, and for telling people that I was from *Modern Bowler* magazine writing a feature piece on Mid-South keglers so they wouldn't bother me any.

I need to show my appreciation to Juanita Wilkins again, too, for not ratting me out those times I was at Plutonium Lanes 'n' Games when she pretended not to see me while she participated in women's league play for her team, the Blood Suckers. Listen, Juanita—and I know you won't ever listen to me again—but a 132 average is *great*. I read somewhere that anyone who can bowl above his or her weight is doing a fine job. Marlon Brando was never worshipped at Hollywood Star Lanes, which served as the

set for *The Big Lebowski*, but then got razed in order to make room
for a school. President William Howard Taft could have never
bowled his weight when he went back to his hometown of Cincinnati and played at Glenmore Bowl, or if he traveled up to Baltimore and played duckpins. In Japan, by the way, sumo wrestlers
are revered until they walk into a bowling alley. There are some
other stories, I'm sure, but I can't think of them off the top of my
head while I'm supposed to be finishing up these Acknowledgments. Anyone on that reality TV show, for example, about obese
people trying to lose weight with the help of a personal trainer
that aired on a network that should be thankful to Ted Turner.

There are a few images that one can never erase from memory,
and my primary one—besides that of Columbus Choice's body
hanging from an oak tree—is that of Chester Clabo's butt pointed
in my direction. I've never thought about how both of them had
the initials C.C. How odd. Anyway, Chester Clabo was my long
snapper at Vanderbilt University, and I would like to thank him for
the indirect way in which he aided me when it came to thinking
up, then finishing, *No Cover Available: The Story of Columbus Choice,
African-American Sushi Chef from Tennessee.* Just in case any scholars
who read my book and are now going through these Acknowledgments don't know the term "long snapper," it's the guy who
hikes the ball to the punter on fourth downs. He's the center, but
with the strength and accuracy to spiral a football twelve yards
back at waist level.

So after I shanked my last punt and got asked to leave the
team, the new punter came in and did the exact same thing. The
chances of that happening might be on par with a guy who has
indelible images of a man hanging from a tree and a guy's rear
end pointed his way, both of whom have the same initials. When
the new punter shanked the ball nonstop, the coach not only cut

him from the team, but also Chester Clabo. The special teams coach figured that, somehow, Chester's delivery—maybe too tight a spiral, maybe too hard, maybe it came in at an awkward angle invisible to the naked eye—caused all of the bad punts. Me, I stayed on at the university and studied up on my history. Chester left school, embarrassed and ashamed. He secured a number of odd go-nowhere jobs for a while until he finally landed a job at the Tennessee Aquarium at One Broad Street in downtown Chattanooga.

Listen, anyone writing a biography the scope and intensity of *mine* knows that he or she must, at times, "get away" from the subject matter, and when I needed to do so, I found a way to get to the Tennessee Aquarium, which isn't but about 79.38 miles from here, according to MapQuest, which I just had to look up in order to keep the goddamn fact checker off my back. There's a town in between called Soddy-Daisy. Get on that MapQuest thing and look it up yourself to see if I'm lying.

Anyway, Chester Clabo and I had stayed in touch over the years—he says he has an image burned into his brain of my staring at his ass—and when I had to go over to the aquarium where he worked as a ticket taker/bouncer, he let me in for free. I'd go in there and stare at the bonnethead, epaulette, brown banded bamboo, and sand tiger sharks. I don't want to get all metaphysical or mystical about it, but their utter menacing beauty gave me a certain strength to forge on with *No Cover Available: The Story of Columbus Choice, African-American Sushi Chef from Tennessee,* I feel sure.

Anyway, thanks, again, to Chester Clabo, for hiking me awkward balls, which made me shank them, which sent me directly to the Vanderbilt library, which got me interested in the history of the area, which led me to Columbus Choice. I am forever grateful, and look forward to more visits to the Tennessee Aquarium, then later to those questionable bars you frequent like Lamar's, or

My Uncle's Place, or Lupi's, or even that strip joint that made me sad to enter because I knew I'd run into Juanita Wilkins, part-time phlebotomist.

I would be remiss to forget whoever it is in Oak Ridge that runs the free summer concert series downtown so that everyone in Roane and Anderson counties can experience some culture. Listen, the first time I encountered the Amazing Hundred Member Marching Jew's Harp Twangers, I worked on *No Cover Available: The Story of Columbus Choice, African-American Sushi Chef from Tennessee* over at the library. I struggled, and couldn't find anything in the stacks that might offer to me what I deemed necessary knowledge as a biographer, at that point. I still have no clue what "Squid in the pot without the squid" means, which is what Columbus Choice had typed out under the Homemade Soups part of his menu.

As I sat there at the study carrel holding my head in my hands, I thought I heard a thousand old-fashioned twin-propeller fighter jets buzzing overhead. I thought I heard a thousand small school children all yelling into a window fan. I thought I heard a thousand bee hives stacked together at dusk when the workers come home. I thought I heard the emergency broadcast system playing a low-pitched siren so as to not alarm local dogs. Maybe one of the nuclear reactors is about to blow a la Chernobyl, or Three Mile Island, or the others one that have probably been kept secret by various governments around the world. Perhaps some kind of aboriginal tribe passed through armed with their melodic and sacred didgeridoos.

I heard what I thought had to be a thousand Buddhist monks Oming their lungs out.

But like I said, it was only the Amazing Hundred Member Marching Jew's Harp Twangers out of western North Carolina performing their spectacular tribute to Led Zeppelin. What brought me onto the library's steps was the opening to "Whole Lotta Love." Walking down to Historic Jackson Square, I fell into step with "Heartbreaker," and by the time I took a seat on the ground amidst forward-thinking members of the community who'd brought along folding lawn chairs with them, the band—made up mostly of ex-hippies who now worked as bankers and architects and lawyers in Asheville—went straight into "Living Lovin' Maid."

Sitting cross-legged, Native-American-style, on the grass, the sounds that the Amazing Hundred Member Marching Jew's Harp Twangers helped me realize that A) anything's possible; and B) Columbus Choice would've dug them playing these Om sounds over and over at his restaurant.

After what I imagine will be an extensive and demanding book tour, I might write a scholarly treatise comparing Buddhist monks to Appalachian musicians adept at producing the soulful, resonating backbeat hums of the Jew's harp. I won't make any promises. There's no telling how many innocent victims will be lynched by that time, good people whose stories need to be known by all.

You would think that a biographer consumed and obsessed with the story of Columbus Choice would not have time for trivialities. It is true that during the decade that I worked on *No Cover Available: The Story of Columbus Choice, African-American Sushi Chef from Tennessee,* I did not join the Oak Ridge Fitness Center and work out daily. I didn't go for long treks on a mountain bike, though there are some wonderful trails in and around Frozen Head State Park. I didn't get involved with those TV reality shows, or many of the situation comedies. Who thinks anything's funny whatsoever after thinking about Columbus Choice's life every waking moment for approximately 3,650 days, when he wasn't thinking about Abby's grievances in the marriage?

I didn't become absorbed with learning Spanish, though I should've. I didn't watch major league baseball, attend the Chattanooga Lookouts minor league games like my old long-snapper buddy Chester Clabo did only because he had a crush on a woman who worked the Cajun boiled peanuts stand, or collect baseball cards. I didn't play video games, online poker, regular poker with ex-colleagues from Tennessee Valley Community College, drive up yearly to Lexington to watch the Kentucky Derby, or squirrel away money for scratch card tickets and daily lottery drawings.

I never ran, unless I felt that someone chased me—and that happened more times than I could count, probably because there are people out there who don't want me to tell Columbus Choice's story. I didn't take up painting or sculpting or whittling. Not once did I think it necessary to learn how to play a guitar or trombone in order to become a well-rounded person, though I might've started playing a Jew's harp if I'd've ever run across one. But I didn't. When I had a car, I didn't spend every weekend washing, waxing, and detailing the thing.

I didn't write poetry.

But I cannot honestly say that I didn't occasionally veer from my main focus. Whenever possible—whenever I had access to an electric outlet, television set, and VCR, I lost myself in the cutting-edge, miraculous, absurd film productions of writer-directors Jim Jarmusch, Ethan and Joel Coen, and David Lynch. I don't think it takes a protégée and/or devotee of Dr. Sigmund Freud to understand that perhaps I needed to "actively participate" in such masterpieces as *Blue Velvet, Down By Law, Raising Arizona, Eraserhead, Elephant Man, Broken Flowers, Night on Earth, Barton Fink,* and the *Big Lebowski* in order to feel that my life wasn't as horrendous as it could be. *Miller's Crossing. Twin Peaks. Mystery Train.* I suppose this notion goes all the way back to Aristotle, but last time

I checked he didn't have a medical degree and background in psychiatry à la Sigmund Freud, and all that crap about "catharsis" that they teach in the English courses.

Now, I understand that I could be accused of sucking up to these absolute geniuses, but after reading *No Cover Available: The Story of Columbus Choice, African-American Sushi Chef from Tennessee*, I think that anyone would easily say, "You know, that would make a great movie!" Hell, it would make *two* great movies, if you ask me. First off, there could be a regular bio-pic of the life and times of Columbus Choice. I doubt that any filmmaker in his or her right mind would want to call the thing—even if it became one of those Hallmark movies aired on the Lifetime or Oxygen channels—*No Cover Available: The Story of Columbus Choice, African-American Sushi Chef from Tennessee*. You couldn't even get all that title out on the screen hardly. I'm surprised the art department at the publisher didn't flinch and say they didn't want to put out a dust wrapper with nine point font all across the top. Anyway, the bio-pic could be, I've been thinking, called something shorter, like *Columbus*, or *Choice*, or *Columbus Choice*, or *Fresh Fish and Mantras*, or *Hang, Stab, Shoot*. And then it'll have "Based on the work of Stet Looper," down at the bottom, you know.

So, you got that. And then another movie could be the one of my life while I *wrote* the biography *No Cover Available: The Story of Columbus Choice, African-American Sushi Chef from Tennessee*. It would start right off inside my History 101 class at Tennessee Valley Community College, and then maybe go through some flashbacks involving my shanking a punt over my teammates' heads on the sidelines and into the bleachers like the time we played Ole Miss, and then maybe I could do a voiceover, you know, and so on. I'd call that one something like *Tennessee!*, or *Oak Ridge*, or *Between Harriman and Oak Ridge*, or *Legal Pads and Sterno*. Or *Juanita*.

I would've liked to have thanked the great movie director Robert Altman, but he went off and died. His movies made me feel better about myself—especially *Nashville*, seeing as it's in the same state as where I live. So no thanks to good Robert Altman. I *am* remiss in thanking Robert Altman. You know why I don't go to funerals? Answer: Those people aren't going to mine.

Juanita Wilkins, phlebotomist, says I can't forget, and need to thank, Roman Polanski in this list. So what the hell, okay, though I can't think of one of his movies that made me feel better. Maybe they're not on videotape yet. Maybe they're on that DVD thing that everyone's talking about down at the library.

And there must be other directors I'll think of later.

While I'm alluding to the this-makes-me-feel-better-about-my-self-and-therefore-I-got-the-opportunity-not-to-get-into-full-blown-manic-depression mode, I want to thank the Tennessee Valley Recreation League Baseball Association, and particularly the team sponsored by one of those interdenominational churches run by a guy with a goatee and a high school diploma who used to do a lot of crystal meth before the Lord told him to become a minister and spread the word. I'm not making it up when I say that the place was called the Second Coming United Ministries, and the poor little ten-year-olds had S.C.U.M spread across their uniforms like badges of dishonor. Another S.C.U.M.! How weird is that?—first the Southern Confederation of United Militia, and now the Second Coming United Ministries.

Anyway, these kids were absolutely dreadful. Not even Michael Ritchie, who directed the classic movie *The Bad News Bears*, could've brought any hope or humor into these children's lives. If you've ever seen little kids out in the outfield staring up at the sky, or chasing butterflies, or looking into the stands forlornly because their fathers didn't show up, or picking their noses, or talking to themselves, or holding their peckers thinking that no one can see them out there, or pretending that they're running a standard muscle car through the gears, or running over to tackle one of the other outfielders on the team because of seasonal confusion disorder—if you've seen this, and multiply it by ten, then you'll understand the Second Coming United Ministries Fighting Laymen, whom I'm pretty sure had been instructed to speak in tongues while in the field. How can a kid speak in tongues? If you got those kids to speak in tongues at the same time that the Amazing Hundred Member Marching Jew's Harp Twangers went into something like an instrumental version of "Smoke on the Water," I do believe that specters would emerge from inanimate objects and take over the planet.

On a side note, I always thought they should've been called the Suckers, or the Bags.

Anyway, I could've never finished Columbus Choice's bio, I doubt, without watching the S.C.U.M. Fighting Laymen lose games, on average, by twenty runs. I don't know why, but that touchy-feely rule employed in more liberal, understanding, foresightful No Child Left Behind states wherein if a Little League team gets behind by seven or ten runs then the game's over—places like South Carolina, even—never found its way to this particular region of Tennessee. I'd go watch a game and then always go back to wherever I lived at the time and crank out something like a thousand words pertaining to Columbus Choice. If baseball season lasted year-round, and the Second Coming United Ministries Fighting Laymen played daily, I would've finished the biography in a hundred and twenty days.

I want to thank the Second Coming United Ministries' choral director, Ms. Emilia Perkins, for a couple things. First off, although I do not believe in that Bible stuff whatsoever, except perhaps the story of Job, I have found it uplifting to listen to Ms. Perkins's choir selections, which lean over into what might be called the "African-American gospel." Those songs where everyone's clapping, swaying, and wailing out things. I have no evidence as to whether Columbus Choice enjoyed this kind of music. As a child, I know for a fact that he attended an A.M.E. church. Before his stint in the military, he probably attended Sunday and Wednesday services like most people in the South. Anyway, when I hear the Second Coming United Ministries choir—it's purely a coincidence that I happened by the front door of the ex-storefront on Sunday mornings—it causes me to know that there's a joyous reason to give the world something like *No Cover Available: The Story of Columbus Choice, African-American Sushi Chef from Tennessee.* And I'm happy that it makes people like Juanita Wilkins, phlebotomist and soprano, happy to be singing, gyrating, and verging toward seizure.

I'm grateful to goatee-wearing high school graduate ex-meth addict Reverend Frankie Spigner for sending off to one of those places in order to get a license to marry people.

Fearless and curious dogs have enough problems, but a dog forced to live in questionable places—say, at the Frozen Head State Park Campground, drinking tainted water straight out of the stream and eating renegade campers' leftovers that fall out of trash bins—surely risks more diseases and parasites than the normal suburban-living poodle. My dog Dooley wouldn't still be here if it weren't for the good people at Intervet manufacturing all the way over in Vienna, Austria, and distributed by Intervet, Inc. of Millsboro, Delaware. To be more specific, I want to thank Intervet for their wonderful product, Panacur C, a canine dewormer with fenbendazole granules. Listen, all those other over-the-counter prod-ucts *might* work for roundworms and hookworms—and I stress "might"—but Panacur C eradicates those tough-to-kill whip-worms that live in the soil, plus tapeworms. You'd think that a dog wouldn't get bored living at a campground, but he does, at times. What does he do when there are no squeaky toys around with which to play? He eats dirt. He digs for moles, and he eats dirt. And gets whipworms.

People who read long biographies out there, you do not want to be stuck in a two-person pup tent on the banks of Flat Fork Creek with a dog suffering whipworms. I won't go into great detail, but the whipworm's effects on a dog's alimentary canal is about the same as what happens to a human after a barium enema, or after drinking a glass of Epsom salts, or after drinking the most tainted water possible down in Mexico, or after eating some good Christian family's left-out-in-the-sun-too-long macaroni salad and potato salad on a picnic table while they go for a hike up to the lookout tower in order to view the Cumberland Plateau in one direction and the Great Smoky Mountains in the other and to thank God for giving them such a spectacular existence.

It would be remiss of my not mentioning this: Panacur C, which comes in 1-, 2-, and 4-gram packets (one gram per ten pounds of dog body weight), carries a warning that goes "Keep this and all medications out of the reach of children." I guess it's some kind of FDA approval law. I don't want to become relent-lessly graphic, but right before I finally sold *No Cover Available: The Story of Columbus Choice, African-American Sushi Chef from Tennessee,* when things were looking bleakest, maybe I had no other choice (no pun intended) but to keep Dooley's medication "within my reach."

An amateur psychologist—which means any person living on this planet only the width of a piece of paper away from being a "certified" psychologist—might say that I cried out for help. This is just to say, as that poet wrote in that famous poem, that I took the last of the dewormer. And now I have one less problem to worry about when I'm on a jet, flying around to book signings and festivals.

Goody's 520 Milligram Powders, made by Goody's Pharmaceuticals over in Memphis, with their Tamper Evident Safety Overwrap. BC Powders. Aleve. Tylenol. St. Joseph's Baby Aspirin. Rite Aid Lightly Coated Easy to Swallow 325 Milligram Aspirin Tablets. Bayer, of course. Excedrin. Advil. Anacin.

I need to thank all of these products. Deep down, I know that Columbus Choice would want to thank a number of anti-inflammatory agents, too.

Flora, my mother's cousin—which makes her my second cousin, I believe—deserves my thanks for giving me a book of etiquette for my high school graduation present. While every other family member gave me money, fancy pen and pencil sets, and study lamps, Flora understood that I needed Amy Vanderbilt's tome so that I might learn social skills. I understand that she only decided on the etiquette book after I had eaten potato salad with my hands and kept my elbows on the picnic table after one of those family reunions, but it's as if she possessed some kind of extra sensory perceptions. It's as if she knew that I would one day go on book tour and be required to attend fancy dinners in my honor with local newspaper book critics, mayors, city council members, NAACP bigwigs, card-carrying members of the Southern Poverty Law Center, and bodyguards to protect me against hate group morons. Second Cousin Flora—who died, oddly enough, in a Japanese restaurant when she mistook a giant chunk of wasabi for a length of avocado, had a coughing fit, then a well-meaning diner nearby thought she choked and during his attempt to perform the Heimlich maneuver broke her ribs, which punctured one lung, which got her sent to the hospital where she caught a staph infection and never got released alive—somehow had a hunch that I would make a fool of myself should I not know which fork to use, or if I reached the wrong way and drank from a tablemate's water. So thanks to Flora, and to Amy Vanderbilt, and in a weird way to the guy who squeezed too hard performing the Heimlich maneuver, because now I know that there's a fellow traveler roaming this planet who understands how best intentions usually go unrewarded at best. A good Taoist knows that aphorism that comes out translated something like "Never do anything, so that everything will happen as it should." It's unpronounceable in the Chinese or Mandarin or whatever dialect a good Taoist might employ. It sounds like "Oooooway er Booooo-weway," and this dishwasher who used to work for Columbus Choice evidently said it all the time when he stuck those dipping-sauce bowls into the Hobart.

I'd like to give a shout-out and offer my props and raise the roof to Sportstar for their ingenious product, Eye Black Stick-Ons (with marker for writing your own message). You've seen these things primarily beneath the lower eyelids of college and professional football players. In the old days, sometimes I blamed a shanked punt for my faulty, old-school eye black consisting of beeswax, paraffin, and carbon. Maybe I had too much on my hands. Maybe it worked so well that the football's lace's disappeared, and I didn't connect my foot to the ball correctly. Anyway, at times I felt, while writing, like I couldn't concentrate due to the glare of the lamp when I lived in a house, apartment, or trailer. I got headaches from having to squint so much while writing at a picnic table at the Frozen Head State Park Campground. I thought to myself, What would help me out in regards to this situation, outside of spending good money on a pair of, say, Suncloud Habit Polarized PS UV Protection sunglasses, which is what I'm going to buy and wear while skipping around the country on the imminent book tour?

Sometimes when I came across conundrums such as this I went walking down at the rec center baseball fields in order to unknot my brain cells. I don't want to call it a miracle, or an act of God or whatever they're calling it these days, but on this particular occasion, with no money to buy sunglasses or eye black, I entered the empty baseball diamond, looked down, and saw two black strips with "Proverbs" printed on one, and "23:14" on the other, right there on the ground next to first base. I'm no soothsayer, but I did take a logic course one time and I envisioned two outs in the bottom of the ninth, boys on base, and a kid grounding out to end the game. Then he ripped off his Sportstar Eye Black Stick-Ons (with marker for writing your own message), and went crying back to the dugout.

I don't want anyone having to cross-reference my Acknowledgments. Proverbs 23:14 goes like this: "Thou shalt beat him with the rod, and shalt deliver his soul from hell." Little League baseball is getting a little too serious, if you ask me.

Anyway, I stuck those eye-black strips atop my own upper cheekbones, and looked straight into the sun. Who invented these things? I thought. I thought, If I had any say in it, I'd nominate this man or woman for one of those Best Invention of the Twenty-first Century lists.

I walked to the empty dugout, where I sometimes found spare change, or a catcher's mitt, or unopened candy bars, and—Lo!—that same kid, I assumed, had left eighteen stick-ons *and* the marker right there on the wooden bench. It was a prize worth $5.99 times .90, seeing as ninety percent of the package was usable.

I looked around, put the package down my pants, and got out of there as quickly as possible before some beaten-with-a-rod kid returned with his twice-angry father.

Call me nostalgic and superstitious and a rationalizer, but I began writing about 3,500 words a day *minimum* while wearing Stick-On eye black. I wrote about Columbus Choice's purported illegitimate child living somewhere in Vietnam. I wrote about the time Columbus Choice was accused of using Chicken of the Sea in a hamachi roll. Then one day things came to a halt writing-wise and I got out that marker—up until this time I'd written things like "Abraham" on one, and "Lincoln" on the other, or "Martin Luther King" on one, and "Jr." on the other. Anyway, when the struggle returned, I wrote, of course, "Fuck" on one, and "Me" on the other.

And went out for another one of my walks, down to the rec center.

I want to thank Deputy Marion Pelt, of the Roane County Sheriff's Department and volunteer coach for one of the Tennessee Valley Recreation League Baseball Association, for believing my story, and for gently leading me off the premises while all those mothers and fathers yelled "He's a pedophile!" and "He's a child molester!" and "That man over there has a rod to spare on our children!" et cetera.

So if it weren't for the Sportstar people and their fine product, and Deputy Marion Pelt, I would've probably never finished my tome. So I thank them endlessly and somewhat apologetically for appearing to use stick-on products for personal gain, though I didn't mean to do so. Because I felt threatened later on in public, I pretty much stayed in my tent for the next month or so, writing, writing, writing. Finishing up. Doing what I didn't even know that I'd been called to be done. I wouldn't have ever finished Columbus Choice's biography if I'd never—rightly or wrongly—felt as if a lynch mob of my own waited for me to come out in public.

I will wear eye black at my book signings, should I lose my Suncloud Habit Polarized PS sunglasses, say, while skimming over one of the lakes in my new used Sea Ray.

I would be rueful to exclude my appreciation to John Cage for his groundbreaking piece 4'33". Silence and brevity. As I wrote *No Cover Available: The Story of Columbus Choice, African-American Sushi Chef from Tennessee,* it occurred to me often that there weren't enough writers out there who understood silence and brevity. Nor editors. Politicians. Everyone. Having John Cage's 4'33" running through my head on most days probably kept my biography stripped down to less than 2,000 pages, which would probably run about 660,000 words, which would mean about 3,540,000 characters not counting the spaces, which would mean about 4,340,000 characters counting the spaces. John Cage, you have, even in your death, become a beacon for the Environmental Movement, by indirectly helping me from killing off trees. Maestro!

I extend my gratitude to Rube Goldberg.

I cannot be remiss in forgetting the influence of Mr. Ray Guy— *Professor* Ray Guy—on my entire life, from front yard punt-offs with neighborhood kids (sorry about the window, car panels, bird feeder, and dog, Mrs. Irwin!) when I sailed my Wilson or Spaulding footballs high over telephone lines into next-door lawns back in Forty-Five, right on up to how I live my life today. Ray Guy— the only punter to have ever been drafted in the first round, who averaged 42.4 yards per punt over a thirteen or fourteen year career, who never had a punt returned for a touchdown, who graduated from the University of Southern Mississippi (not that far from where I received my low-residency master's degree in Southern culture studies at Ole Miss-Taylor), who wears three

Super Bowl rings proudly, who had five punts go over sixty yards *in one season*, who had opponents test his balls for helium because they hung so long—made all of those Pro Bowl teams, and he's not in the Hall of Fame in Canton. Now, I must keep Ray Guy in mind should, perhaps, my book *No Cover Available: The Story of Columbus Choice, African-American Sushi Chef from Tennessee* end up getting a lot of attention, sell 100,000 copies, then never win the Pulitzer Prize or National Book Award.

I would like to thank the Pulitzer Prize and National Book Award selection committees for their on-target selections *in every category* over all these years.

Anyway, a thousand thanks to Ray Guy, professional punter, who stayed on my mind every time that my long snapper, Chester Clabo, hiked the ball back to me, and then I didn't have a 42.4 yard punt, and had countless punt returners catch the line drives and return them for touchdowns when I didn't shank the thing off into the bleachers. Thanks for fucking up my mind and causing me to shank all those punts, Ray Guy, which got me kicked off the team at Vanderbilt, which drove me straight to the library, which got me interested in the life of the mind, as they say—or at least what that mass-murderer Charlie character says to Barton Fink in the classic movie *Barton Fink*. I couldn't have done Columbus Choice justice without you, Ray. Maybe one day I'll come down to Georgia or wherever you live in retirement and have a punt-off with you. I hope you don't have neighbors.

Ronaldo Rash was a regular at the VFW, listening to Mighty Max, and I want to thank Ronaldo for making me appear almost normal when it came to dealing with Drink for Free Ladies Night: "Hey, you ever have a Rash on your vagina?" Ronaldo used to say to women. They'd go, "No! No, I'm a clean, STD-free woman!" because it's impossible to see capital letters in regular everyday spoken words. And he'd go, "Well, would you like a little Rash on your vagina?"

I wouldn't have met Ronaldo had I not misread the sign out front that first time and thought it meant, "Drink for Free Ladies Night," as in "If You Win Some Kind of Drinking Contest, then You'll Get a Free Lady."

I am oddly grateful to Mr. Randall Brewer (father of two) at Nationwide Insurance for providing Mr. Joe Smythe (father of four) with personal injury coverage. And I want to thank Nationwide for "settling out of court." Listen, to the end of my days I'll argue that A) it doesn't matter if a person's intoxicated when he's walking across the street legally; and B) if a man (Mr. Smythe) and his wife (Mrs. Smythe) find it necessary to have four children in five years, even if they're Mormon or Catholic or other cult members or whatever, then they (the Smythes) must understand that they just can't drive around the Tennessee Valley with their heads craned into the back seat looking at their babies in car seats to make sure they all have their pacifiers shoved into their mouths. I mean, I know one must show some responsibility as a parent, but one must show even more responsibility as a *driving* parent.

The money I got for the settlement allowed me to A) continue *No Cover Available: The Story of Columbus Choice, African-American Sushi Chef from Tennessee;* and B) limp back to the Atomic Arms apartments where I had enough electrical outlets to plug in a laptop and type up what I had handwritten. And eat. And watch some TV so I could get back in touch with pop culture. And later make the mistake of going up to every obese person I ever came across and say, "Hey, aren't you on *The Biggest Loser?*" like an idiot and get punched with a slow right-cross, which made me realize that I needed to stay inside more often and finish *No Cover Available: The Story of Columbus Choice, African-American Sushi Chef from Tennessee.*

Which made me call up Juanita Wilkins and say, "I know that I threw you out of class that time and embarrassed you to the point of making shit up to my department chairman and the dean, but I hope—seeing as you're a good Christian—that you believe in forgiving people, and seeing as you're the only person I really know here in town with any kind of background in medicine, because you're a certified phlebotomist and all, could you please come over here and take a look at the hematoma on my eye socket?"

It's not as hard to thank unknown people as it may seem. I wish to offer my gratitude in advance to the kind, hard-working, detail-oriented comrades at the Library of Congress, in charge of "cataloguing-in-publication." I can only be presumptuous here, but I'd be willing to bet that y'all are more anal retentive than copyeditors, what with having to make sure my name's spelled correctly, and you got down the year of my birth right, and so on. Who gets to decide all those little taglines about the book's major themes in the CIP data? I would put down Biography/History/African-American History/Customs of the South/Social Life/Secrecy/Military History/Food/Tennessee/Town Life/Alternative Lifestyles (but not that way)/Buddha/Nuclear Power Predicaments/20th Century/Racism/Raw Fish. Feel free to add anything else. I won't mind if you put in there something like "Punting."

And y'all have to be comfortable and well-versed in math—ISBN numbers are really getting up there in regards to digits, aren't they? It isn't like the old days, when the first printed book ever had "ISBN 0-1-1-1" down there on page iv. What was that book, anyway? Was it the Gutenberg Bible? Was it one of those ancient Chinese texts that didn't survive? Was it something by

Joyce Carol Oates, or maybe even the actress Shirley MacLaine—who would be perfect for playing the part of librarian Gloretta Knoblock in a movie version of *Columbus Choice*—in a previous life?

These are questions way beyond my abilities to answer them. These are questions that can only be answered by a Supreme Being, and the outright amazing employees at the Library of Congress. Bless you all, prematurely!

Not that I've ever read every word that he wrote, but I want to offer my undying support to Frederick Exley—who got brought up in New York, though I understand him as a southern writer—and who somehow spanned the gap between fiction and nonfiction way back in the 1960s, long before all this ruckus occurred about people who said they wrote nonfiction that ended up being fiction, and all these people who wrote fiction that ended up being nonfiction. Frederick Exley had a thing for football in his work *A Fan's Notes*. Well, I think it's pretty obvious that *I* had something to do with football. Frederick Exley sometimes drank too much and made some inappropriate decisions. *I* have drunk too much and made inappropriate decisions. Frederick Exley spent a lot of time in mental institutions, and living on his widowed mother's couch, or his aunt's couch, or friends' couches.

I never got the opportunity to go that far, but I still have time.

Columbus Choice, as I pointed out in the chapter, "Choice Moments with Huddling," considered his most soulful and inspirational and calm moments as occurring on Sunday mornings, right before NFL kickoffs, when he prepared his sushi counter and awaited for the after-church masses to enter in need of The Halftime Report Roll, his biggest selling foot-long that included fish *and* pepperoni, plus *lotus root* that everyone around thought was just a hardened fancy yellow tomato or bell pepper.

Could it be that Columbus Choice met his untimely and disastrous death due to playing tricks on people? I hope not. What kind of God could hold it against him for hoping that the Lotus root might bring about a harmony to the people of lower middle central Tennessee? That just wouldn't be fair, if you ask me. Poor Columbus Choice. If only he'd been brought up in a time when whitey allowed black men to feel comfortable about college. If only he'd been able to punt a football, and make it to college on an athletic scholarship. If only his Protestant congregation held enough sway to keep him from joining the Army to kill people in Southeast Asia, then returning to open up a sushi restaurant, which made him become viewed as an enemy to short-sighted, long-winded, no-toleranced rednecks like the Plemmons brothers. If only...

My platelets feel like miniature, flawed, unbalanced tires, bumping unevenly through my circulatory system. I hear them droning, a constant *Om*, as if that marching Jew's harp band plays in the distance. Or they *clack*—like a pebble stuck in the deep treads of an otherwise good radial. I am grateful to the good pharmacists at Chase Drugs on Roane Street in Harriman for allowing me to come in and check my blood pressure a couple times a day, though I admit I've been remiss in doing so since having to finish up this Acknowledgment page. Maybe it's time for some blood work from a qualified phlebotomist, working for a certified hematologist, running an oncology and hematology clinic in Oak Ridge.

Now it's time.

No one in the publishing industry can say that I don't deliver.

I hope I didn't forget anyone.

ACKNOWLEDGMENTS

I wish to thank everyone at Dzanc, especially new editor Guy Intoci. For putting up with me, still, Glenda Guion. For agreeing that I should not bow to the pressure of writing another novel—and that no writer should try to outguess what publishers may or may not want in the future—and for sending the last two manuscripts to Dzanc, I wish to thank the late Kit Ward, agent. I am grateful for the magazine and journal editors at the publications where most of these stories first appeared.

I would be remiss in not mentioning gratitude to the John Simon Guggenheim Foundation.